No Face
to Murder

Miss Edith Howie

No Face
to Murder

Edith Howie

Coachwhip Publications
Greenville, Ohio

No Face to Murder, by Edith Howie
© 2022 Coachwhip Publications edition
Introduction © Curtis Evans
Front cover: Church steeple (Library of Congress, Prints
& Photographs Division, Theodor Horydczak Collection,
LC-H814-T-C07-020)

First published 1946
Edith Howie, 1900-1979
CoachwhipBooks.com (print) / Coachwhip.com (epub)

ISBN 1-61646-526-3
ISBN-13 978-1-61646-526-1

MURDERS END IN LOVERS MEETING:
THE MYSTERIES OF EDITH HOWIE

Curtis Evans

Dear miss Howie

I saw a picture in the family circle and liked the looks of you. Thought I would like for you to correspond with me. I am single not been married but would like to if I could find the rite girl ha ha. Maybe that you. I hope it is. Please write to me. Send picture of your self and I will do the same. I would like to come up and see you if that all rite with you. I have been in Dakota a few years now and liked it all rite. How is crops. They look good here. I am 43 years old and have brown eyes and dark haire and weigh 175 and 6 feet tall. Write. Tell me all a bought your self. I will cease now.

A friend

When an August 1941 profile in the Sioux Falls *Argus-Leader*, the leading newspaper of the Great Plains state of South Dakota, described Edith Howie as an "unpretentious person, quiet, small-featured and trim," with auburn hair, "deep blue eyes and . . . small, tapered . . . unusually beautiful hands," Edith, an unmarried woman of forty-one years who lived quietly in Sioux Falls with her parents, had just published her maiden mystery novel, *Murder for Tea*, about the fatal poisoning of the town vamp at a literary luncheon. The novel had appeared in *Three Prize Murders*, a trilogy of tales which had received honorable mentions in publisher Farrar and Rinehart's second annual Mary Roberts Rinehart mystery contest, named for America's preeminent woman crime writer (one of her sons had co-founded the company); and it had been highly praised in the *New York Times Book Review* by Isaac Anderson, who pronounced it "as puzzling and as entertaining a mystery as one could desire." (The previous year Elizabeth Daly had entered her debut novel, *Unexpected Night*, in the first Mary Roberts Rinehart mystery contest, in which she, like Edith Howie the next year, was a runner-up.)

Living up to her "unpretentious" reputation, Edith Howie wryly noted to her *Argus-Leader* interviewer, Lois Thrasher (who the next year would transfer to the *Chicago Daily News*, where she became night editor in 1945), that so far her greatest putative perk of fame as an author consisted of receiving myriad marriage proposals from importunate "mail-order bachelors," like the gentleman quoted at the top of this introduction, who had eagerly espied Edith's picture in *The Family Circle*, a women's household magazine distributed for free at the once omnipresent Piggly Wiggly grocery store chain. Another of Edith's male mystery admirers rang her up at home on the telephone one night, obviously inebriated and gushingly praising her books. When he failed to make any headway with the object of his fervent devotion, he rang off, angrily admonishing her, "I guess your books aren't so good after all!" Edith, resistant to the charms of such men, remained single for the rest of her life. Yet she enjoyed an impressively full creative existence, allowing her to give rewarding expression to her twin true loves: professional writing and amateur acting.

Between 1938 and 1946 Edith wrote eight mystery novels, seven of which were published in the United States and the United Kingdom as well as other countries (there are some particularly nice Spanish-language paperback editions); and during this time as well, and for many years afterward, she was one of the leading lights in Sioux Falls' community theater, both writing plays and performing in them. After her retirement from acting in the 1970s Edith reviewed local productions for the *Argus-Leader*, publishing her final review (*The Fantasticks*) in March 1979, just two months before her death at the age of seventy-eight. Although her career as a mystery writer was a brief one, lasting less than a decade, Edith during this time established herself as an American exponent of regional mystery and became as well a pioneer of the "cozy" detective story, where the tone remains light amid larcenies and criminal mayhem fails utterly to falsify the adage "murders end in lovers meeting."

******

Edith Christy Ann Howie was born on July 12, 1900, the eldest of three children of William Henry Howie and Christy Ann McLean, natives of Ontario, Canada of Scottish derivation. Shortly after the couple's marriage on April 12, 1899, they moved to Bradley, a town of fewer than 350 souls in the northern part of the raw, decade-old state of South Dakota, where Edith entered the world. William Henry Howie was the son of Cyrus Thompson Howie, an Oxford Mills farmer and Wesleyan Methodist, while Christy McLean was the daughter of Hugh McLean, a Maxville furniture store owner, Presbyterian and freemason. For four years prior to his marriage William had been a member of Canada's Northwest Mounted Police and at the time of his nuptials he managed a cheese factory in

Maxville. He carried on this latter occupation in Bradley, also adopting his wife's faith, before moving with his
growing family in 1905 to the city of Sioux Falls, South
Dakota, the state's largest city, located on the bank of the
Sioux River in the far southeastern corner of the state,
tucked between Minnesota and Iowa. For many years there
he sold farm machinery for International Harvester Company. In this capacity he was often away on the road, plying
his vital trade among Great Plains farmers, but his family
became staunch members of Sioux Falls' First Presbyterian
Church, where Edith in the 1920s served as an organist.
"Always an organist and never a bride," self-deprecatingly
comments a character in one of Edith's later mystery novels, which was true enough in her case.

Edith's father lived a more outwardly eventful life. For
eleven months between June 1924 and April 1925, William
Howie served, at the request of his highly-placed friend,
Mayor Thomas Mckinnon, as chief of police at Sioux Falls,
which then had a population of about 30,000 individuals.
In 1925 Chief of Police Howie reported that the police
department had made 1135 arrests during the previous
year, about 4% of the population. The great majority of
these arrests were for minor violations of liquor laws and
traffic ordinances, although there were also eight cases of
burglary, seven of bootlegging, five of bank robbery, five
of prostitution, four of grand larceny and four of forgery,
as well as two rapes and an assault. Happily not a single
murder was reported that year. "Nashiona (aka Sioux Falls)
is small town Middle West and doesn't go in for murders,"
asserts the narrator of *Murder for Tea* with unintended iro-
ny. "It isn't that sort of town." Most of the other offenses
with which Chief Howie and his men had to deal, like
discharging firecrackers within city limits and bathing
outdoors in the nude (i.e., skinny-dipping), admittedly
strike one as disarmingly minor.

Hanson & Leigh Photo
Chief W. H. Howie

As Halloween approached in October 1924, Chief
Howie issued a stern reminder to the city's boisterous
youth that pranks were only tolerated on All Hallows' Eve
itself, while the commission of acts of actual damage to
people's property would most definitely be prosecuted.
Rather more seriously, Chief Howie the previous month
warned local representatives of the Ku Klux Klan that his
department was prepared to make "wholesale arrests" of
any masked persons parading through city streets. During
the Twenties, which saw a national resurgence of the Klan,
South Dakota, like other Midwestern states, was, as one
authority puts it, "plagued by cross- and circle-burnings,
tar-and-featherings, and mass rallies and parades, including one attended by nearly 8000 people," mostly with the
goal of intimidating the state's Catholic population. Perhaps it was this sort of thing which prompted Chief Howie
to resign from office after having served for less than a
year. He had been long retired from policing in 1934,
when John Dillinger and his gang dramatically robbed
Sioux Falls' Security National Bank, in the process pump-
ing eight bullets into a local motorcycle cop.

During his short tenure the Chief had done his part
to make Sioux Falls safe for law-abiding people like his
daughter Edith, who lived a virtuous and placid life in the
city, presumably eschewing even illicit firecracker lighting
and skinny-dipping, not to mention acts of grand larceny.
In addition to her performances at the organ and piano at
public programs (she confided that she had relinquished
any hope of becoming a concert pianist on account of the
"smallness of her hands"), Edith in the 1920s was active,
along with her slightly younger sister Bessie, in the local
chapter of the Delphian Society, an international organization which promoted women's cultural education. For a
time Edith, who attended writing classes at the University
of South Dakota in Vermillion but never took a degree,

succumbed to the vogue for archaic Old English names and self-consciously styled herself "Edythe," but happily she abandoned this affectation.

During the Thirties just plain Edith Howie became active in Sioux Falls' community theater and began publishing short stories in magazines, including *Good Housekeeping, Ladies' Home Journal, Liberty* and the Canadian *Chatelaine.* In 1938 she completed her first mystery novel, *Treeholme House.* The novice mystery writer submitted the manuscript to Doubleday, Doran's Crime Club imprint, who snobbishly turned it down, sadly, on the grounds, Edith later wryly confided to *Argus-Leader* reporter Robert Gunsolly, that "four of the five persons murdered in the book were servants." Instead the tale appeared later that year, spiffily illustrated, in the Canadian magazine *Maclean's.*

Undaunted by her limited success at mystery writing, Edith in 1939 began simultaneously writing two new mysteries, which she entitled *Murder for Tea* and *Santa Claus Died.* She submitted the two manuscripts to Farrar and Rinehart, who accepted both works and published them within a few months of each other in 1941, *Tea* in August in its *Three Prize Murders* volume and *Santa* in December (appropriately enough), with its title altered to the rather more anodyne *Murder for Christmas.* Presumably the publisher was leery of traumatizing, with Edith's original blunt title, dewy-eyed innocents desirous of raking in their annual seasonal haul from Saint Nick.

Both *Murder for Tea* and *Murder for Christmas* are light "couples mysteries," in which a husband and wife are confronted with murder, respectively during a tea party at a literary luncheon and at a country house Christmas gathering, where, reminiscent of Ngaio Marsh's popular Seventies mystery *Tied up in Tinsel,* a man dressed up as Santa Claus is violently done to death. *Tea* takes place in Edith

Howie's fictional Great Plains city of Nashiona, an imaginative rendering of Sioux Falls, which also appears under the same name in one of Edith's later mysteries, *Cry Murder*. Conversely *Christmas* is set in rural New York State, perhaps as a sop to Plains wary editors, who once queried her having some of her characters travel twenty miles without encountering a single house. Edith worked on her first two published mystery novels in tandem, taking up one as she became stuck with the other, a process which she again employed with *Murder at Stone House* and *Murder's So Permanent*, both of which were published in 1942, and *No Face to Murder* and *The Band Played Murder*, both of which were published in 1946. *Cry Murder* appeared singly in 1944.

Once she had her characters and their milieu set firmly in her mind, Edith would begin writing, even though she claimed that typically she had no notion when she started of who her actual murderer would be. She might change her mind on that matter more than once as she wrote. All of her mysteries are brightly narrated by chatty young women, either married or well on their way to wedding their crime-busting beaux by the end of the story. While arguably not the most rigorously plotted of Golden Age mysteries, Edith's detective stories deliver the entertainment goods to likeminded readers, in the ingratiating manner of the modern "cozy" mystery.

In his reviews of Howie's mysteries in the *San Francisco Chronicle*, prominent American reviewer Anthony Boucher emphasized their amorous underpinnings: "Ross Langdon doubles as love interest and detective. . . . Good reading for the romance public. . . . (*Cry Murder*); "Randolph Garrison is more efficient as a lover than as head of homicide, but the telling and the church background . . . are pleasing." (*No Face to Murder*); "Jewel thefts, love and marihuana tie into the murders of two girl vocalists with a big-time band. . . . Colorful, unassuming and pleasant" (*The Band Played Murder*).

Five of Edith Howie's seven published mystery novels are set in cities on the Great Plains, including the three reprinted by Coachwhip (and reviewed by Boucher above): *Cry Murder, No Face to Murder,* and *The Band Played Murder. Cry Murder* concerns killings and attempted killings which take place in Nashiona among a little theater group putting on a trial run of a play by a famed New York playwright (and former Nashiona native). The first murder, of hateful diva actress Nola Powers, takes place at the Olympia Theater, for which the author likely had been inspired by Sioux Falls' own Orpheum Theater, a beloved institution still standing today.

The Orpheum opened in 1913 and staged vaudeville acts until 1927, when it was sold and converted into a second-run and B-movie theater. By the time Edith wrote *Cry Murder* sixteen years later, the theater had fallen into disuse and been abandoned, but in 1954 the building was purchased and renovated as a stage theater by the Sioux Falls Community Playhouse, of which Edith was an important member. Mary Thorpe, the narrator and heroine of *Cry Murder*, memorably describes the Olympia Theater with WASPish middle-class distaste as follows:

> The Olympia was an eight hundred-seat theater that, once in use almost exclusively for vaudeville and stock, had, with their passing, degenerated into a third-run movie house. . . . Cheap hotels and cheaper restaurants surrounded it and its audiences were drawn quite frankly from that class of people who scorned to pay the 'forty cents and tax' price of first-run theaters and were willing to wait for their pictures. One visit there, during my noviciate

in town, had been enough for me. The place
had been poorly lighted and smelly, the screen
a flickering disgrace. The seat to which I'd
been ushered had been broken and sagging; I
was suspicious of the probability of mice, or
their big brothers, rats; while overhead the
tireless dance of two creatures, which could
have been none other than those anomalies of
the animal kingdom, bats, had appalled me.
My first visit had been my last.

Appropriately Edith stages the most atmospheric section of her novel here, when Mary goes there to meet Nola
and encounters . . . well, read it for yourself and see! The
case ultimately is solved by Mary's love interest, handsome
private detective Ross Langdon, although not without
Mary's help. Also contributing to the case is folksy Chief
Hanover of the Nashiona police, whom Mary explains had
"been a small groceryman before he picked off the plum-
iest of Nashiona's appointive jobs." Somewhat defensively
Chief Hanover tells Mary and Ross: "[W]hile maybe you're
thinking I'm only a dumb old fogy who got the job of
police chief in Nashiona by reason of being a good friend
of the mayor's, you want to remember I've held onto that
job mainly by getting results. And results are just what I
aim to keep getting." Mary describes the Chief as a "short,
stout, ordinary-looking man in a wrinkled gray suit whose
waistcoat was crossed by an old-fashioned watch chain. He
had thinning gray hair, a somewhat straggly gray mustache
and eyes that were shrewd and sensible behind gold-rimmed
spectacles." The description matches that of Edith's father
when, at age fifty-two, he headed Sioux Falls' police force.

The *Fort Worth Star-Telegram* delightedly described *Cry
Murder* as "a typical murder mystery, the sort everybody
enjoys," with "appealing characters and situations and an

atmosphere of eerie danger and suspense that marks the most satisfying type of mystery thrillers." In its review the *Argus-Leader* spotted similarities between Nashiona and Sioux Falls, including the fact that with the advent of the Second World War, Nashiona's population, like that of Sioux Falls, had virtually exploded. Observes Mary in the novel:

> Nashionites consider that they dwell in a metropolis, which I suppose they do—it being the largest city within the border of two sister states—but nowhere has there been normality since Pearl Harbor, and Nashiona was no exception to the rule. Close against the boundaries now sprawled the mushroom growth of the huge army school. . . . No one knew just how many soldiers were stationed there in the rows of wooden, tar-paper covered barracks but the number hovered somewhere between the twenty and thirty thousand marks. . . . the soldiers formed a little city in themselves.
> . . . sweethearts and wives . . . simply picked up their belongings and moved to Nashiona on the chance of finding accommodations that would enable them to spend a few more precious months with their loves ones. . . . Every apartment, every hotel, every rooming house was jammed to its roof top. Rents had risen—temporarily, for a freezing order was imminent—to unprecedented levels. Tourist homes and cabin camps . . . were being rented upon a monthly basis. At the edge of town a flourishing trailer city had sprung up over-night.
> It was all pretty breath-taking. . . .

In real life, Sioux Falls in 1942 became the site of the Army Air Forces Technical School, which over the course of the war trained nearly 50,000 hostilities-bound men in radio communication, Morse code, and aircraft identification. The school enabled Sioux Falls finally to recover from the lingering effects of the Great Depression, lessened the city's Plains parochialism and launched a building boom which lasted well into the 1950s, as many recruits remained there after the war, married and started families. Much of this phenomenon is captured, albeit fleetingly, in *Cry Murder*—not the least of the novel's felicities.

No Edith Howie novel appeared in 1945, but in January 1946 the author published *No Face to Murder*, which, like *Cry Murder*, is set during the war, in 1944, with wartime scarcity rather more advanced. (In *Cry Murder*, characters are still able regularly to consume waffles and grapefruit for breakfast and chocolate cakes with chocolate icing for dessert.) *Face* takes place in the Great Plains city of Dorchester rather than at Nashiona, but Dorchester, like Nashiona, sounds a lot like Sioux Falls, or possibly Sioux City, Iowa, about ninety miles south of Sioux Falls, where Edith's sister, Bessie, a bank cashier, had moved and Edith frequently visited. The novel's St. Thomas' Episcopal Cathedral seems quite a lot like Sioux City's St. Thomas' Episcopal Church, imposingly constructed in the Richardsonian Romanesque style and completed in 1892.

In the novel double slashing murders, respectively of the church caretaker and the organist, incongruously take place at St. Thomas' Episcopal Cathedral, in an opening surprisingly reminiscent of P. D. James' lauded 1986 crime novel *A Taste for Death*, where two people, a homeless man and an MP, similarly are found dead at St. Matthews' Catholic Church, their throats cut. Despite its uncharacteristically grim opening circumstances, however, *Face* ultimately bears a much greater resemblance to

Agatha Christie's *The Murder at the Vicarage*, peopled as it is with a charming cast of principal characters, including the young church secretary narrator, Tess King; church dean Alec MacDonald and his wife Ruth; Bishop Walters, who takes an interest in the case; and Randolph "Ran" Garrison, the handsome head of the Dorchester police department's homicide division and Tess' love interest.

Drexel Drake of the *Chicago Tribune* deemed *No Face to Murder*, which in my view is the author's finest mystery, a "well-written yarn" with a "well-planned puzzle," while noted crime writer Dorothy B. Hughes in the *Albuquerque Tribune* praised the "English atmosphere to this Midwestern mystery," tipped off by the name of the city in which it is located, as well as the "authenticity" of its church setting and the "quite nice feeling to the whole . . . along with the bite of small-town nastiness." For her part Avis DeVoto in the *Boston Globe* gave the novel an unqualified rave review, selecting it as her mystery of the week. "An unusually penetrating picture of a small community, with a double murder in a church as the highlight. Practically every member of the choir, around which the story is built, is a suspect," DeVoto wrote. "Inspector Ran Garrison, assisted no little by his girlfriend, who is also the rector's secretary, and a cooking bishop come through with all the answers, just too late."

Ten months later came *The Band Played Murder*, Edith Howie's final published crime novel. While with *Cry Murder* and *No Face to Murder* Edith had been able to draw heavily on her own familiarity with theater and church milieus, with *The Band Played Murder* she had to bone up on swing music, dance bands and "crooning" by reading back issues of *Downbeat* at the Sioux Falls Carnegie Free Public Library. Her protagonist and narrator, Connie Waring, another would-be concert pianist, is persuaded to serve as a last-minute substitute singer in Gale Ullman's

—Harold Photo.

Edith Howie with her nephews Billy and Gary

band. When murder beats the band at the city of Harriston during its annual Harvest Festival, Connie, who discovers the dead body, finds herself a person of interest to both local police and the actual murderer. The devoted Edith Howie reader can be certain there will be ample love interest in the novel as well.

The Band Played Murder is another enjoyable Edith Howie mystery, pleasingly more sympathetic and informed about its subject than Ngaio Marsh's Swing, Brother, Swing, which appeared in print three years later. "Reading Ngaio Marsh's Swing, Bother, Swing," wrote crime writer and composer Edmund Crispin disgustedly in 1966. "Poor, and if she's going to try and write about jazz bands, why can't she find out something about them? 'Tympanist,' indeed." Edith did rather better in this regard than Ngaio, although like Cornell Woolrich in his notorious 1941 crime novella "Marihana," the author propagates the myth that the drug can immediately transform people into murderous maniacs. (One guesses that Edith, like the heroine of her story, had never personally tried it.) The Lexington Herald deemed Edith's "swinging" novel "a bang-up yarn that does not drag a paragraph throughout the whole 243 pages," while the Knoxville Journal avowed: "It's an unusual background and a well written story told in the first person by a girl who is as confused by life in a dance band as most readers would be."

After Band came silence. Edith accepted a position as a librarian at the Carnegie Library and continued working on mystery writing, but she never published another novel, criminous or otherwise. In 1951 Argus-Leader reporter Bob Gunsolley wrote that Edith was simultaneously working on not two, but three, mysteries, the most promising of which concerned an identical twin sister who, after awakening in bed with a choking sensation, later that morning learns that her twin was strangled during the night. Of course she sets out to find her sister's killer. Apparently Edith completed neither this novel, nor the other two which she was writing (one of which took place among a horsey set in Kentucky bluegrass country), although by her own admission she remained a "rabid mystery fan," getting first dibs on all the new mysteries at the public library.

After the deaths of her parents Edith in 1960 retired from the library and moved to Sioux City to live with her sister Bessie in a two-story, foursquare Craftsman-style house, which still stands today. She remained active in Sioux Falls little theater, for decades indulging her own "taste for death" with parts in such mysterious plays as the chiller *Night Must Fall*, the farce *Arsenic and Old Lace*, the ghostly *The Innocents* (the stage adaptation of Henry James "The Turn of the Screw") and a 1969 performance of Agatha Christie's *And Then There Were None*, arguably the most renowned murder mystery of them all, where, at nearly seventy years of age, she played coldly pious spinster Emily Brent, who memorably gets figuratively "stung" to death by a "bee."

In real life Edith Howie passed away, a decade after this performance, at the age of seventy-eight on May 1, 1979. Her younger brother, William Lawrence Howie, a photography enthusiast who four decades earlier had advised her on the properties of potassium cyanide for her first published mystery novel, had predeceased her in 1961, while her sister Bessie expired in 1996, at the age of ninety-three. "Reviewer, Thespian Here Dies," read the headline to Edith's 1979 obituary in the *Sioux City Journal*, omitting mention of her mysteries until the body of the article, in which it was briefly noted that "she had eight books and 40 short stories published. Stories by Miss Howie have been widely published in the United States, England and

Australia, and have been frequently translated for publication in Norway, Denmark and Spain."

Having noticed that copies of Edith Howie's novels were quite scarce and highly collectible, I wrote in 2012 about the author's *Murder for Christmas* at my vintage mystery blog *The Passing Tramp*, while two years later Edith was profiled in a series of articles by *Argus-Leader* features writer Jill Callison. Finally in 2022, over eighty years after the publication of her first mystery, Edith Howie's books are again back in print, as part of the remarkable ongoing reclamation of worthy crime writers from our past. Death for Edith Howie, it seems, came not as the end, but rather an intermission.

NO FACE
TO MURDER

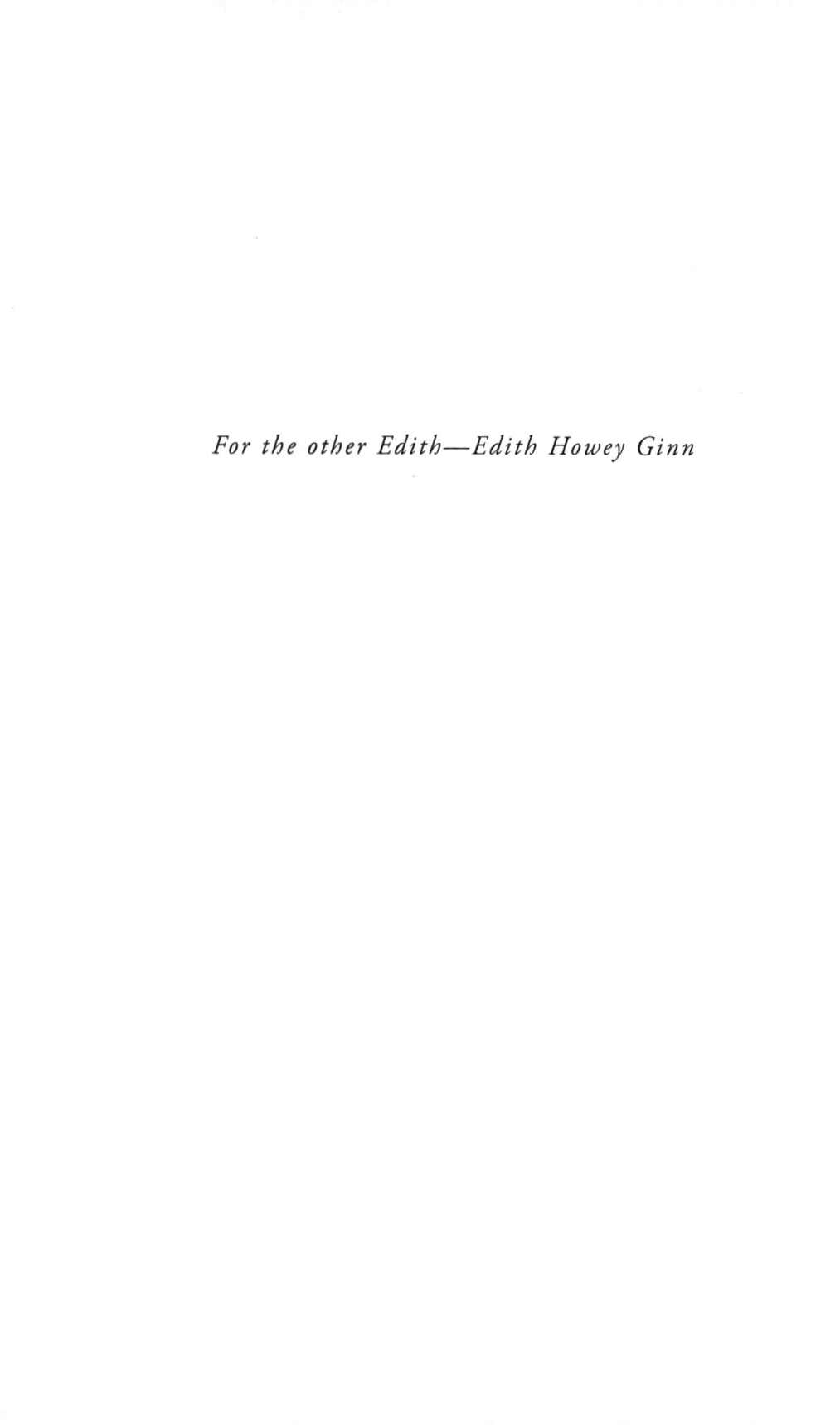

For the other Edith—Edith Howey Ginn

1

I am still secretary at St. Thomas'. I will be until Friday next when I lock the doors for the last time and hand my keys to Alec who will, in turn, present them to Miss Hallie Robertson. Miss Hallie is gray and brusque and unimaginative. Today, when she came in to check over office supplies, she made it plain that murder—even murder at St. Thomas—was no more than a word to her, something that the Dorchester papers had chosen, regrettably, to feature. "Murder!" she had sniffed. "What's murder other than death in a violent form and goodness knows death is natural enough. No, my dear, I don't intend to let this bother me. Frankly, I see no reason why I should!"

Well, that's all very well. The church is satisfied—Miss Hallie is sixty if she's a day and altogether the most suitable kind of a secretary for a young good-looking minister—and I—well, I have nothing to worry about. Marriage will take care of my future but I am certain that, for a time at least, St. Thomas' will know me only on Sundays when, garbed in my trousseau best, white-gloved and prayerbooked, I once again shall occupy what has been known for years as the old King pew.

I know that I should be happy. There is nothing now of which I need be afraid. They have all told me so and I

agree. Our murderer will do no more harm. No one practices on the organ now, and the doors into the chancel and
the body of the church are locked and Alec keeps the key.
There is no admittance to my office save by the straight
narrow flight of stairs that rises directly from the north
door, and my desk faces the entrance. Set in the carpet at
my feet is a buzzer that rings simultaneously in a dozen
parts of the church and that will, should need arise, sum-
mon the janitor within a second or two. We have a new
janitor now—a dignified gray-polled Negro. With the
perspicacity of his race, he senses my uneasiness and so is
never out of range of the buzzer's summoning. Yesterday,
inadvertently, I trod upon it and he came pounding up
the stairs, his eyes rolling in their ash-black setting and a
hatchet, snatched from a nail beside the furnace, clutched
in his trembling old hand. We had a good laugh over the
episode but I am convinced that our laughter arose more
from relief than good fellowship.

No, it is not the days so much that matter. Spring is
coming early this year and already, in March, we have hints
of swelling buds and the freeing of ice-locked streams.
Tulips are pushing green spears through snow patches and
one of these days forsythia will drip golden rain against
the gray church walls. Day lingers a little longer each
evening but I am away by four. It was the only proviso I
made. "I won't stay there after it begins to get dark," I told
Alec. "No matter whether my work is done or not, I go."
And I have kept that promise.

Everyone has been more than kind—Alec, Ruth, Bishop
Walters, those of the congregation with whom I have come
in contact. They ask no questions, volunteer no information. They tell me only that I am young, that time blurs
all things, and that I will forget. I hope with all my heart
that they are right. I want it to be so.

Winter is a busy season in church affairs. You scarcely recover from the pageantry and extravaganza of Christmas before you are committed to the extra services and confirmation classes of Lent. Ash Wednesday was just behind us, I remember, that day it all began, and Alec was tired. Tired and jittery. He came over that afternoon and part of the time he sat on the corner of my desk, poking his pipestem at the spoiled copies of mimeographed letters I'd been getting out, and part of the time he paced back and forth, hands in pockets and an ear cocked to where, through the half-open chancel door, a Bach fugue rolled in waves of sonorous sound. That the music failed to give him pleasure was evident. Listening, he frowned.

Alec is the Very Reverend Alexander Francis Ross Mac-Donald, D.D., Dean of St. Thomas' Cathedral, Episcopal, the oldest church in Dorchester and, indeed, in our section of the midwest. Alec is very tall, very dark and very young, too young some of the parish thought when he came to us, fresh from a year of study abroad. Some of the old die-hards still regret his youth—he is just over thirty —but the consensus of opinion is that his three years here have been good ones. His wife, Ruth, was my school chum and is still my closest friend. I suppose I know them as well as anyone in Dorchester.

Which was one reason why I was so acutely aware of Alec's restlessness that February day. It was beginning to be dusk, my neck ached from cutting stencils, and I found the music that rolled over us, beautiful though it was, insistent rather than soothing.

I remember I banged my typewriter carriage over at last and glared at him. "Alec, if there isn't anything you want here, for pity sakes go home where you'll be wearing out your own carpet. This one is thin enough in all conscience!"

"I know," he said meekly. "And I don't want anything. I only came over with the kitchen knives. Ruth said they were dull when she was helping cut sandwiches last Tuesday so I went to work on them." He smiled at me, that

nice smile that verged on a grin. "They're sharp enough now."

"That's nice," I said. "The Guild can give you a vote of thanks. I suppose Oscar couldn't have done them?"

"Oscar—" He bit off what he'd meant to say, began again. "Oscar said he was busy."

Oscar was the dour Norwegian with whom St. Thomas' had been burdened for thirty years or more and, if Alec would admit it, one of the scratchiest patches in his suit of life.

I said, "Well, if you're still looking for odd jobs, there's that other typewriter—it needs cleaning. Or if you care to stamp envelopes . . ."

He said, "Thanks. I'm going home." But he still lingered. He jerked his head toward the chancel door from which the music had again surged forth tremendously. "Has she been here long? All afternoon?"

I nodded. No question as to who was meant. Carol Tolliver's touch on the organ was unmistakable. There was no one else in town who could, or would, have attempted the *Bach Fugue in E Minor*. She was playing it magnificently.

"There's heat in the church today," I said. "Choir practice tonight. And she's giving a recital in a month, she told me."

"She can play," he agreed absently. "Too bad she's such a little—minx."

I didn't comment on that. "Minx" was by far the kindest term I'd ever heard applied to the child. Mothers of sons eligible for marriage had called her much worse and, now that the majority of such sons were safe in Uncle Sam's keeping, rumor had it that it was the young wives of Dorchester who were showing perturbation.

So far it was all very hush-hush and underground. There was nothing you could really put your finger on, but there were tales of stolen noontime car rides along little frequented country roads. Dr. Carter's wife was authority for that. "I saw Carol myself—her and that young baritone from the Methodist church. They were parked—just off the highway. And he has such a nice little wife! What on earth are the Tollivers thinking of?"

There'd been other stories as well. Something certainly had happened to the winter series of violin recitals announced by Victor Czerny, brilliant young director of the Dorchester symphony orchestra. The first one had gone off as scheduled with Carol presiding at the piano, but all subsequent dates were canceled. The story was that Mrs. Czerny had insisted upon playing the latest accompaniments and that her technique was, to put it kindly, inadequate for the style of music her husband effected.

There were a dozen other such tales that involved such figures as the head of the high school music department, the song leader of the luncheon club for which she played, and even the director of the St. Thomas choir. Just what basis of fact there was for these stories no one knew but Carol herself, and she wasn't telling.

Alec was shrugging into his overcoat. "There's a movement on to oust old Dennison and put Carol in as organist here," he said as he adjusted his scarf. "Heard anything about it?"

I stopped folding letters. "No," I said carefully. "I haven't. But I'm not surprised."

Nor was I. Charles Dennison had been organist at St. Thomas' for more than thirty years. An indifferent musician when at his best, he now waged a losing battle with failing eyesight and arthritic joints. But he clung stubbornly to his organ bench.

"Charles Dennison," I said slowly, "will have a fit!"

Alec was staring at the floor. He said, "Yes. Well. The argument is that if we don't take her, some other church will, and that since she's a communicant here . . . Then there's the theory that the church should encourage its own young people, as well as the idea that Dennison's had it long enough. I don't know—there's some talk about her going away to study."

"Frederick Brastock's behind this, I'll bet," I said inelegantly. Brastock, a newcomer in Dorchester, had been made choirmaster of St. Thomas' the fall before through sheer nerve and the fanfared announcement that he was opening a studio for voice culture on Canal Street. Music committees do odd things at times.

Alec said, "Well, Brastock's in it, of course—he and Dennison have been rowing all fall. Remember the midnight service at Christmas? But, actually, it was Harvey Thurston who came to me. There's been an anti-Dennison faction for a good many years and now it seems there's an organized group swinging in behind the Tollivers."

I said, "Oh, dear, why do old people cling to things so determinedly? I believe Charles Dennison would rather die than give up the organ. It's his only claim to a position of importance in the world, to say nothing of the financial angle. He only gets forty dollars a month here but I imagine that's more than half his monthly income. Poor old creature! If they let him go, it will break his heart. Alec moved uncomfortably. "I know. But there's something to be said on the other side too. Of course, if the talk about Brastock and her is true . . .

"She's in the choir anyway," I pointed out. Nature, which had richly dowered the child, had given her a pleasant singing voice. "Short of throwing her out . . ."

Alec sighed, "Oh, well. I'd probably better see Brastock. Whoever it was who called the choir the war department of the church surely knew what he was talking about!"

Sound from the organ had ceased. I gestured toward the half-open chancel door. I said, "Do you think—?" and Alec said loudly, "I'm off. Ruth said you were coming to dinner, Tess. I'll see you then."

"And that," I thought grimly, listening to the rapid clatter of his footsteps in retreat, "is no doubt a man's idea of a graceful way out when confronted with a delicate situation. But—drat him!—he's left me holding the tag!"

He had, too. Simultaneously, with the slam of the street door, the heavy oak of the chancel door swung wide and Carol Tolliver stood on the threshold, her eyes licking over the room.

She said, "Oh!" in manifest disappointment. "I thought Dean MacDonald was here. I wanted to talk to him."

I sat and looked at her. She was a pretty thing even in these days of almost universally pretty girls. I suppose she was twenty and she wore the preposterous habiliments common to her age and sex: softly plaited skirt, brown and blue; thin blue sweater, blue socks and grimy saddle shoes; the inevitable string of imitation pearls. Her heavy blond hair fell in natural ringlets well below her shoulders and her eyes were green-gray jewels set in an incredible length of black eyelashes. Tilted nose, rounded chin, each was perfection embodied in flesh. Only her rather ugly hands and feet were out of key. But the hands, at least justified their existence. They were square and strong—pianist's hands.

"The dean *was* here," I said at last. "But he's gone home. If it's important, why don't you go over and see him there?"

"Oh, no," she said and, smiled. It wasn't a normal twenty-year-old smile. It had an amused, tolerantly understanding quality that infuriated me. "I don't think so. Dear Ruthie wouldn't like it. You don't think *I'm* welcome in that house, do you?"

I knew what people meant by "seeing red" then. I wanted to shake the little idiot, slap her out of her heroics once and for all. I did nothing of the sort. I sat and glared at my typewriter until the red tides subsided, and then I said slowly, "I thought you were going away, Carol. Why don't you go?"

Again she gave me that quick unchildlike glance. "You'd like that, wouldn't you? Everybody would. But I'm not going. I can't. I haven't any money."

I suspected that was true. The Tollivers belonged to the rank and file who depend solely upon a monthly salary for their existence. In this case, it was a very modest one. Mr. Tolliver was bookkeeper at the Dorchester National Bank.

"Couldn't you borrow the money?" I hazarded. "Once you got away, there'd be scholarships. You're thinking of Rochester—the Eastman School, aren't you? Perhaps they'd help if they understood the circumstances."

"I suppose you think I want to stay here," she said sulkily. "Oh, I'll go—sometime. Don't worry about that. But not without money. Dad can't let me have any—it takes every cent he makes to keep us going. If I could get a job—if they'd even give me old Dennison's place here—I could save that money. In a year I'd have something to start on."

"Charles Dennison's been organist here a long time. He has his friends too, you know. I wouldn't count—"

"Okay—okay." She sounded good-humored now. "That what the Very Reverend thinks, huh? Well, wait and see!"

Once more I took a good grip on my temper. "I don't speak for the dean," I said. "I'm only giving you my opinion. As for the rest of it—your going to Rochester—I'm not sure that couldn't be arranged. I belong to a club—we have a scholarship fund. Perhaps if I talked to the committee . . ."

"Peace in our time, huh?" She was actually laughing at me. "Don't look so shocked, Miss King. All of us kids read the papers. All right—you go ahead, see what you can do.

And don't make a mistake about it—I'd go tomorrow if I had the money. You don't think I like sticking around here, do you? All the old cats gossiping and the men . . ." She used a wide gesture. "I'd do anything in the world to get away!"

How much of that was true, I had no way of knowing. It had the ring of truth, though, and I found myself looking at the girl with new eyes. Suppose we'd all been wrong about her. What if she'd been the pursued and not, as the feminine contingent wanted me to believe, the pursuing? She had genius, beauty of a sort, and wherever you went there were men unscrupulous enough to want to exploit such things. She was gay and young and men grew weary of their wives . . .

I slapped the cover down over my Remington. "Don't give up hope," I told her. "We'll see what can be done."

"Gee, thanks." She was the complete schoolgirl again, "You quitting now?"

I said that I was. These letters had to go out that night and it was nearly five-thirty and quite dark outside. "Aren't you through?"

Again that short abrupt transition from childhood. "You're never through in music," she said. "I guess I'll run down to the Café Rouge for a sandwich and then come back. I can still get in an hour or so before the choir gets here. All right if I leave the organ unlocked?"

"I wouldn't." The organ had just been rebuilt and was the pride of St. Thomas' music committee. "Stick the key here in my top drawer—I'll leave the desk unlocked and you can get it when you come in. Sorry, but I'll have to lock the door at the foot of the stairs. You'll have to come in through the basement."

"That'll be all right," she said absently. "I'm not afraid. Oscar'll be somewhere around."

Oscar would. He had his own apartments in the basement, not far from the kitchen, where he spun out his own queer existence. He was a bachelor of sixty-odd, grizzled and taciturn, but he was to be trusted. No fear of Carol getting past his lair without him seeing her, and once he knew her to be inside he'd keep an eye on her.

Or so I thought.

I'd donned hat and coat by this time. Now I caught up my purse and stack of letters. I said, "It's twenty minutes to six right now. I've got to fly." I did, too. I had the letters to take to the post office, groceries to buy, and I wanted to run out to my own apartment for a minute before going to the MacDonalds'. Dinner there would be at six-thirty, Ruth had told me, but it was usually late. Nevertheless I had no time to waste. "Come along with me—why don't you?"

But she hung back. "No, thanks, Miss King. I've got to lock the organ and . . . Never mind about me. I'll go out the other way and I'll tell Oscar I'm coming back."

But for all my need of haste I lingered until I heard the bang of the organ top going down and the quick slap of her feet along the carpeted aisle. I even went to the chancel door and watched to see light glow at the top of the basement stairs and listened to the far-off noises of her descent. I waited until I heard her close the door at the foot of the stairs before I turned away, uneasy in spite of myself. I wondered if I should have gone with her, seen her safely out of the church. But, no—it was all right this way; it had to be. Oscar was somewhere in the basement, and she knew every inch of the church as well as I did. There was nothing to be afraid of—there never had been.

Shrugging, I went down my own flight of stairs, clicked the switch that lighted them, and pressed the catch that locked the outer door. It was fifteen minutes to six. I quickened my steps. If I were going to make the MacDonalds' by half past six, I'd *better* hurry.

2

The Deanery snuggled close to the church, the only house in the block, for St. Thomas' owned all the property with the optimistic notion of some day being able to rebuild. It was a rambling red-brick house, older by a dozen years than the church. It was far too big for Alec and Ruth and their nine-months-old twins, but an Episcopal minister must and does expect a constant stream of visitors, and the place served.

Now, as I climbed the hill, the lights from its unshaded windows were like beacons of welcome. I had passed some of the pleasantest hours of my life within its walls.

There were no guests tonight. The long length of Alec was relaxing before the open fire. He wore smoking jacket and slippers—the jacket, dating back to his Oxford days, was of dark blue flannel with the arms of some college embroidered on its pocket—and the air was pleasantly scented with the good tobacco he affected. The evening paper, reduced to separate pages, was scattered around him—a sure sign that his relations with home and the world were good.

According to custom, I hadn't rung—I'd simply opened the door and walked in. Equally according to custom, Alec didn't rise. He looked vaguely in my direction and grunted something that might have been a greeting and probably was no more than an acknowledgment of my presence. For my part, I didn't bother him with words. I hung my coat in the closet under the stairs and prepared to hunt for Ruth on my own.

It wasn't necessary. Before I'd passed beyond range of the fire, the swinging door between pantry and kitchen slapped shut and Ruth came in. She wore a postage stamp apron and she looked flushed and harried.

She said, "Hello, Tess," and flopped down on the nearest chair. "Oh, yes, a new one," she said in answer to my raised eyebrows. "Worse than the last—she doesn't know from nothing! If the war ever ends and I can get decent help again . . ."

Alec broke up that line of conversation by saying, "Hah!" and rattling his paper. I jumped but Ruth only sighed.

"It's Russia probably," she said. "He fights every foot with them and the way he quarrels with the radio announcers is something scandalous. If the bishop ever hears him . . . ! I always did think profanity wasn't so much a matter of words as it is a tone of voice."

I laughed. I like Alec but Ruth is my joy. She is the exact opposite of her husband, as fair as he is dark, and, while Alec's good looks depend upon boyish charm rather than upon regularity of feature, Ruth balances on the edge of beauty. She is all gold and amber, hair and eyes, with a skin like warm cream. Mentally, too, she differs from Alec whose thought processes are always sharp, instant and logical, whereas I've heard parishioners complain that "Mrs. MacDonald is so very vague." I do not agree. Vague she is not. Her ways of arriving at conclusions may appear obscure and roundabout but their essential rightness can and often does challenge Alec's swifter and more direct methods. It is Alec's delight that she is so often reasonless and yet completely right.

"How are the infants?" I asked after a pause during which Alec grunted, "Tokyo—huh!" by which I judged he'd moved to other circles of combat.

"Fiends," Ruth said and shut her eyes. "Simply fiends. Original sin has entered into them. But definitely. Wait until you hear. Sandy has always been such an angel about taking his food—they both have. Well, today he learned how to sputter. Cereal, orange juice, cod liver oil, milk— he'd get it into his mouth and then go spffftt! and out it would come—over me, over himself, over the high chair, the floor—oh, it was terrible! I took a bath after every feeding and the worst of it is I don't think I got anything down their throats. If they could walk, I bet they'd be down raiding the ice box right now!"

I laughed and Alec, from behind his papers, emitted something like a snort, but Ruth only sighed again.

"The whole day's been like that. Cold, and Alec like a wild bear—underfoot all the time." (For some reason, Thursday is Alec's day off from ministerial duties.) "I don't know what's bothering him—he won't tell *me,*" Ruth said righteously. "And then, when I finally get him out of the house—about five—who should show up but Mrs. Harvey Thurston if you please! She's all worked up about the Guild and what it ought to be doing and isn't, and she wanted my advice and you know how good that is!"

I did. Ruth had been an indifferent Presbyterian when she married Alec.

"So I said yes and no and I think it would be lovely— it's something about a gift; communion linens or some- thing—and then about half past five Alec came storming up the porch steps—I heard him if she didn't—and then he never came in! I think he looked in through the window and saw her and . . . He says he went for a walk! But, I ask you, is that a way for a *minister* to act?"

"We have our weak moments, my dear," Alec said dryly and flapped his paper over.

Ruth shrugged. "So there it was five-thirty and I thought surely she'd go—but no, she stayed. And then it developed that what she really panted to talk about wasn't the Guild and its doings at all but Carol Tolliver. Mrs. Thurston's worried. It seems that Carol's been making passes at Mr. Thurston or Mr. Thurston's been making passes at Carol—"

"Really, my dear!" Alec gave up all pretense of reading. He arose in outraged ministerial dignity and stood, tall and straight, upon the red-brick hearth. "I doubt if Mrs. Thurston expressed it in quite that way."

Ruth opened her amber eyes widely at him. "It was what she meant. I wasn't a minister's wife until I married you, Alec, and I'm willing to work at being one, but I refuse to give up my vocabulary. 'Making passes,' one or the other, was what it amounted to. Naturally she thinks it's Mr. Thurston but she blames Carol. I won't tell you what she called her but it was Freudian and nasty. She says Mr. Thurston's been acting queerly all summer, talking about lending Carol money to go on with her musical career and saying that she wasn't appreciated in Dorchester. Lately he's been worse than that—just talking, I mean, is nothing—but Carol is always telephoning him at home, and once she came to the house and Mr. Thurston took her into the library and shut the door, and they were there for a long time and when they came out Mrs. Thurston was sure Carol had been crying. And Mrs. Thurston said that when she asked her husband he wouldn't explain, just told her to mind her own business for a change. She went all to pieces when she told me that. She says they've been married for twenty-five years, happily until now, and if anyone thinks she's going to sit back and watch while a chit of a girl breaks up her home . . ."

"Oh, good grief!" Alec said between his teeth. It's the strongest expletive he allows himself and he uses it only in, moments of extreme perturbation. He took his old pipe, dug savagely into its bowl, packed it with tobacco and lit it. He took three or four furious puffs and then stuffed it absently into his pocket. "All right—I was wrong. I had no business running away and I'm sorry you got let in. But, as a matter of fact, I had a good reason for not wanting to face the lady just then."

"Take that pipe out of your pocket," Ruth ordered calmly, "or you'll be on fire in a minute. Your apologies are accepted. I think myself she'll have cooled off by tomorrow. Today was the result of an accumulation—the straw that broke the camel's back, so to speak. It was one of her dear friends who'd furnished a list of dates—luncheon with Mr. Thurston, the suspicious proximity of Mr. Thurston and Carol at a movie palace—"

"Stop it!" Alec ordered. With dignity he removed the pipe, with dignity knocked out its smoldering contents and placed it on the mantelpiece. "I can reassure Mrs. Thurston—I think I can. Without violating a confidence, I am certain that I can explain—"

"Splendid," Ruth said. "I hope you've got an equal confidence about your power for explaining why you happened to be dining Carol at the Café Rouge at the moment Mrs. Thurston was unburdening herself to me."

Which speech revealed Ruth at her most typical. She drops her bits of information with the devastating effect of block busters. The interesting part of it is that it's done in mischief rather than in malice, but the world-shaking is accomplished nevertheless.

Alec looked dumfounded. Also foolish. He said, "Whaat? How do you know?"

"I've spies out," Ruth said serenely. "Don't goggle so, darling. I knew fully three minutes before you came in.

No, I won't tell you who told me. It would simply prejudice you against a most worthy lady. And, of course, it wasn't just to spill gossip that she called me. She merely mentioned it in passing."

"I know who it was," Alec said grimly. "I saw her and there's nothing worthy about her. She's a pestiferous, gossiping busybody and you know it. Something else to talk about—you bet she had!—but this was the milk in the cocoanut, the—"

He had to stop then for the latest incumbent of the MacDonald kitchen had arrived to lean perilously against the swing door and intone doubtfully, "Dinner's ready, I guess, M'is MacDonald, if you want it."

The burden of proof was upon us. We moved forward.

Dinner was just what you might imagine. Flowers and candles, Ruth's contribution, and unseasoned, overcooked food, sloppily served, from the kitchen.

We talked polite nothings except for the moment when Ruth remarked, "If the infants had had to cope with this, I wouldn't have blamed them for ejecting it. But the cereal was all right—I cooked it myself. Never mind, darlings. Coffee and sandwiches after choir practice. We'll make up for it."

Dessert, a soggy apple pie, was soon over and we were back in the living room. Alec, with formal politeness, lit Ruth's cigarette and mine, and then took up his stance on the hearth.

"I presume," he began, "that I may now attempt an explanation?"

"Not to me," I said hastily. I stood up. "It's none of my affair. Besides—look at the time. I've got to go."

"This won't take a minute," Alec said ponderously and Ruth said, "Don't be silly, Tess, you've lots of time. Of course you want to hear. I certainly do. And all I've got to say is that what I'm going to hear had better be good—and I mean *good!*"

Alec glowered at her.

"If you're expecting Tess to do jury duty for you," he began stiffly, but Ruth cut him off. "'I'll be judge. I'll be jury, said cunning old Fury—' Never mind, pet. Nobody's blaming you. We know all about Carol Tolliver and her little tricks."

But Alec wasn't to be placated. "But you don't—that's the whole difficulty. I came back here to the house after I left you, Tess, though how Ruth found that out I don't pretend to know. I'd been feeling rotten all day and I wasn't up to facing Mrs. Thurston, so I decided to walk around the block and perhaps her car'd be gone when I got around again. It wasn't, and I went down past the church for the second time. That's when I saw Carol.

"She'd seen me coming and she waited for me. She said she wanted to talk and there I was. I couldn't bring her up to the house with Mrs. Thurston there, and I wouldn't take her into the church, and we couldn't just stand there. She had no hat and just one of those thin reversible coats, and it was cold by that time with a raw east wind that means snow before morning if I know anything about it. I asked her where she was going and she said to the Café, and I said I'd walk along with her. So I did." He stopped then, failed to continue.

Ruth gave him a quick look. "That makes dull enough telling, darling," she said gently.

"It was dull enough," he said grimly. "I walked with her—what is it?—three, four blocks but we didn't talk much. You can't, lurching along a slippery street with the wind howling in your ears. That's why I went into the Café with her. She sat down and ordered, and I had a cup of coffee, and then, somehow—everything fizzled out."

"You mean she didn't want to talk to you after all?" Ruth probed.

"She didn't tell me anything," Alec said slowly. "Oh, don't look like that—I think she intended to and then, for some reason, changed her mind. You know, as a rule, Carol's pretty sure of herself. She knows what she wants and she's—well, coldblooded about going after it. But to-night she wasn't like that at all. She seemed upset—nervous—no, there's even a stronger word. Jittery, that's it."

We digested this. "Oh, well," Ruth said at last. "I don't like them—the Tollivers. Mr. Tolliver is what my father'd call a dour man. As for the mother—" She made a gesture that disposed of the mother. "They're the sort of people who'd jump at the chance to go riding in your automobile, and then sue you for everything they thought they could get if you had an accident."

Having nothing to add to that, I kept still. I was wondering what in the world could be bothering Carol. Not money, surely—the Tollivers never had had much and, so far as I knew, they hadn't lost what they had. One of her clandestine love affairs gone wrong, perhaps. Or an outraged wife threatening reprisals. A baby in prospect—I doubted that. There was a shrewd streak in Carol. She wasn't the type to toss virtue away without getting full value for it. And just how and where the Thurstons fitted in . . .

Suddenly I had an idea. I said, "Do either of you remember when Blair Thurston was home last?"

I certainly hadn't intended to start anything, but non-intent is no excuse. Apparently I'd done it just the same. Their minds withdrew from mine so swiftly that I could almost feel the wind of passing. For just a minute there it was as though we were strangers and I had trespassed, unwittingly perhaps, but none the less unforgivably, upon some secret preserve.

Not even a glance flickered between them. There was only that queer breathlessness of silence, and then Alec said slowly, "Blair Thurston—whatever made you think of him?"

It was a little thing but it hurt. To find a barrier raised where never barrier'd been before . . . I got up and crossed to the hall closet where I'd left my coat. "No particular reason," I tossed over my shoulder. "I just happened to think of him."

Ruth followed me into the hall. "Word association," she said brightly. "I expect a psychiatrist or psychologist or whatever they are would make something of it. Like a lie detector. You know—where they say one thing and you answer another."

I agreed rather grimly. "We might play Truth some-time," I suggested. "You can get almost the same effect." At once I was ashamed. I came to the door of the living room and looked at Alec. "If you'll give me the list of hymns," I said.

"I'll get them—they're on the desk," Ruth said and de-parted.

I waited—Alec, having a large acquaintance with hymns, is capable of picking the most gosh-awful ones, usually unheard of in Dorchester and with a good average of elev-en verses or so which we sing to the bitter end. Frederick Brastock, the choirmaster, liked to have the numbers for practice, going on the assumption that the choir, at least, should be familiar with them. It was one of the few points on which we agreed.

Alec had come into the hall now and was regarding me thoughtfully. "No need to take any of this too seriously," he suggested, and I said, "Certainly not. I'm not a fool," and then Ruth came back with the hymns and it was time for me to go.

I promised to come back afterwards, give them an idea of the state of the public's pulse, as Ruth put it. "If Ran

Garrison is there, bring him along," was her parting shot. "We owe him some hospitality."

I parried that one neatly. Randolph Garrison was a new, very good-looking young man who had been imported, at considerable expense, to head the homicide department of the Dorchester police force. A particularly vicious scandal that had shaken not only city but state was responsible for his appointment. He was also a baritone and one of his first acts upon arrival in Dorchester had been to join St. Thomas' choir. On the strength of a half dozen movie and dinner dates, Ruth was convinced of his interest in me. I suspected her of wanting to further it with the match-making instinct inherent in women. I was even in favor of the furthering myself but I didn't want her to know it.

"If Ran Garrison is there," I said and laughed at her, "he can bring *me* here!"

We left it like that.

3

True to Alec's prediction, it was snowing when I came out of the house. The wind from the north drove the fine icy flakes in stinging pin pricks against my face. Already enough snow had fallen to cause drifting, and visibility was bad. The street lights and distant neon signs showed only as rounded blobs of light.

"A rough night in the Ozarks," I told myself as I drew the collar of my coat across my mouth. "I doubt if there'll be many out for practice but I'm not going to worry. If it gets too bad, I'll beg a bed from Ruth."

I had approximately a block of facing the wind to get around to the side door of the church—no good trying to cut across the lawn; a close-planted hedge of honeysuckle prevented that. I was gasping and breathless when I finally pushed open the door into the warmth and still security of the little entranceway that led upstairs.

The big roundish room which is my office by day is also used as the choir room. From it, on ordinary Sundays, by means of a door that opens into the body of the church far to the right, our brief processional wends its way. It contains—besides my office equipment—music files, oaken wardrobes for storing vestments and a grand piano about whose triangle Frederick Brastock, choirmaster of St.

Thomas, was now aligning a double row of chairs into a rough semicircle.

He vouchsafed me a single sulky glance but he didn't speak. Ours was a stormy feud that had had its inception the first night of the fall practice when he had evinced the singular belief that my position as church secretary automatically made me choir flunkey as well. Disabused of that notion, he had taken defeat badly. Since I steadfastly refused the responsibility for furniture rearrangement and since Oscar, accidentally-done-on-purpose, always forgot, he had to do it himself. He only tolerated me because there was a scarcity of contraltos in Dorchester, but his manner said distinctly that he didn't have to like doing it. He was a dapper, rather small man with snapping black eyes and hair, a fair example of the type of musician who, by shrewd exploitation of a small talent, has made what might be termed an outstanding business success. Certainly there were better, more conscientious voice teachers in Dorchester, but none so widely advertised.

Since our relations were those of armed neutrality—the music committee who considered that they paid their choirmaster enough so that he could move a few chairs if necessary, and Alec, being my authorities—I said, "Good evening" and left it to him to take it or leave it. He left it, unless a grunt could be construed a greeting.

Not so his wife. Mrs. Brastock was a little woman, a faded blond, thin and worried-looking. She was fussing over a pile of music sheets, sorting them by titles. She smiled brightly at me. "Good evening, Miss King. Isn't it a terrible night? I do think you were so brave to come."

"Not so brave," I said, bringing into view my heavy artillery on the chance that Mr. Brastock was going to be as nasty as the glint in his eye portended. "I was just next door. I had dinner with the MacDonalds."

"Oh, how nice for you!" Mrs. Brastock fluttered, but her husband's growl cut her off. "The dean send over those hymn numbers?" It was a question he asked every choir practice night in the hope, I suspected, of some day catching the two of us out.

I said that the dean had and produced them. At once Mrs. Brastock snatched them out of my hand. "I'll look them up," she said eagerly. "I can tell if they're familiar or not. Oh, dear, I do hope that they are!"

The worry in her voice made it appear a matter of national importance and, without conscious thought, both Frederick Brastock and myself stood stock-still awaiting the word.

It came. "Oh, they are!" she said. "All of them. Isn't that nice? I do think Dean MacDonald finds some of the oddest hymns. Do you suppose it's because he was educated in England?"

I said I didn't know. The fact was indisputable, but I suspected that the result arose less from British influence than from a deep interest and appreciation of the literature and hymnology of the church. I've known ministers who couldn't carry a tune. Alec possessed a ringing bass voice and frequently, when his ideas of tempo differed from the assorted ones of organist, choir and congregation, he not only carried tunes but ran away with them.

"I do wish the rest would hurry," Mrs. Brastock murmured. "Of course, if Mr. Garrison does come," she glanced archly at her husband, "we could have a quartet."

Frederick Brastock only grunted and I stifled a smile. One of the choirmaster's boasts is that he can teach anyone to sing and the consensus of opinion in Dorchester is that, in his wife, he has provided a horrible demonstration of his powers.

The beaver of my coat was heavily spotted with moisture. Thinking that it looked as though we were in for

a long wait and that I might as well make myself comfortable, I took the coat off, shook it and then draped it
over my desk chair. I was standing on one foot removing
an overshoe when the door into the chancel opened and
Charles Dennison walked in.

I'd known he was there. Ever since I'd come in my ears
had been assaulted with the peculiar, not-to-be-mistaken
combination of organ stops—*Vox Humana, Celeste* and *Vox
Angelica*—to which he was addicted. He called them the
"Heavenly Choir" and appeared to believe that their nasal
quiverings were of sufficient attraction to counterbalance
the childish mediocrity of the melodies he gave them to
voice. He was a little dried leaf of a man, well over sixty,
bald and almost toothless. His left hand was so crippled
with rheumatism that he had the use of but three fingers,
but those three scuttled over the keyboard with the agility
of spiders.

Only heaven and the music committee of St. Thomas
knew why we were saddled with him. Sentiment, presumably, for they certainly could take little pride in either his
reputation or performance. He did not even possess a large
personal following—than which there are few things that
loom so high in the minds of music committees. He was
cranky, untidy and taciturn and the average person disliked him on sight. Tonight he took in the room with one
glance, then shuffled in my direction. Behind his glasses,
his light little eyes were malignant.

"You tell that Tolliver girl," he rasped, "that if she
wants to keep on practicing on this organ, she's got to quit
leaving it open and running!"

I said, "What?" rather stupidly. "Are you sure? Because
Carol never does . . ."

She didn't either. We've had plenty of students practicing there who'd been careless about lights and switches,

but Carol Tolliver was not one of them. To her the organ
was the same as a living thing and she cherished it.

He was glaring at me. "Of course I'm sure! Didn't I say
so? When I came in about seven there was no sign of her,
but the lights were on and the organ unlocked and the
motor running. I guess that proves it!"

I guessed it did. Carol, at the moment, was the only
person privileged to use the organ. I said, "She was still in
the church when I left tonight. She was on her way downstairs to see Oscar. Then she was going to get something
to eat and come back to work until choir practice. Are you
sure that she hadn't just gone downstairs for a minute?"

"She wasn't here," he insisted stubbornly. "There wasn't
a sign of her—hat or coat or anything. Wasting electricity
like that and the motor heating up—some day it'll burn
out on you and it'll serve you and that dumb Oscar, who's
too lazy to watch it for oil, good and proper!"

Since I was not disposed to answer that, he looked
around for a new subject to quarrel about. He found it
in the chairs that semicircled the piano. "What in time's
going on here anyway?" he demanded querulously. "Going
to practice out here tonight? What's the matter with using
the organ?"

"We will—later," Brastock assured him smoothly. He
was well aware that such suavity of manner was the surest
way to goad the old fellow to extremes of anger and he
utilized the knowledge in the hope of sometime profiting
thereby. "We're going to work on the Easter cantata and
some of the choir members feel that it is—er—easier for
them to hear the separate parts with the piano."

Dennison looked at him suspiciously and then let it go.
"All right," he grumbled. "I don't mind, but if they knew
anything about music . . . The Easter cantata, you said?
Maybe I better take a look at it myself."

He sat down at the piano and began to rattle off something that had a vague likeness to the opening chorus. Frederick Brastock closed his eyes in apparent agony but he said nothing. There was no good. One of his crosses was that the music that appeared upon the sheets Charles Dennison propped before him and the music that emerged from beneath his fingers bore only a superficial resemblance one to the other. Too old to feel the urge to practice, too self-complacent to feel the need, the old man depended upon his wits to carry him through. They accommodated him well. He was a sight reader second to none, a rearranger of some ability, and a faker par excellence. He always got by, but with such a narrow margin that, invariably, he left you doubting your own sanity, despairing of the discrepancies you'd caught between eye and ear, wondering who was wrong—you or he?

He was still grumbling. He left off playing to demand, "Where's the light? It's too dark over here. How'd you expect me to read notes when I can't see them to read?"

Frederick Brastock muttered something under his breath—something about he didn't know what the hell good *reading* notes did if you didn't intend to play them after they were read. Aloud he spoke with calm. "Miss King, may we borrow your desk lamp?"

I got it for him, helped him to find an outlet into which to plug it. I didn't like the man but there were times when he had my sympathy. This was one of them.

Feet thumped upon the stair just then and Bill Carter, first of the choir members to arrive, blew in, hat and overcoat powdered over with snow. He was a big black bear of a man who had come to Dorchester the spring before to open a loan company. No one knew him very well but the Brastocks made a big fuss over him because of his low, growly bass voice, the only real bass the choir possessed. For my part, I didn't like the man. He did entirely too much laughing and joking with the high school girls in the choir. Georgia Brastock had told me she understood there was a "Mrs. Carter" somewhere in the offing but thus far none of us had seen her.

"Whew!" he said as he shouldered out of his wet overcoat. "Not a bad night—if you're going to spend it at home. Bet you a nickel, Brastock, nobody else'll come tonight."

"You lose, then," Frederick Brastock said imperturbably, and even as he spoke the others began to straggle in. Eight or ten sopranos, three altos, the two tenors upon whom every other church in town was casting covetous eyes, four bassos of assorted voice and ability. One by one they divested themselves of outer garments, offered their impressions of wind and weather, and then slumped into the chairs clustered about the piano. I suppressed a smile at Leota Erickson's unobtrusive entrance. She had literally slipped in—between two of the heavier-set members of the choir. Poor Leota—she was about fifty years old, a school-teacher, and punctuality was an obsession with her. It must have been a terrific blow to her pride to be this late. Frederick Brastock adjusted his music stand, rapped on it with his baton.

"We'll begin with the chorus on page twenty-four," he said. "Altos take up the lead—we'll omit the solo. All right—one, two, three, four—sing!"

The others obliged but not me. Carol Tolliver had not come. Neither had Ran Garrison. While the rest of the altos in company with the tenors droned an assertion that "there was a green hill far away," I sat and worried. Not about Ran Garrison—he was old enough to look out for himself. But Carol's absence bothered me. The things that Alec had said had been disturbing—well, not so much what he'd said, for he'd actually known nothing, but the things that must underlie such knowledge, give it foundation.

What in the world had happened to the girl? It wasn't
like her not to appear at choir practice, particularly on a
night like this when she was already in the building. And
apparently she had been, if Charles Dennison was to be
believed. Mentally I went back over the story. She'd been
ready to leave when I was. I had heard her lock the organ.
I had watched her as she went down the aisle toward the
basement. Alec had met her shortly afterward, left her in
the Café Rouge. She had come back to the church, re-
opened the organ, set its motor running.

Frederick Brastock was scowling at me, but I didn't
care. Let him scowl. The door at the foot of the stairs
shut with a bang and I nearly broke my neck trying to see
who was coming. But it wasn't Carol. It was Mary Collins, snow-covered and vociferous with apologies to which
Brastock listened in icy silence.

She took the chair next to mine and at once began to
rattle questions at me in a piercing whisper. Wasn't it perfectly awful weather out? She'd had to stand on a corner
for hours waiting for a bus and when it finally came she'd
had to stand all the way down town. Didn't I think the bus
service was terrible since the war? Was she awfully late,
and had we been practicing long, and what page were we
on anyway?

I answered her, conscious of Frederick Brastock's glare,
as quietly and briefly as I could. Mary was one of those
people created for the express purpose of driving choir
directors out of their minds. She was a thin, undernour-
ished woman of thirty-odd who spent her days in a bookkeeper's cage at one of our chain groceries. With nothing
to differentiate herself from the common herd, she had
long ago found satisfactory distinction in delicate health.
According to her, she balanced eternally upon the edge
of a nervous breakdown. Perhaps she did—I wouldn't
know. Certainly there was nothing healthy-looking about

her thin, straggly hair that not even a permanent could tame, her pale eyes blinking behind thick lenses, her heavily-veined, paper-dry hands. Just looking at her was enough to make me shudder. She exemplified so perfectly all I hoped I'd never be.

The rehearsal dragged on. We passed from chorus to chorus but I scarcely noticed. I was beginning to be definitely worried by this time. No need to be, I assured myself, except that Alec had alarmed me and, after all, what did he *know?* Nothing. It was entirely possible that the girl had been taken ill or that she'd been called away, only . . . It wasn't like her to be careless about the organ.

I was seriously considering making an excuse to go downstairs and interview Oscar when the telephone rang shrilly. It didn't take Brastock's jerk of the head to get me over to my desk. I had the wild idea that the caller might be Carol.

It wasn't. The voice was a man's, low, guarded, faraway and disturbingly familiar. I knew it and yet I didn't, I was so busy trying to identify it that the words spoken hardly registered.

"Is this the church? I'd like to speak to Miss Tolliver."

Automatically I said, "She isn't here."

"Not there?" The voice gathered volume. "Are you sure? But she is—she told me to call her there."

"Well, she's not," I said flatly. "Perhaps she'll be in later. Would you like—"

"Listen," the voice interrupted. "This is important. Would you mind looking around? Maybe she's downstairs."

"She's not here," I said again. "Who is this, please? I can have her call you . . ."

There was no answer. Only a click. The person at the other end of the line had hung up.

Regardless of the curious stares I was getting from the rest of the choir, I jiggled the receiver up and down. When a bored voice responded, I said, "Central, we were cut off. Would you ring that number again?"

"What number were you calling?" The voice was worse than bored; it was completely indifferent.

"I don't know," I said. "The call came here. I was cut off."

"Just a minute, please." I waited through a series of clicks. Then Central spoke again. "I'm sorry. The party who called you has hung up."

I'd known that myself. Disgusted, I disconnected and stood for a second puzzling over that voice. It *had* been familiar. I'd heard it before. But when? Where? Man's or woman's—I wasn't even sure of that. Its quality was light for a man, heavy for a woman. It could have been a boy, perhaps. Could it have been one of her brothers? Was that why it was familiar? Only in that case, why the attempt at secrecy? I gave it up.

The choir were surrendering their cantatas, filing toward the chancel where the finishing touches would be placed upon Sunday's anthem. Charles Dennison was the first through the door, Brastock, save for myself, the last. When he saw me coming, he paused and waited. "Who was that?"

I shrugged. "Someone for Carol Tolliver. She's not here."

He looked at me queerly. "So it would appear," he said dryly and went on.

I followed.

St. Thomas' is old and the choir stalls, at festival times, are inadequate for the size of our choir. There are three rows of stalls on each side, the first two on the same level, the last, which is used by the men, raised one step. Behind that last row, on the side on which altos and bassos sit, is a narrow, carpeted space between stalls and organ. Beyond this, oaken doors lead into the recesses of the organ. Here temporary chairs can be placed if needed. On the opposite side, the organ console, which is movable, stands flat against the wall behind which are more organ chambers.

I took my customary seat, third in the row of contraltos—there were five of us now. I opened my copy of the proposed anthem—Dvorak's *Blessed Jesu*—saw that it was uninterestingly familiar and once more gave myself over to meditation. It had been a dull, dispiriting, uneasy evening. I wondered if it would grow better or worse when I returned to the MacDonalds'. I wondered what Alec would say when I reported on the latest in the Carol Tolliver mix-up. I wondered—and then immediately caught my breath in tremendous relief. Why, of course! What was the matter with me? There was no mystery any more. It was solved. Carol had gone to Alec. She had wanted to talk to him. Perhaps her need—alone there in the church—had become too pressing to be denied. That could be the reason she'd gone so precipitately, forgetting even to turn off lights or power. It would explain, too, the absence of her outer garments. Probably, when I got to the MacDonalds', I would find her there. It was even possible, I thought, building it up, that I'd passed her in the thick of the storm when I was on my way to choir practice. At once, I discarded that. It was a lovely theory but it just wouldn't work. I knew that I'd seen no one on that lonely walk, that no one had passed me by.

Brastock was satisfied at last, indicated that we were dismissed. Poor man! Choir practices were the only times when he got the chance to crack his whip. On Sundays, Charles Dennison, with his back safely to choir and choirmaster alike, went his own sweet way and swept the rest of us with him.

All around me, the others were stirring, the women gathering up purses and gloves, the men pushing toward the choir room where the lighting of going-home cigarettes was permissible.

Mary Collins joggled my arm. "Are you going to stay here all night?" she demanded. "If you are, I wish you'd let me past."

"Sorry," I said and stood up. My purse was tight in my right hand but, as I turned to go, my anthem, held loosely in my left, slipped from my fingers and fluttered over the top of the pew back.

"Oh, bother!" I said. "You'll have to wait a minute." I knelt on the seat to retrieve it.

Even in the act of lifting it, I could feel its sticky wetness. I thought, "Queer—someone must have had a lot of snow on their feet . . ." and glanced at it casually. And then more closely, in horror and disbelief. For it was no snow that had dampened this corner. It was something red and viscous—like paint—only it wasn't paint. No paint looked like that. No paint felt like that. With a shudder I looked at my fingers. They were red and sticky too.

It was then that I screamed.

4

Afterwards I could have kicked myself, I who'd always been proud of my coolness in an emergency. At that, screaming was no worse than several of the other things that happened, and I had good excuse.

The scream did things to the others. Even now I have only to close my eyes and I can see them again—the men crowding back; Charles Dennison swinging about on his organ bench and peering over the top of his glasses; Frederick Brastock letting the music stand he'd been adjusting fall with a crash; Georgia Brastock's open mouth and wide, frightened eyes.

Brastock was the first to recover. He said, "What the—? Miss King! What's the matter? What is it?"

I had managed to sit down. I said, "I don't know," but it was more to convince myself than because I believed it. I stared at the fingers of my left hand. "I don't know," I said again.

Mary Collins was looking over my shoulder. "I do. It's—I think it's blood," she said and promptly fainted.

I looked at Brastock who was standing in front of me. I held out my hand. "It's back there," I said. "On the floor. I dropped my music."

There was a diversion then. Phil Smedley, a nice pink-cheeked youngster whose draft board had rejected him for a heart murmur, said, "But—but that's where *I* sat—back there." As though impelled, he let his eyes go downward. "Look!" he said, and with the word his voice cracked, jumped half an octave. "I must have stood in it! I'm—I'm making footprints!"

He turned lime-green, clapped his hand over his mouth, and fled. In the temporary silence we could hear the desperate plunging of his feet upon the stairs.

It was a new voice that broke the silence. It said, "Sorry to be so late but it couldn't be helped. And, by the way, what's going on here anyway? What have you been doing to Smedley? He almost knocked me down— Oh!" The voice paused briefly; when it resumed again it had a slightly official tinge. "What's happened to Miss Collins?"

The belated Ran Garrison had arrived.

There are those who think Randolph Garrison an exceptionally attractive young man. There are others who call him wooden and expressionless. I had never seriously considered the question but at that moment, standing there, snow heavy upon his shoulders and upon the brim of his soft hat, he looked beautiful to me. He was sense and sanity in what had become a lunatic world.

"She's fainted," Frederick Brastock said of Mary Collins. He sat down heavily, as though his legs had failed him. "Look, Garrison—you're the police, aren't you? I think you're the one who's going to have to tell us what happened. All I know is that Miss King dropped some music into what seems to be a puddle of blood. . . ."

Ran Garrison listened to our tale without comment. He looked at my hands, at the anthem with its sticky thick blotches, at the heel and toe marks that Philip Smedley had left upon the soft pile of the carpet. He leaned over the back of the pew and scrutinized the floor. "All right," he said at last. "I don't know what you've got here but we'll find out. Someone go after Smedley—see that he comes back. A couple of you men carry Miss Collins into the choir room—see if you can revive her. The women had better go too. Not you, Miss King. I may need your help."

I was fighting down a nausea as real as Smedley's. I said, "My hands—can't I wash them?"

"Is there a lavatory up here?"

I shook my head. "I'll go downstairs. Someone can come with me."

He said, "No!" quite firmly to that. "For the present I think we'll all stay where we are. Here!" He whipped a clean linen handkerchief from his pocket and dabbed it in the snow puddles that were melting on his hat brim. "See if you can manage with this."

I took it gratefully, began to scrub. He looked down at me, spoke gently. "You'll have to move, you know. We want to carry Miss Collins out."

So I did. Into the pew in front of me. None of the others had moved as yet. I had an instant's glance at their faces, strangely unaltered. Later on, when they knew, horror would come. Now they revealed only the fascination that the unknown engenders.

Ran Garrison was trying to clear them out. "Will you all go into the other room, please? Mrs. Brastock, won't you lead the way? I'm sure Miss Collins will need your help. If you'll just wait quietly, we'll report as soon as possible."

They went, reluctantly. I didn't turn my head but I heard the shuffle of their feet, heard Ran's voice, "Brastock, will you stay? I may need someone . . ."

Charles Dennison was standing before me. I saw the unpressed bagginess of his trousers, his cracked, unpolished shoes. He bent down, bringing his face within my vision's range. His breath, fetid and sickening, was on my cheek. He said, "Look—that Tolliver girl—think maybe it's her?"

There it was, the thing I hadn't wanted to think about, out in the open. My hands were clean now, the handkerchief encarmined. I pushed it away, far from me. I said, "Don't. I don't know. I don't want to think about it."

"Maybe you're going to have to," he said shrewdly. "She didn't come to practice but she was here—tonight. I told you I found the organ running."

"I know," I said. "You told me. I think you'd better tell Mr. Garrison too."

He chewed on something in the mysterious depths of his cheek—candy I supposed. He was addicted to small balls of sweetness; carried them loosely in his pockets. "Maybe I will," he said thoughtfully. "And then again—maybe I won't have to."

With that he joined the others behind me. I heard the shake of wood against wood and then Ran Garrison's voice. "I'd like to get this pew out of here."

"You can't," Brastock said wearily. "Not without tools. It's bolted to the floor."

"Oh, well, let it go," Ran said. "I thought it would give us more room. But perhaps the door will open wide enough . . ."

The door! What were they talking about? What door? But I knew. There was only one.

"There's nothing to open it with," Ran was saying. "I'll have to force it. Got a knife?"

I managed to find words. "If it's the organ door you mean," I said drearily, "it's locked." And then, fearfully, "Is it?"

Ran came around beside me. "Yes," he said gently. "There's a trail of blood leading to it. I'm sorry. Do you have the key?"

"Yes," I said. "Yes, I have the key. I'll get it."

I almost ran out of there. Into the big room where the others waited.

They looked at me and their faces shouted questions. I
had no answers for them. I said, "It's—whatever it is—is
back in the organ chambers. I'm getting the key."

Queer how your eyes function. Even as I fumbled for
the heavy chain of keys, securely hidden behind box files
in the lower drawer of my desk, I was seeing them. They
had laid Mary Collins upon some chairs. Someone had
opened a window and Georgia Brastock was patting snow,
taken from the ledge, against her forehead. Philip Smedley
huddled in a chair beside the door. His face was green no
longer but it might as well have been.

I found the keys. I said, "I don't know—Mr. Garrison
didn't say to but I think someone ought to call Dean Mac-
Donald and tell him what—what's happened." I turned
then and fled.

Ran met me at the chancel door, took the keys. He said,
"Go back, my dear. You needn't stay . . ." and I said, "But
I can't—I've got to know."

I did, too. There are worse things than not knowing.

I stayed out of their way, back against the communion
rail, but I heard the rasp of the key as it went into the
lock, the grating swing of the door as it opened. There
was an instant's silence and then a quick drawn breath,
Charles Dennison's queer little cackle. "By the great gollies! It isn't her after all!" and Ran's instant, "Isn't her?
Who? What do you mean?"

I said, "Who—who is it?" It was Frederick Brastock
who answered me. He said, "It's Oscar. The janitor. His
throat's been cut. From ear to ear."

I looked then through the angled oaken door. I saw the
raw wood of wall and scaffolding, blue denim that huddled against the bellows. There seemed to be a great deal
of blood . . .

I didn't need to stay any longer. I knew now. I could
go. My feet stumbled a little. I had to hold to the sides of
the chancel door as I went through.

It was just the same in the big room except that Mary Collins was sitting up. The first thing I saw was the dark, terror of her face, the first sound I heard her voice.

"Did they—what is it, Tess?"

"It's Oscar," I said dully. My legs had completely given out. I reached for a chair, sat in it. "Someone cut his throat."

There was fear in their faces now, horror, as I'd known there would be. They knew now. Before it had been an intangible thing, impersonal, although I think we'd all accepted the premise that the red tide must mean murder. But it could have been anyone. Now it wasn't. Now I had given murder a face, a name, and detachment failed us.

They were coming now, the others, led by Frederick Brastock. For the first time since I'd known him, he'd lost his arrogant assurance. He looked tired and old. The black of his hair and eyes seemed to have dulled. Even his crisp little mustache appeared wilted.

Ran had Charles Dennison by the arm. He was saying, "But you must have had a reason, surely. What was it?" and the old man was whining, "Does a man have to have a reason to say what's in his mind? I said it wasn't her—that Tolliver girl—and it wasn't. Just detecting, Mr. Garrison, just doing a little detecting and no harm done because I was wrong."

Ran said, "Hum-m" and let him go. He looked at me and said, "Did you tell them?" and, when I nodded, he said, "Good. Now that you all know what's happened, I'm sure you won't mind a little inconvenience. I'm going to call the department and have them send over some men. They'll want to ask questions, take your fingerprints and so on. After that you will be allowed—presumably—to go home."

He didn't wait for comment on that but crossed to the telephone. As he gave the number, the outer door at the foot of the stairs banged and feet came slapping up the stairs.

The feet belonged to Alec. Looking at him, I judged that, while he might be clothed, he was hardly in his right mind for, despite the weather, he wore heelless leather house slippers. I shuddered to think of the walk he'd taken through what must now be deep snow and I wondered how he'd managed to get the slippers past Ruth's eagle eye.

He said, "Ran!" and there was something imploring in his tone. Ran replaced the handset and crossed over to him. He put a hand on Alec's arm.

"I'm sorry, Alec," he said. "We just found your janitor's body. Someone's cut his throat."

"Oscar?" Alec sounded dazed. "Somebody—you mean it's murder?"

"It couldn't be anything else," Ran said evenly. "He was in one of the organ chambers and the door locked on the outside. I didn't move him but I saw no sign of the weapon."

Alec said nothing. He stood quietly, looking past us and over us, and I wondered just how much he was seeing. After a minute he said slowly, "Oscar—the poor old fellow. He never harmed anyone . . ." and with that he walked straight to the chancel door and through it. It closed behind him.

I looked anxiously at Ran Garrison but he made no attempt to stop him or warn him to leave things untouched. Perhaps he knew it wasn't necessary, that Alec's interest was not, at the moment, in temporal bodies.

The police arrived before Alec came back through the chancel door. There were a half a dozen of them and they carried cameras and other paraphernalia. One of them, a stout reddish man, gave a half salute and said, "Doc Morton'll be right along, Chief."

Ran Garrison said, "Good." He went on, giving directions in crisp low tones. He wanted pictures, fingerprinting of the organ doors, the organ chamber interior, the

adjacent pews. The body was to be left untouched until
the doctor arrived. He said, "You'll have to wait a minute." His eyes were on the chancel door.

It opened and Alec came through, the slap of his slipper soles disconcerting upon the oaken floor. He said to
Ran, "Your men are prompt."

Ran said that they were. His tone intimated they'd better be. "I'm afraid we're going to have to let off a few flash
bulbs, dust some powder around." He looked anxiously at
Alec.

The balance between church and state is always pre-
carious but Alec's nod gave consent. He said, "I suppose
you've searched the church?"

Ran said not yet. There hadn't been time. "That'll be
your job, Murphy," he told a lean dark Irishman. "Take
Hanson with you and go over this place with a fine-tooth
comb. Wait a minute before you start. What about doors,
Alec?"

There were three, Alec told him lifelessly. The main
door was locked every night at five unless there was to
be an evening service. This door—he waved a hand at the
stairway—was opened evenings when there was to be choir
practice, guild meetings or the like. The third one led
directly to the basement, Oscar's quarters, and the kitchen.

"But it's locked," he said. "Now. I came out my own back
door, cut across the lawn. I tried it but I couldn't get in."

"Then anyone in the church would have had to leave by
this door?" Ran asked thoughtfully.

Alec shook his head. "They could get out. All of the
doors have night latches."

Ran said, "All right," and looked at Murphy. "You can get
going. I don't expect you'll find anything but you can try."

They started, hesitated, and came back. "Which way
to the basement, Chief?" Alec showed them the door that
led to the north aisle of the church with its corresponding

door into the entrance. "There's a stairway that leads down. You'll want lights. Tess—"

I moved to the board and pressed all the switches down. Some of the lights would be further controlled by wall switches but they could find that out for themselves.

Dr. Morton, a nice, white-headed old fellow whose reputation for cleverness and ability was unquestioned, had arrived. He was the result of one of the reforms Ran had insisted upon: that the medical officer be also a practicing physician. He glanced shrewdly at the silent choir members, wrung Alec's hand, and murmured, "A bad business, my boy—a bad business," and then trotted off in the wake of camera and fingerprint men.

We were alone. That is, as alone as twenty-five people can be.

Ran looked at us and smiled a little. I suppose we did look pretty doleful. "Relax," he said. "This isn't going to be so bad. I don't think any of you killed poor old Oscar. But we've got to have something for the record—names, addresses, telephone numbers, time of arrival—that sort of thing. After that you can go home. Now, who's going to be first?"

I can't say there was a rush of candidates for the honor. I don't know whether they were wary of police procedure, afraid of being dismissed too soon for fear they'd miss something, or just too numbed with shock to volunteer. Eventually it was Miss Erickson who was chosen.

As I sat there and listened to Ran's crisp questions and the muddle of her answers, I thought that questioning the choir was going to be a complete flop. What did they know of murder? Or even of Oscar? Leota Erickson was typical. She'd sung in St. Thomas' choir for the last thirty-five years and I'm not exaggerating. I'd heard her boasting of it often enough. She lived with her mother in a neat little cottage on Vine Street. It was twenty-three blocks from the church and she had to walk, but she never missed a church service or a choir practice. Tonight she'd been a little late—because of weather. She'd come in just ahead of Mr. Smedley and behind Mrs. Winters. She was sure they would remember.

It was evident that she didn't like the idea of having her fingerprints taken but she didn't protest. She couldn't. It would be out of character for the forward-looking educator she claimed to be. "I suppose," she sighed as Ran manipulated her fingers from stamp to record card, "that the day will come when fingerprinting of all citizens will be compulsory."

"No doubt," Ran agreed politely. "Well, I think that's all, Miss Erickson. You can go home."

I had always liked Philip Smedley. Now he gave evidence that my liking was based on something more than instinct. "If you'll take me next," he suggested, "and if Miss Erickson doesn't mind waiting, I can drive her home. I have my car here."

Miss Erickson agreed effusively and Ran, after a questioning glance at the others, motioned toward the chair he'd drawn before my desk. "All right," he said. "Let's see if I've got this straight. You're Philip Smedley, you live at 724 West Sixteenth Street and you're a clerk at the Gunderson Clothing Store. Did you go home for dinner tonight?"

Philip Smedley never answered. At least, not then. He was half rising in his chair. "What's that?" he said. "What is it?"

We all heard it then. Feet that were running in the north aisle. There were confused shouts from the men employed in the chancel and then the small door that led from the body of the church was flung open. Murphy's face, pale and sweating, thrust at us.

"Chief!" he said. "Chief—you better come downstairs. Quick. We found another one—a dame this time—throat's been cut just like the other. She's down in the janitor's apartment—the knife's there too."

Carol Tolliver had been found.

5

It was Charles Dennison who had the first word. He said, "Great jumping gollies, I was right after all!" He sounded awed at his own perspicacity.

Ran Garrison was on his feet. He said, "Cooper, take over here. No one is to leave until I give the word."

Cooper stiffened. He said, "Okay, Chief. Do they talk?" and Ran said, "If they feel like it. For myself, I'm speechless. Will you come, Alec?"

They went out. I heard Ran's call for Dr. Morton and then nothing but receding footsteps. They went at decent sober pace. There was no running now nor need. The tale was told.

Charles Dennison was the hero of the hour and he made the most of it. Over and over he told his story of arrival at the church—seven o'clock for he'd heard the town clock strike as he turned in—of finding, against all regulations, the organ lights on and the motor running. "I shut it off quick," he said virtuously. "Not that it'd have hurt the organ any—it's the motor downstairs, Oscar never watched it like he ought. It takes a quart of oil every week or so and if it doesn't get it, it gets hot. Lots of good motors are spoiled by no looking after. Not that everybody thinks about them . . ."

"Oh, forget the motor!" Bill Carter said rudely. So far as he was concerned, Charles Dennison was no more than a wordy old man; the others might regard him as a landmark of St. Thomas' if they liked. He walked over and stood in front of Dennison. "What made you think it was the Tolliver girl?"

"Well, who else could it have been?" Dennison demanded. "She's the only one they let practice here and now look what's come of it! Maybe now they'll pay attention to me when I tell them it doesn't do the organ any good nor the church neither having youngsters running in and out as they like, wasting good electricity—"

"Oh, rats, Dennison!" Frederick Brastock said. He looked better, almost like himself again. He had lighted a cigarette and was half-sitting on the edge of the desk. "You're completely off the beam! There's not much connection between practicing on an organ and murder. I grant you the fact that she practiced over here—alone—might have made it easier for her murderer, but even so he'd need a reason. She wasn't killed just because she practiced here. Motive—my dear chap—you've got to consider motive. Take my word for it, that's what the police will do." Lazily his eyes flicked over us, came back to rest on Dennison's truculent face. "Better think fast, Charlie. We all know you couldn't stand the kid."

"Why, you—you—" Dennison sputtered but there was no bite in it. It was the weak and futile rage of an old man and he knew it. "If this was twenty years back you wouldn't be saying things like that to me and you know it! And so far's not liking her goes—it seems to me I recollect some talk around that you liked her a little bit too much! And you can just pack that into your pipe and try to smoke it!"

In one fluid movement Brastock came off the desk edge. "Why, you addlepated old gossip!" he began furiously only to be stopped by the phlegmatic Cooper. "Cut it, you two! The chief didn't say anything about free-for-alls. Besides—haven't you guys got any respect for where you are?"

Brastock subsided, glowering, but there was a certain jauntiness in the way Charles Dennison flipped a candy ball into his mouth and looked around with a satisfied nod. It was a minor war but he figured he'd won it.

This episode rather removed any enthusiasm for further conversation which we might have had. Miss Erickson did say, "But of course we don't know yet that it is Carol," but no one responded to her hopefulness.

For my part, I was too sick at heart to want to talk. Perhaps we didn't know and wouldn't until Ran and Alec came back, but reason agreed with Charles Dennison. Who else could it have been? Who else would have known where I kept the organ key or how to distinguish between the switches on the board so that just the right lights would come on?

Suddenly I stiffened. If it came to that, who would know about the keys that were always secreted so carefully behind the file boxes in my deep desk drawer? It wasn't a matter of common knowledge. The doors into the organ chambers were always locked. They had to be. Otherwise the doors swung open and there would be the danger of stray youngsters getting in and damaging the expensive "innards." Oscar would know where to find them, of course, and Alec and I, Charles Dennison certainly, Frederick Brastock perhaps, Carol, the organ tuner who came and went at his own convenience—who else? I didn't know. Any one of a hundred people—women who'd wanted the kitchen unlocked during one of Oscar's infrequent absences from his post; church wardens who developed sudden desires to inspect the furnace rooms or supply cabinets; the Sunday School superintendent without doubt; heaven only knew who else. Probably anyone who'd ever sat in the office and watched me handle them.

I shut my eyes and wondered why the organ doors had been unlocked in the first place. Oh, why skirt around it? That wasn't what I meant at all. What was bothering me was the reason the body'd been placed in the organ chamber. Surely there were better hiding places. Offhand I could think of half a dozen. The body of the church, for instance. It wouldn't have been lighted—not for tonight. A body'd be only a darker shadow among the pews. Or there were Sunday School rooms in the basement, supply closets, vestibules, lavatories—any one of them safer, less vulnerable to discovery. Unless the time element intruded and this was the most convenient . . .

I wasn't a policeman and I didn't know anything about detecting but I decided that, if I had been, the first thing I'd want to know was why Oscar had been upstairs at all.

I let my breath go out on a long sigh. Of course. That was it. Oscar'd been the one who'd unlocked those organ doors. Probably something had gone wrong with the organ. The swell pedal perhaps—there was a screw that worked out every once in a while—and Oscar knew how to fix it. Carol would have called him. To get at the recalcitrant screw, he'd have to unlock the organ doors and climb the little ladder that lay flat against the wall up to the platform that held the wilderness of pipes. He would have left the key swinging in the lock . . .

I was relieved. I even congratulated myself upon my reasoning. It took care of the key question nicely and also of who originally had opened the organ doors.

Only it didn't. Because, although Oscar might well have been the one to open the doors—probably was—he certainly hadn't been the one to close and lock them again.

Nor had he been the one to return the keys to their original hiding place.

Well, there I was. Nowhere at all. As a reconstructionist of crime, I was a brilliant failure! What might have happened wasn't necessarily what *did*.

Someone sat down beside me and I opened my eyes to meet Georgia Brastock's anxious gaze. She patted my hand. She said, "You feel badly, don't you, Miss King? I'm so sorry. Naturally you'd know Oscar better than the rest of us and Carol Tolliver too. Oh, dear, I *do* hope there's some mistake and that it's not her—her body downstairs!"

Well, there'd been no mistake about Oscar's, I thought grimly. And there seemed little doubt that there was a body downstairs. I wondered, given a choice, just who I'd prefer it to be, other than Carol Tolliver. I wondered who Georgia Brastock would prefer it to be. I murmured something inarticulate.

"She was such a pretty little thing," she was continuing. "Frederick—my husband, that is—thought she had a very great talent. He—we both tried to help her. She wanted so much to go away and study and she had no money. You knew that she played accompaniments for Frederick's voice pupils and that he paid her? She was at the studio a good deal. I suppose that the police will want to question us about that."

There was something very sweet and eager about her at that moment. The fact that the information was unsolicited didn't alter the matter. It mightn't even be true. I didn't know about that. But it was evident that she'd heard some of the stories about her husband and Carol and was putting on the best face possible. She was telling a good story. I hoped she got to Frederick Brastock with it before the police intervened. It would be a pity if their stories didn't agree.

I patted *her* hand. I said, "I wouldn't worry. We all knew her. They'll probably have questions to ask of all of us."

I stopped there because the little twitters of talk about us were quieting. The room was dead still. I knew the reason. Ran and Alec were coming back.

They were stern-faced, tight-lipped. Alec stood back against the door. It was Ran who told us, told us in a voice flat with emotion restrained.

It was Carol's body they had found. It was lying on the floor of the living room in Oscar's meager apartment. The door to the apartment was open but the room had been unlighted when Murphy flashed his torch inside. She had been killed in the same manner as Oscar, her throat cut. It had not been an easy death. Slashes on her hands showed how she had struggled to defend herself. Perhaps she had not died swiftly enough, or perhaps the murderer became impatient because there were also stab wounds in her heart.

"If there are some of you who wish to make telephone calls," Ran said still in that clipped cold voice, "you may. I shall have to detain you for some time. There will be the matter of definite times to establish. You will have to answer questions. There was a great deal of blood in the room downstairs. It is unthinkable that the murderer could have escaped unmarked. I shall want to examine your clothing. In the meantime, if you have relatives who may become alarmed at your absence—" He gestured toward the telephone.

Alec was buttoning his overcoat. I went over to him. I said, "Where are you going?" and he looked at me as though I were a stranger. "To the Tollivers."

I could have wept. It was the first time I'd thought of them. I said, "Oh, poor Mrs. Tolliver. She was so proud of Carol. But, Alec— must you go alone? Wouldn't you like me to come too—or Ruth?"

He said, "No. Ruth can go tomorrow." The overcoat was buttoned. He looked vaguely about as though for a hat. He hadn't had one when he came in, and I said, "My dear, you'll have to go over to the house. Don't look—you were bareheaded. I know it. And your feet—you'll have to change your shoes . . ."

He looked down, seeing the slippers as for the first time. The sight seemed to waken him. He said, "Ran, come over here . . ." and when Ran had come, "Look. I'm going to have to go over to the house. That means telling Ruth. I didn't want to do it now but I can't help myself. I've got to have shoes. Will you let Tess come with me? She didn't have anything to do with this—you know that. Carol was alive when Tess left the church—she was with me in the Café after that. Ask Miss Erickson—she'll tell you."

Ah, I thought. So Miss Erickson was the pestiferous old busybody.

"Tess had dinner with us. She probably wasn't the first one here—"

"No," I said. "The Brastocks were here when I came."

"There—you see." Alec moved his hands imploringly. "I wouldn't ask it, Ran, only Ruth's going to be shocked and—and frightened. If I could stay with her but—I don't like the idea of leaving her alone with a murderer armed with a knife ramping around."

"He hasn't got the knife now, Alec," Ran said gently. "We have it."

"I know." Alec looked physically sick for a moment. "He used a butcher knife—one of the ones I sharpened this afternoon," he told me. "I'd left them lying on Oscar's table."

"Alec, for the love of mercy!" I said. I could feel myself going green.

He looked at me absently. "Sorry, Tess. Well, is it all right, Ran? Will you let her go?"

Ran agreed. "The others won't like it but if Carol was alive when Tess left here and you say she was with Ruth and you until she came over for choir practice—"

"The Brastocks can tell you," I said eagerly. Now with escape in my hand, so to speak, I was realizing just how much I wanted to go. "They were here when I came over. Charles Dennison, too."

"All right," Ran said in sudden decision. "You can go. Get your coat."

I flew to obey. The others weren't liking it much, I could tell by their faces, but no one spoke. Alec waited for me by the door, and as I came up Ran was scribbling something on a card. "I've a man down at the door," he said. "Give him this. He'll let you by."

It was still storming. Even on the narrow enclosed stairway we could hear the howl of the wind and, once outside, snow smothered us. The policeman who scrutinized our pass was powdered with white. He was doing a slow walk between the two doors but his footprints blurred from sight almost as quickly as they were made in the snow.

Alec held my arm tightly. "Let's run," he said but we didn't. Running in his present footgear was out of the question.

It was better after we had turned the corner and had the wind at our backs. We could have talked but we didn't. Only once Alec, watching the snow slither before us, said slowly, "They'll get no help out of footprints tonight." I couldn't answer. I only shivered, clutched his arm the tighter.

Then we were fumbling through the drifts that choked the steps, pounding up the porch. Ruth had the door open before we touched it. The hall was warm and safe and quiet. It was heavenly to be there.

Ruth said, "Well, Alec, I'm glad you had sense enough to bring her with you. Tess, you're not going one step out of this house tonight. I won't let you. It's not necessary. We've lots of room. Now, both of you take off your coats and come in to the fire and tell me what all the to-do at the church was about."

I let Alec tell her. It was his job. Ruth said only the one thing—"Oh darling—not in the church!"—before rising magnificently to the occasion. Alec was to take off those ridiculous slippers and his socks, get his feet warm. "Nonsense! Tess won't mind. She's seen feet before. What about bathing beaches?" She'd get his shoes and woolen socks, his galoshes. In the meantime he could drink some coffee; it was ready. She'd telephone for a taxi—of course she would. If he thought she would let him get his car out, go out there to the garage all alone through those shrubs and hedges and tombstones . . .

There was only one tombstone—that of Bishop Wetherell who'd built St. Thomas' and a gentler soul had never breathed—but Alec didn't protest. He simply obeyed orders; it was as though he were glad, momentarily, to surrender his will to hers.

When the taxi's horn sounded, he shrugged on his coat. He said, "I don't know how long I'll be gone. You girls keep the door locked and if you should be frightened call the church. Ran's coming over when he's through but he'll telephone so you'll know when to expect him. Don't open the door to anyone else."

"I won't," Ruth promised fervently, and then he was gone. We watched the taxi's red tail lights dim away into distance and the snow whirl. Ruth clicked the door latches and put up the heavy chain. Then she turned to me.

"Oh, Tess, darling, isn't it awful? What are we going to do? Poor Alec! Poor all of us!"

6

We discovered that night there is a limit to the number of things that can be said upon any definite subject. By eleven o'clock, both our speculation and our information had run out. We had covered the known angles. I began to wish that I'd remained at the church where, presumably, events were still happening. Although the church itself loomed a dark bulk in the center of the swirling storm, discreet reconnaissance had revealed a faint light-glow behind the Crusader window.

"Still there," I said and let the curtain I'd drawn slip back into place:

Ruth was at my elbow. "I wonder if Alec went back there. I'd like to call and find out but I don't dare. It would just make everyone mad. I suppose we'll have to wait."

We went back to the fire and waited. There was nothing else to do.

"Carol was all right," Ruth said suddenly. "I liked her. So did Alec. We never believed those silly stories."

"You were the only ones then," I said uncomfortably, conscious of the same feeling I'd known when Georgia Brastock had insisted, so obviously, upon the girl's defense. I wanted to say, "Et tu, Brute?" and refrained for very shame. But, now that she was dead, was everyone going to jump on the bandwagon and proclaim the child's virtue?

"I think she was drunk—drunk with her own power," Ruth said dreamily. "She was so pretty and she hadn't always been. She wasn't at all when we came here. And then there was her music—that opened doors. She met people and they made a fuss over her—"

"Why don't you say 'men' and be honest?" I interrupted.

Ruth made a gesture. "All right—men. It simply went to her head. And then, all the time, there was that horrible home background. A house in the wrong part of town, a father who never made enough money nor wanted to, a mother—well, the less I say about Mrs. Tolliver, the better—all that rabbit brood of younger brothers and sisters. It's one thing to be rich and beautiful and admired and able to do things. But when you haven't any money and you still can be admired . . . It's not much wonder it all went to her head."

"Nice," I said. "As an analysis. But not much help in explaining who killed her—nor why."

"That's the part I hate," Ruth said with a shiver. "What I mean is, Carol's dead. There's nothing we can do about it now—to bring her back. We can only hurt—the living. Drag out secrets that were better not to see the light of day."

"Probably," I said. "But it'll be done. I saw Alec's face and Ran's. There was no compromise in them."

"I can talk to Alec," Ruth began doubtfully but I stopped her. "You're mad," I said. "You can't stop Ran. Alec couldn't. This isn't just a church squabble. It's murder. Ran's got the authority of the law behind him. He won't care who gets hurt so long as justice is done."

"Justice," Ruth said in a queer voice. "What's that?"

"An anodyne," I said promptly. "What's the matter with you anyway? I'll admit I'm not keen on a murder investigation myself but neither do I care for the idea of a murderer running around loose. I work in that church—remember? You act as though you were afraid to find out who it is."

"I am," Ruth said. "Tess, I don't suppose it could have been Oscar after all? It would make things so much simpler."

"It wasn't Oscar," I told her. "Not unless his spirit was able to project itself through a keyhole and become material enough to lock a door and hide the key. In the place they've always been kept."

"Of course it could have been a tramp," Ruth said brightening suddenly. "I know there've been tramps. Alec told me. He and Oscar found traces. Sandwich crusts and greasy papers."

"Nice time to tell me," I remarked with a shudder. "Murderers and tramps—I can see I'm going to be awfully comfortable around St. Thomas' after this. That is, if I ever go back. I rather think my resignation as of this moment is indicated."

"Don't worry—you won't have to go back until it's safe," Ruth comforted. "Alec'll think of something. You can work over here. Besides, all of this—the tramps—was quite a while ago. When we first came. Oscar's kept a close watch ever since. But it could have happened again. Tonight was sure to be a terrible one—anyone could tell that—and churches are warm. If you wanted shelter—"

"If I wanted shelter I could get it without resorting to murder. No, I think we might as well skip the tramp. He leans too heavily on coincidence. First we'd have to *have* a tramp—and they are darn few in these days of war jobs and employment for everyone—and then we have to have the particular kind of tramp who is infected with a blood lust—"

"But it could have happened," Ruth insisted stubbornly. "I mean, things like that *do* happen. I've read about them. Suppose he saw Carol and knew she was alone and attacked her. If she'd called Oscar and he'd found her—"

"No good," I said. "Oscar was locked in the organ. No tramp could have known about my keys."

"Oh, dear," Ruth said forlornly. "I suppose not. Still, if it was Oscar who took the keys out in the first place and left the drawer open . . ." I kept silent, and she went on more eagerly, "Tess, it could have been like that! If Oscar were fixing something in the organ, he'd be out of sight, wouldn't he? It would look as though Carol were all alone—"

"I don't know," I said. "Maybe. Only—well, I've got another idea. How do we know we're not going at this backwards? We're taking it for granted that someone wanted to murder Carol and that Oscar was killed because he got in the way. Why couldn't it have been the other way round? That Oscar was the one who had to be killed and that Carol—"

"Was there and saw!" It fairly burst from Ruth. "But—but, Tess! That makes her death so horrible, so unnecessary."

I shrugged. "Whichever way it goes, one of these deaths was unnecessary. Because I can't see any link between the two. Can you? What do you know about Oscar by the way?"

"N-not a thing," Ruth was fairly stuttering by this time. "Right now I can't even remember his last name. Probably Alec knows. He was always so cranky—Oscar—that I stayed away from him as much as I could. I never asked him to do anything for me, he was so ungracious about it. That's why I asked Alec to sharpen the knives . . ."

Mention of those knives made my teeth grit. "I don't like murder," I said. "I wish Alec had put those knives in the kitchen where they belonged. If he had . . ."

Ruth's eyes widened but she said firmly, "If he had, it would have been something else. What I mean is, you don't have to have a knife to commit murder. You can strangle people or shoot them or bash them over the head. Of course, bashing is awkward. There's apt to be blood."

"There *was* blood," I said. "For mercy sakes, let's stop talking about it. Can't we make coffee or something?"

So we did. There were sandwiches made so Ruth mixed a pan of brownies. At least we could talk about them until they were safely out of the oven.

Ran and Alec came at about two o'clock. They telephoned first so we were at the door to watch them struggle up the hill. It was still snowing. The world was blank and blind, lost behind a swirling mist of white.

They were so worn and tired and silent that we were suddenly shy of them. And shy of words. We hurried into activity, piling logs on the fire until it crackled furiously, bringing in the tea wagon loaded with food, pouring coffee, steaming, from the thermos jug.

Ruth was the one who first asked questions—not me; I'd told myself I wouldn't, not if I never learned what had happened. Ruth, however, had no such scruples. She drew a large floor cushion close to Alec's chair and sat down. She put her hand on his knee. She said, "Darling, was it so terrible?"

He glanced down at her, his mouth grim. "Well, what do you think? Mrs. Tolliver was pressing a dress in the kitchen—for Carol. Mr. Tolliver was clearing a path out to the street. It was just about time for her to come from choir practice, he told me. The children were asleep—at least they were until I arrived. Then—they got up." He stopped, gazed unseeingly into his coffee cup. "It was the first time," he went on after a moment, "the first time I've had to do anything like this. Sudden death, yes—often. That's different. Love seems to carry within itself an expectancy of fear. You dread that something will happen to the people you love and when it does happen—well, you accept it. But this—murder—no one is prepared for murder!"

Ruth said, "Oh, poor Mrs. Tolliver! Was she alone, Alec?"

"No. Luckily her sister from Minneapolis is here on a visit. She seems a sensible woman. She took charge. I told her you—we—would come back tomorrow."

"Of course," Ruth said softly. "And Mr. Tolliver? What about him?"

"He wouldn't believe me," Alec said. "Not at first. When he did, finally—well, he insisted on going down to the church. That's why I had to leave the rest of them. I couldn't let him go alone."

"It was just as well he came," Ran said, speaking for the first time. "It saved me from barging in on the mother."

I forgot my resolves. "Did he—would he tell you anything?"

Ran shrugged. "Well, he was pretty much shocked, poor devil. He broke down completely when he saw her. He kept saying, 'I never wanted her to play the organ. A piano you've got in your house but when you have to do your practicing alone in churches—'"

I shivered in spite of myself. I'd never been afraid in the church myself. I'd never even thought of being. Of course I'd often heard noises—wood that creaked and settled, odd rattles from the heating apparatus, far away thuds and bumpings—but they'd never meant anything. I'd found the church a friendly place. Now I wondered if I ever would again.

Some of the tension had gone out of the room. The waiting was done with and knowledge counted so little against the fact that our men were here, within finger touch, and safe. I knew a moment's astonishment. It was the first time I'd admitted even to myself that Randolph Garrison *was* my man and I found myself staring at the flat planes of his face and wondering how and why. He

wasn't good-looking, not in the accepted sense. His hair
was black and slightly unruly, his eyes gray-blue, start-
lingly light against a skin so tanned it knew no winter's
fading. His mouth was wide, mobile, his nose straight; the
thin line of a scar ran jaggedly above one eyebrow. There
was nothing you could criticize, the face was balanced in
all its parts, well assembled. But a veil lay across it. It was
closed, secret. You could retire behind such a face, know
yourself inviolate, secure from the world's prying, and in
that instant of revelation I envied Ruth. She would always
know what Alec thought, experienced, while I . . .

Ran had taken a small black notebook from his pocket
and was flipping through its pages. Now he laid it down
with a sigh. "She was twenty years old," he said, "and what
I know of her has been written on two pages. It's not much
of an obituary."

Ruth came to alertness with a jerk. "Well, what I know
would fill a book. Or several books."

Ran shut her up. "What you know or what you think—
what you've heard? There's a difference."

Ruth subsided. "You're right. I don't really know a single thing. It's all gossip. But there's been a lot of that."

"Gossip helps sometimes," Ran said absently. "But I
think for the present we'll stick to facts. You were one of
the last to talk to the girl, Alec. Wasn't there anything she
said—?"

"I've been trying to remember," Alec said. He looked
tall and dark and somber as he stood with his back to the
blazing log fire. "We didn't say so much. Walking down
town we couldn't—there was too much wind. Oh, we talked a little—about her music. Ever notice how much nicer
she was when she got on the subject of music? It was as
though she changed identities—became more sensible—"

"You're a blind baby," Ruth murmured, "but I adore
you. The girl was clever— I always gave her that. Why

waste feminine wiles on a minister when the intellectual approach . . ."

Alec's glare was disapproval.

"The Café was crowded. There were other people at our table. It was obvious we couldn't talk there. I think she was disappointed but she only said we'd better skip it, that she had no intention of broadcasting her troubles even though the whole world was bound to hear sooner or later. Then she said a funny thing. She asked me if I'd ever started anything I couldn't finish. She said, 'Well, I have. I didn't mean to—I thought it was my own affair but . . . You know that Bible verse that's something about sowing the wind and reaping the whirlwind? Well, take it from me, I'm the gal who's done that very thing!'"

"Reaping the whirlwind, eh?" Ran repeated thoughtfully. "That's all, was it? No idea what she meant?"

"I tried to find out," Alec said wearily. "She froze up, told me to forget it, that she'd been a fool to think she could talk it out. She said, 'You know, Dean MacDonald, you can be pretty sure about yourself—what you want and how far you'll go to get it—but you never can tell about somebody else.' That was all. My coffee came and I drank it. I thought she was glad when I stood up to go."

"Glad?"

"Relieved, then. As though I'd made things easier for her by going."

"Why?"

"I don't know. It was just an impression."

"Anyone you knew in the restaurant?"

"I don't know," Alec said again. "There might have been. It was crowded. I wasn't taking census."

"Miss Erickson was there," I said grimly.

"I remember," Ran said. "All right." He riffled through the book again, made a note. "I'll ask her."

"What makes Miss Erickson an authority on people I know?" Alec was haughty.

"She's an authority on everything," I said vindictively. I'd gone to school to Miss Erickson. "There isn't anything she doesn't know."

"That should be helpful," Ran said absently. "I'll talk to the cashier at the Café. And the waitresses. One of them might know if the girl ate her dinner alone. Or if someone else joined her after you went. At least they could establish the time she left the restaurant. Dennison said he arrived at the church about seven o'clock. The time lag is short." He tapped irritably with one finger. "What time did you leave her, Alec? Know?"

Alec frowned. "It must have been shortly after six—five or ten minutes. I'd been home for quite a while when Tess got here. That was around half past six."

"Tess—oh, yes." Ran looked at me directly then. "You talked to her at the church, didn't you? What did she say to you?"

I shrugged and reached for a cigarette. "Nothing significant. I wasn't very nice to her—I've never liked her. She—oh, well, I asked her why she stayed in Dorchester and she said it was because she didn't have the money to get out. She said I didn't need to think she didn't want to go, that she'd do anything to get away. Perhaps," I said thoughtfully, "that's a clue."

"If it is, it's very well disguised. Anything more?"

"Oh, I suggested that a club I belong to might help her. That was all. We parted amicably enough. I was in a hurry to get to the post office and I had some shopping to do before I came here. I asked her if she wanted to leave with me—she'd said something about getting a sandwich down town and coming back to practice—but she said no, she had to lock the organ and that she'd go out by the basement door. I waited until I heard her going downstairs before I left. I don't know why. I was uneasy. All of a sudden the church seemed very dark and—oh, menacing. A presentiment, I suppose. I'd never felt that way before."

"What time was this—when you left?"

I tried to think. "About twenty minutes to six. I know I thought I'd have to hurry if I were to get my shopping done."

"That would be about right," Alec said unexpectedly. "It was a quarter to six when I met her. I remember looking at my watch and thinking that Mrs. Thurston couldn't stay much longer. I thought probably once more around the block would do it. That's how I happened to run into Carol."

Ran's eyebrows lifted skyward. "You were avoiding Mrs. Thurston?"

"I was."

"In the name of . . . Well, never mind that. But why?"

"Does it matter?" Alec was at his stiffest, most unapproachable.

"I think it might." Ran paused, then went on more softly, "If it had anything to do with Carol's marriage . . ."

"Marriage!" This was Ruth but I was right behind her. "You mean Carol Tolliver is—was married?"

He nodded slowly. "Yes. To Blair Thurston. Don't look at me like that, Alec. It was her own father—old Tolliver—who told me. He said that beside himself only you and Thurston knew. That was why you didn't want to talk to Mrs. Thurston, wasn't it?"

"Yes." It came from Alec in a sort of groan. "She didn't know but she was getting close to the truth. That's why I didn't want to see her. I didn't want to have to answer her questions. That's Thurston's job. I like him—he's a fine man—I'd do a lot for him. But I draw the line at lying to his wife. It doesn't come within my province."

Ran was watching him carefully. "Any chance that the marriage was what Carol wanted to discuss?"

"I doubt it." Alec was going slowly now, weighing each word. "I hadn't married them. So far as she knew, I wasn't supposed to know about it. It was Thurston himself who told me. Besides, to the best of my belief, whatever problem there was had ceased to exist. Thurston had assured me it was all settled. Satisfactorily."

"Satisfactorily," Ran repeated. "Hmm. Then there *had* been a problem. Satisfactorily from whose point of view, I wonder. Thurston's?"

"From Thurston's certainly. There was to be an annulment. But also, I surmise, from Carol's. According to Thurston, the girl had admitted the marriage to Blair was only for one purpose—to obtain sufficient money to leave Dorchester and continue her musical education.

"In other words," Ran said pleasantly, "blackmail."

"Blackmail," Alec agreed with a sigh.

7

There was complete silence then. No one spoke. No one asked questions. Not even Ruth. I remembered the electricity of that moment after dinner when, so idly, I'd spoken Blair Thurston's name. Alec had known then, of course. But what about Ruth? Had she known—or guessed?

"It's no fun to be the one who's left out," I said plaintively. "Isn't anyone going to bring me up to date? I seem to have missed an awful lot."

Ran's eyes went to Alec. Alec shook his head. "What I know was told me in confidence," he muttered.

Ran shrugged. Nothing doing there and he knew it. Alec has a stubborn streak.

"Ruth?"

"I don't *know* a thing, Ran—really I don't." She made a wide gesture. "With me it's been simply a matter of putting two and two together. It came to me all of a sudden tonight when Tess mentioned Blair Thurston. I thought possibly that Blair could be the explanation for Mr. Thurston's interest in Carol. I knew she and Blair saw a lot of one another last summer. And of course it would explain Mrs. Thurston too—if it was being kept from her . . ." Her voice trailed off.

Ran looked at me, grinned. "Well, Tess, I seem to be the information kid. What I know came from Tolliver—

it ought to be straight enough. If I go haywire, Alec can check me."

"I didn't marry them," Alec said. Virtue sat on his shoulders. "I heard of it the first time the other day. Thurston came to me. Naturally I offered to speak to Carol but Thurston said no, he would prefer I didn't. I —gathered that Carol didn't want me to know about the—the marriage."

It was an opening and Ran pounced. "But that could have been what she wanted to talk to you about?"

"It could have been," Alec agreed. He sounded tired. "But I don't think it was."

Impressions are nothing to argue about—there's never any sure ground for your feet. I said, "Oh, forget him and his scruples! Go on, Ran—tell us what Mr. Tolliver said."

He hesitated, made up his mind. "All right—you're entitled to know, I guess. Besides, the papers will have if tomorrow—the marriage, not the rest of it. It was when I took him down to see the body. We'd covered it with a clean sheet from Oscar's chest and he lifted one corner and then let it drop. He said, 'I guess it came cheaper this way.' Now that's an odd thing for a man to say when he's standing over his murdered daughter so I asked him what he meant, and this is what he said: 'She married the Thurston brat around Christmas time and his father's been trying to buy him out of it ever since. But with her dead they're sitting pretty. They won't have to pay anything at all now—see?'"

"Oh, dear!" Ruth said. "I never thought too much of Ed Tolliver but with his daughter dead if all he can think of is money . . ."

"Now wait a minute." This was Ran. "I asked him if, by that, he was accusing the Thurstons of murder and he told me to figure it out for myself. Then he looked at her again and this time there were tears in his eyes. He said,

'The money couldn't have meant anything to them—they got plenty. She didn't want much—only enough to clear the mortgage on our home and to get her started with her music—'"

Alec got up abruptly and walked out of the room. Ruth looked after him with a sigh. She said, "People get too much for him at times. Go on, Ran."

"Nothing much to go on to. I got the story as painlessly as possible. It seems that Carol and young Thurston were married last December as a last-minute gesture before he was inducted into the Navy. There was a farewell party and dance with, I suspect, considerable liquor. At any rate, the suggestion was made and acted on."

"But what about marriage laws?" I objected. "I thought you had to file notice, have blood tests and so on."

"Not in our sister state," Ran said grimly. "Just the two of them went—in young Thurston's car. There was no—honeymoon. By the time they got back across the line, it was time for Thurston to report to his draft board. He was sent out that same morning."

"Leaving Papa Thurston to hold the sack," I said. "Lovely."

"Papa Thurston didn't know anything about it," Ran told me sternly. "Carol told her own people but swore them to secrecy. It wasn't until she had received her first allotment check that she went to Thurston and put her cards on the table."

"I wonder if the allotment didn't have a good deal to do with the marriage," Ruth said dreamily. "Have you ever seen the Thurston scion, Ran? He's tall and white and pimply. No one could love him for himself alone. But for fifty dollars each and every month—to say nothing of Thurston père being the richest man in Dorchester . . ."

Ran was eyeing her with amusement and something like respect. "People never get you down, do they, Ruth?"

"No-o," she said thoughtfully. "I don't believe they do. Perhaps it's because I stay on their level. My head isn't in the clouds. I don't expect more of them than they can give me. And fifty dollars would really mean a lot to the Tollivers, Ran. They're horribly hard up. There are six children beside Carol—she's the oldest—and Mr. Tolliver's only a bookkeeper in a bank—Thurston's bank, too, as it happens. They've had to almost *scratch* sometimes to get enough to eat. They're the kind of poor I'm sorriest for—you know, the respectable, keep-up-a-good-appearance-no-matter-what-the-cost kind. The kind that wouldn't go on relief no matter what happened. Their pride would keep them from it."

"Umm." Ran had put away the little black notebook and was leaning back, his eyes half closed. "Still the girl's music must have cost them something."

It was my turn. "Not a great deal, I think. People are usually pretty kind to the geniuses of this world and there wasn't much doubt about Carol from the start. She not only had talent, she had the ability to work hard and not waste opportunities. Her first teacher gave her lessons for nothing. I suspect most of the others have followed suit. Then she's been able to earn quite a bit herself—on the radio, playing accompaniments, substituting for other organists, playing for funerals. She worked a couple of summers at the dime store. I don't think she burdened her family to any extent. I imagine what she earned was sufficient to pay for her music and her clothes and other incidentals. But I doubt if she could save anything. Perhaps she didn't even try. She was always good to her family. That was her weakest point. She wasn't single-minded enough. Genius ought to be ruthless so far as talent is concerned. She wasn't."

"Sure of that? That marriage had all the earmarks of clear headed calculation. So far as I remember, the word 'love' doesn't enter in."

"Oh, doesn't it?" Ruth said. "Look—she was trying to kill two birds with one stone—get herself established in the field of music and help her family financially by paying off the mortgage on their home. If that wasn't love—love for her family—what do you call it?"

"There were two killed all right—but not with a stone," Ran said grimly. "And somehow her plan back-fired. She wasn't the killer but the victim."

Alec stalked in just then with an armful of wood. He looked very stiff and unapproachable. I kept an eye on him as I asked, "What about Mr. Thurston—how did he take it?"

"I haven't seen Thurston yet," Ran said. "That'll come tomorrow. But from what Tolliver said he was considerably upset. He would have liked to have had the marriage annulled but that was out of the question. The two principals were of age and in their right minds. So there remained nothing to do—since in his opinion the marriage must not be allowed to stand—except to come to financial terms, Carol having delicately hinted that such a solution was possible. When, less delicately, she named her price, Tolliver said he thought Thurston would have a stroke. Not that it was so much out of line—five thousand dollars—"

"Tolliver!" I said, bewildered. "You mean that he was in on the conference?"

"The first one, yes. It took place at the bank. Thurston hauled him off his stool, or whatever it is bookkeepers sit on in banks, with the idea of using him as a whip to keep his daughter in line. But Tolliver got stubborn. It was Carol's show and so far as he could see, she was capable of handling it. Then, too, I imagine he was a trifle dazed at the prospect of having his mortgage wiped out. So he kept still or threw his weight on what, to Thurston's point of view, was the wrong side."

I tried to imagine meek, graying Ed Tolliver defying the bull-like Thurston and couldn't. I said, "It's a wonder Mr. Thurston didn't kick him out of the bank."

"Oh, no," Ruth interposed dreamily. "If he had, there'd have been talk, and there mustn't ever be talk about the Thurstons. Mr. Tolliver had worked for that bank for a long time. Then, too, if he lost his job, the story of the marriage would be bound to come out and—well, it would be awkward."

"The secrecy angle seems screwy to me," Ran yawned, "Suppose two kids *do* run off and get married—what of it? It happens. Parents aren't always consulted. It seems to me that if both sides had been a little more sensible about it . . ."

"There's more to it than that," Alec said. He had suddenly decided to be cooperative. Or perhaps it was just that, since we already knew so much, he thought a little more wouldn't hurt. "There are other Thurstons in the state, distant cousins who are more conservative than—than our Thurstons. They are also, I believe, very well-to-do and they have a daughter—"

"Oh, for goodness sake, Alec!" Ruth suddenly lost patience. "Stop beating about the bush. They're rich and they've got a daughter and Harvey Thurston likes money and he's got a son. It's as simple as A-B-C. A marriage is arranged."

"Was," Alec said with the ghost of a smile. "You're overlooking the marriage that already has—er—occurred."

"I overlook nothing," Ruth assured him. "More conservative Thurstons—dear me! I'm glad I don't know them. How about Blair? Didn't he have any voice in the matter?"

"Apparently he's had it," Alec said, still with a hint of a smile. "I've—er—seen a picture of the lady. You might say she was not in Carol's class."

"Oh, well, conservative or not, I suppose it could be smoothed over, kept quiet," I said. "But why—in that case—didn't Harvey Thurston jump at Carol's offer? Five thousand dollars isn't so much, not when you're a reputed millionaire."

"You don't get to be a millionaire by throwing around five thousand dollars," Ran opined sagely. "Besides, according to Tolliver, the negotiations hadn't broken down. They were only stymied temporarily. Thurston had gotten as far as offering five thousand dollars in war bonds—cash value thirty-seven hundred and fifty. Carol had turned that down. The mortgage on the Tolliver house was three thousand. That would have left only seven hundred and fifty to launch her on her musical career. And with a divorce the fifty-dollar-a-month allotment would cease."

"Only seven hundred and fifty—what did she want?" I grumbled. "Lots of careers are launched on considerably less than that."

"She wanted money," Alec said quietly. "All she could get. It's not nice to contemplate but there it is. She had a hold on the Thurstons. She intended to use it for all it was worth. What's more, it was my impression that Thurston intended to meet her terms. He had a reason. Blair was about due home on furlough."

We all thought about that. Ran said, "I wonder—you don't know at exactly what time he was due to arrive, do you?"

Alec shook his head. I said, "But—oh, I think he's here now. I mean, someone called the church tonight, during choir practice, and asked for Carol. I said she wasn't there."

I stopped then, remembering how mistaken I'd been, how dreadfully she had been there.

"Recognize the voice?"

I shook my head. "No. It was vaguely familiar, that was all. Telephones distort voices sometimes, don't they? I suppose it could have been Blair Thurston."

"I think a call at the Thurston home is indicated," Ran said evenly. "An early one."

Alec had been standing by the fireplace. Now he brought one hand sharply down upon the marble mantelpiece. "This is ridiculous!" he said and his voice bit at the words. "Harvey Thurston is a church warden, a man of honor and integrity. What you imply is monstrous. I cannot permit—"

"Easy!" Ran said softly. "Murder is a brew full of strange ingredients. You're taking this too seriously. You forget that these people are strangers to me. I'm simply trying to gain perspective."

Alec wasn't to be pacified so easily. "From somewhat prejudiced sources."

"As if you could be prejudiced when Carol was concerned," Ruth murmured. "All right, darling—let's wash out the Thurstons. Goodness knows there are plenty of others. There's the Brastocks and Charlie Dennison— oh, all *right*, Alec! Charlie Dennison's an old man and he wouldn't kill a fly, but just the same he hated Carol. He was scared stiff she'd get the organ away from him. Then there's the Czernys—she breathed fire last fall when Carol played so many accompaniments for her husband— and there's Phil Smedley—"

"No!" I said. This was news to me. "What about him?"

"Nothing," Ruth shrugged. "He was wacky over her, that's all. Absolutely besotted. Didn't you ever notice?"

I hadn't. I considered it and then shrugged in my turn. "Oh, well, he's one Ran won't have to worry about. He hasn't brains enough to be a murderer."

"Is that so? Sometime you take a look at his ears and his thumbs," Ruth advised darkly. "He had blood on his feet, didn't he?"

"Anyone would have," I said uneasily, not quite sure why I thus aligned myself for defense. "He was standing in it."

"I know. But it'd be a lovely explanation for—for any other blood that happened to be on him."

Alec moved deliberately. "You'd better cut it out. Speculation won't get you anywhere. Nor maligning people's characters. Aren't you forgetting one of the salient pieces in this murder? What about Oscar?"

"I hadn't forgotten," Ran said promptly. "I'd not gotten around to him, that's all. Now that you've brought him up—well, what about Oscar?"

I looked at Alec and Ruth and they looked at me. It was humiliating but it was true. We didn't know one single thing about Oscar—we never had.

There was a frown between Alec's eyes. "His last name was Johnson," he offered feebly. "He was here at St. Thomas' when I came—that was three years ago. He was a cross-grained old fellow—seldom had a decent word for anyone, but he was efficient and he kept the church clean. And he'd been here a long time. I suppose they put up with him because of that."

"St. Thomas' needs a pension system," Ran observed. "Sentiment can be carried too far. All right—you said a long time. Anybody have an idea how long?"

"Well, he was janitor here when I was a little girl," I offered doubtfully.

"Family?"

None that I ever heard of. Oh, he might have had some in the old country—Norway, you know. He sometimes got mail with foreign stamps."

"Friends?"

"Some," I said cautiously. "Not very nice ones, I'm afraid. Lots of them looked like plain ordinary bums to me. I think he picked them up in cheap restaurants down town. He was a great friend of that Brannigan—the one they call Red—who's always trying to reform some thing or other. He'd come up to the church afternoons to see Oscar and then I'd smell coffee and hear them talking."

"I know Brannigan," Ran said thoughtfully. "Calls himself a socialist or communist or something, doesn't he?"

"Well, Oscar was a kind of communist," I said. "You know—the sort that's always 'agin' the government. He and I argued quite a lot in his loquacious moments, which didn't come often. You know the sort of thing—the country's going to the dogs and will so long as we let the 'Wall Street' boys run it. Since the war he's been worse than ever. A complete isolationist and Roosevelt-hater. Since Pearl Harbor he's been quieter."

"He doesn't sound too enticing," Ran said with a grimace. "Perhaps tomorrow when we go through his stuff . . ."

"Tomorrow's here," Alec said firmly. "It has been for some time."

Ostentatiously he took a large plated key from the mantel and began to wind the eight-day clock.

We laughed but we took the hint. We went yawning to our beds.

8

Ruth's knock awoke me. The bedside clock said a quarter past ten but to me it was still the middle of the night. I stretched and rolled over to blink at the tawny mass of her hair, warm and colorful in the cold grayness of the room.

She said, "Sorry to wake you, honey, but Ran's been gone for hours and Alec wants to go over to the church. He thinks you'd better go with him."

I envisioned the pile of mail that always waited on my desk, and I agreed. Yawning, I fell out of bed, blundered into clothes.

Out of doors it still snowed. There was no hint of the storm's lessening. The wind was a shriek that rattled windows and tossed white flakes into thickening veils. From the tall church chimneys, thick smoke drifted, darker even than the leaden sky. I wondered who had stoked those fires, who tended them. Remembering Oscar, who never would again, I shivered.

Downstairs Alec was just finishing his coffee. He looked at me as though he'd seen me somewhere before, said, "Good morning," not too enthusiastically, and then vanished into his study.

On the floor the twins wobbled together in their play pen. They greeted me with shouts of joy. Then Frances whammed Sandy over the head with a wooden monkey and he retaliated by poking her in the eye with a pencil. Joy turned abruptly to woe.

"Oh, stop it, children!" Ruth came through the swing door balancing a tray. "Here you are, Tess—orange juice, toast, eggs, bacon. The coffee's fresh. I just made it. If you want anything else, ask for it."

"Anything else!" I said with scorn. "What sort of a breakfast do you think I usually eat?"

"Not enough," Ruth said promptly. "You're too thin. Sandy, if you don't stop that howling, there'll be a murder in the parsonage as well as one in the church!"

At once she caught herself guiltily. "That's the sort of thing I'm always saying and I shouldn't. It's never really meant anything before. Now, after last night . . ."

"Forget it," I said, more hardily than I felt. "You'd better bring me up to date. What's happened so far?"

"Telephone calls," Ruth sighed. "I think everyone who ever went to St. Thomas' has called. Including the bishop . . . long distance. I don't see how *he* found out so soon. I wanted Alec to have the telephone disconnected but he said no, so I've given him the pleasure of answering it. Once he's out of the house . . ." She made a sort of thumbs down motion with her right hand. "Oh, and reporters—we've had two of them."

"Nice," I said and poured more coffee. "Who's over at the church now?"

"Policemen, I suppose," Ruth said vaguely. "And Ran must be somewhere around. Dr. Kennedy—the Congregational minister—sent over an old fellow who used to do their janitor work. He's at the church now. There have to be fires, you know. We can't let the pipes freeze."

I looked at the clock. It said a quarter of eleven. "You've had a busy day so far. Do you mind telling me—have you been to bed at all?"

Ruth glanced pointedly at the twins. "Do you think those hyenas sleep?" she asked bitterly. "No child of mine goes on a schedule after this. They feel too obligated to follow it."

The study door opened and Alec emerged. "Are you ready, Tess? Then if you don't mind . . ."

I went for my hat and coat. When I came back, Ruth was patting a muffler about Alec's neck. She kissed him. "Do be careful, darling. I'd hate to have to bring up the twins alone."

"I'll be all right," he told her. "Sorry I can't give you any idea when I'll be back. But I'll call you."

Ruth raised resigned eyebrows at me. There went her chances of disconnecting the telephone.

The full force of the wind caught us as we opened the front door. It sent us staggering and breathless back against the house wall. Someone had swept across the porch but already a new layer of white had formed. Beyond, the walks were badly drifted.

Alec jerked his fur cap farther down over his forehead. "Come on, I'll break trail. You'd better stick close."

We proceeded on those lines—King Wenceslaus-page fashion—past the church and around the corner. It took a long time. My hands, in woolen mittens, felt frozen. As for my ears, they had simply passed out of existence.

"In weather like this, we could do with a system of tunnels," I grumbled as we toiled up the steps to the side entrance. Someone had shoveled here. Alec only grunted.

Then we were within the entry way, gasping as our lungs adjusted themselves to the sudden warmth, stamping the snow from our galoshes. The door at the top of the stairs opened and a policeman peered down.

"It's all right," Alec called. "It's I—MacDonald—and Miss King."

"Oh, yeah," the policeman said. "The chief said you'd be along. Come on up."

Nice—inviting us into our own bailiwick. We went up.

All the time I was shrugging out of my coat, shaking the snow from it, hanging it up, I kept looking around the room. I don't know why I expected it to be different, but it wasn't. Even the chairs still held their semicircle about the piano.

I think Alec felt the same. He, too, was peering about as though for evidenced upheaval. "Have you been over this room?" he asked suddenly.

The policeman shrugged. "All we want. But it wasn't no good. Lots of prints but I guess that don't mean nothing in a place like this."

It didn't. An ordinary day might bring thirty callers.

"How about the knife? Get any prints off that?"

The policeman guffawed. "Only yours." He seemed to think that funny. Alec's face froze.

"This thing," said the policeman, crossing the room and laying his hand on the metal locker that held the choir robes, "was locked. We didn't take time to bust it open. Thought maybe one of you'd have a key."

"It's a combination lock," I said. "I'll open it. But it's queer that it's locked. No one ever shuts it tight."

I brought the letters into line, turned the door handle. I had an instant's qualm as I threw the doors wide but there was nothing to see. Only the close-packed robes, each on its hanger.

The policeman pulled out one or two, let them fall back. "Nothing here." He sounded disappointed. Alec and I weren't. We breathed separate sighs of relief.

The telephone rang just then but, before Alec could move, the policeman grasped it firmly. "I'm taking the calls," he said. "Chief's orders."

"Good," I thought. "That'll save me something."

It didn't save Alec. After a few perfunctory questions, the policeman handed over the telephone. Alec said, "Who is it? Oh, yes. I see . . ."

I sat down at the desk and began to sort over the mail. The policeman, hands behind his back, stood and watched.

It was the usual run of mail. Appeals for money, bulletins from various organizations, a few bills, notices of meetings—like all ministers, Alec is hopelessly involved in civic affairs—letters from soldiers and sailors in camp and overseas. A music catalogue addressed to the choirmaster of St. Thomas'. Sunday School supplies—those were late. Two letters for Oscar Johnson—one a bill, the other with a foreign stamp and censored. I laid them aside.

Alec had just finished his conversation when Ran, followed by another man, came up the stairs. Ran looked tired but he smiled at us. "Hello—hello," he said. "Do you know our District Attorney? Miss King, Dean MacDonald—Mr. Elrod."

The District Attorney was lean and dark and hatchet-faced. Also young. The same wave of reform that had given Randolph Garrison to Dorchester had swept Elrod into office. He bowed at me, shook Alec's hand firmly.

"Sorry about this, Dean MacDonald," he said briskly. "Dreadful thing to have happen. Especially in a church. However, we hope to make things as easy for you as possible. Perhaps I should tell you what we've done so far." He lounged on the desk corner. "A coroner's jury will view the bodies this afternoon. The inquest will be tomorrow at ten o'clock. Bad day—Saturday—but there wasn't a chance of getting our people together today in weather like this. I understand the funerals will be held tomorrow?"

"Carol Tolliver's—yes," Alec said slowly. "As to Johnson's—well, there may be some delay. Very little is known about the man. If we can locate relatives . . ."

"We're going to his apartment now," Ran said. "Look it over. That's not been done yet. I'd like Tess if you don't mind. There may be things she can tell us."

"Certainly," Alec said. I thought he looked relieved. He had opened his overcoat but not removed it. Now he buttoned it again. "I'm going over to Tollivers," he said briefly. "And I expect I'd better see Thurston."

"I talked to Thurston this morning," Ran told him. "The son will be in on the night bus."

That was all. But a long look passed between the two men. Then Alec moved abruptly. "About telephone calls . . ."

"Hanson"—this was our policeman—"can take them. All right, Tess. You'd better bring some pencils and a note-book. And if you've some spare envelopes . . ."

I saw Oscar's letters. I handed them over. "These came this morning."

Ran took them eagerly. The bill he shrugged over, slipped into his pocket. The other letter he slit open. Almost at once he replaced the single flimsy sheet of paper. "Nothing there. Uncle Olaf is well—they've all been well and happy. They don't want for anything. The food is good—all the lies they have to tell to get past the censors. Come along."

It was odd but during the five years I'd spent at St. Thomas' I had never been inside Oscar's apartment. A bell in my office summoned him upstairs. If, for any reason, I had to go down to find him, I only tapped at his door which was, invariably, locked. It was disturbing that it took murder to give me entrance.

I don't really know what it was I expected to see. Something ghastly—blood, evidences of a struggle. There was nothing. Two rag rugs laid, for obvious reason, down the center of the faded rose-patterned carpet, an old-fashioned library table moved aside until it blocked the rolltop desk. That was all.

The first thing that impressed me was its cleanliness, the second the room's evident comfort. No church guild had furnished this with odds and ends of discarded furniture. What was here must be Oscar's personal property, chosen to fit his needs. There was a davenport and chair, old but comfortable. An ancient Morris chair, its leather cracked along the seams. The roll-top desk. An up-to-date and very expensive radio with a record attachment A carved Norwegian chest still faintly revealing splashes of rose and blue. A wicker fernery. Pots of hyacinths just coming into bloom.

The bath was minute but spotlessly clean. The bedroom contained only a chest of drawers, a chair and a dilapidated steamer trunk, an iron three-quarter bed. The kitchen, equally spotless, had a small frigidaire and an electric stove. There were crisp curtains at the single window, two red geraniums in tomato cans. On the stove was Oscar's coffee pot, half full of turgid brew.

"Well, this shouldn't take so long," Ran said. "Want to start on the desk, Elrod? I'll take the bedroom. Tess, if you want to try the chest over there . . ."

I advanced reluctantly. I never had pried among other people's possessions, and this was more than curiosity. Under the circumstances, it was desecration.

The chest wasn't locked. The top came up easily. Inside the workmanship was intricate. Built into the sides were drawers, trays and pigeonholes. It made me think of a pencil box.

There was nothing in the main part of the chest but a blue suit of wooden-feeling material, a woolen scarf, half a dozen mothballs and a Norwegian Bible. There was nothing in the pockets of the suit. The pigeonholes held letters. They were all in Norwegian and, as the dates were in the 1920's, I replaced them where I'd found them.

Most of the drawers were empty. One held photographs, yellowed old things, bent and broken at the corners. They looked like family group pictures to me.

I was refolding the suit preparatory to returning it when Elrod's low whistle brought me around to look at him. He was scowling at several small bank books.

"What the devil sort of money did you people pay Johnson?"

"Sixty a month and this apartment," I said promptly.

Ran spoke from the doorway. "Why?"

"I might want the job myself. This—this very remarkable janitor of yours appears to have been banking upwards of three thousand dollars a year for the past six years. During the ten years before, when he opened the accounts, he didn't do so well. A measly eight or nine hundred."

Ran said, "Whew!" I did a little hasty multiplication—twelve times sixty—and "whewed" myself. "What are his balances?"

"Something over twenty-six thousand. Twenty-six thousand four hundred and fifty-three dollars and nineteen cents. I wonder why the nineteen cents," Elrod said pensively. "He might have kept that out for stamps. You know, Ran, this has all the earmarks of being the miracle of our generation. A janitor who banks a fortune on a salary of sixty dollars a month . . ."

"Forget the miracle," Ran ordered grimly. "What I want to know is where he got it *to* bank."

"Couldn't it have been dividends or something like that?" I offered feebly. "He might have owned stock—oil or gold . . ."

"I've bought oil stock myself," Elrod told me. "I'm a sucker for salesmen. None of mine ever paid off in three-thousand-dollar hunks."

Ran shrugged. "We may know more when we've talk-ed to the banks. Go ahead—you're doing all right. The bedroom's a blank—nothing but clothes. How about you, Tess?"

"Nothing," I said doubtfully. "Old letters—very old; nothing later than 1925. There's a few pictures . . ."

Ran leaned over my shoulder to look at those, replaced them without comment. He said, "Sometimes these things have a secret drawer." His hand moved in the depths of the chest. There was a loud click and a shallow drawer snapped forward. It held nothing but a gold watch and two plain gold rings.

Ran laughed softly and let the drawer swing back. "All right, Tess—close that thing and see if you have any luck with the table. I'm going through the record cabinet. Then we'll take the kitchen."

But even when the table and cabinet were proved innocuous, Ran remained unsatisfied. He was poking among the cushions of the davenport when Elrod's grunt brought him up to attention like a bird dog on point.

"Found anything interesting?"

"Another bank account. His salary checks went into this. The record's clear—sixty a month. He didn't spend much—there's over two thousand here. Nice going."

"I could bear to know who gets it all now," Ran said.

"Keep your shirt on," Elrod advised cheerfully. "I'm not done yet. God knows what I'll still turn up. Not that the man kept anything worth while. A more useless bunch of truck— Why didn't he burn this along with the rest?"

Ran, on his way to the kitchen, stopped abruptly. "What do you mean by that?"

Elrod leaned back in his chain "It's obvious, isn't it? Miss King says he received mail—where is it? I haven't found any letters. Have you? There's nothing here but bank statements and circular letters. Not a scrap of personal stuff. But there's a furnace in operation a couple of doors from here, and he had every opportunity to shovel the stuff in."

"Could be," Ran said, "But there's still the kitchen." He didn't sound hopeful and he had reason. The kitchen yielded little. We opened one cupboard door and viewed modest supplies of staples. Another showed a hit-and-miss collection of dishes. A third door opened upon pots and pans. Drawers held silver, cooking utensils, towels. There was one locked drawer . . .

The drawer was a large one. At least fifteen inches deep. Ran took keys from his pocket, surveyed them doubtfully. "None of these is right. I seem to remember another in that chest . . ."

He got it, slid it into the lock. The key turned smoothly. Ran jerked the drawer forward.

I don't know what Ran's reaction was but, for myself, I could hardly believe my eyes. Surely we were looking at one of the strangest collections ever assembled by the hand of man. There were a number of silk umbrellas. There were women's handbags, children's purses; single gloves and pairs of mittens. There was a six-inch pile of beautifully laundered handkerchiefs. There were compacts, key rings, glasses cases and prayer books. Bracelets and woolen scarves and a child's red sweater.

"For the love of Mike!" Ran said. "What kind of a treasure trove is this?"

"Treasure trove nothing!" I retorted. "This is the lost-and-found department. That's Mrs. Fred Gregory's pin-seal purse and—oh, look! There's Miss Erickson's false teeth!"

Ran peered at the ghastly semicircle. "Miss Erickson's false teeth—great goldfish! How do you know?"

"How shouldn't I know?" I asked scornfully. "She made fuss enough about losing them. It was—oh, two years ago, during Christmas vacation. She had to have all her teeth pulled, and of course she didn't want anyone to know. Dr.

Burns pulled her uppers and put a plate right in, but he left two or three teeth in her lower jaw and attached the lower plate to them with clamps. It wasn't very comfortable, I guess, so she slipped the teeth put during service and wrapped them in Kleenex and put them in her purse. Or so she said. Anyway, when she went to look for them again, she couldn't find them. She came to the office next morning and told me about it and swore me to secrecy. I had to act as go-between with Oscar who insisted he'd never seen them. Miss Erickson was furious—I suppose it meant eighty or ninety dollars to her—but there wasn't anything to do. Oscar said he hadn't seen them and that was that."

"Oscar was something of a liar," Ran grunted. He stirred the contents of the drawer with one finger. "Why do you suppose he hung on to this stuff?"

"How do I know?" I asked wearily. "Oscar did all the picking up in the church. If he said a thing wasn't there, why we took it for granted it wasn't. It was his job. I remember Mrs. Gregory's purse though. She felt badly about losing it. She said there was fifty dollars in it."

"It's not there now," Ran said, investigating. "Part of the twenty-six thousand-odd, no doubt. Seems to me Oscar's developing quite a character. Liar and thief—"

"Who's a liar and thief?" Elrod demanded behind me. "Look, you two!—I've struck pay dirt. That is, I've got something. You wanted a will, Ran—here it is. Drawn up about a year ago by our top legal firm—Grayson and Cameron. All signed and attested to. It leaves everything of which Oscar Johnson dies possessed to—hold your hats, folks! Here comes the joker!—to Carol Tolliver if she is still living *at the time of his death!* If she predeceases him, it goes to his old friend, one Charles Patrick Dennison! Now, what do you think of that?"

9

I was the first to recover. "But Carol's dead," I said. "Does that mean that Charles Dennison gets it now?"

"The sixty-four-dollar question," Elrod murmured. "Lawyers probably. I can almost smell the smoke and hear the shouting. Who died last anyway, Ran?"

Ran looked harassed. "How should I know? On the face of it, the girl since the knife was found beside her. Maybe Doc Morton can tell you, but I doubt it. According to him, they were killed within minutes of one another."

"Johnson first and then the girl," Elrod mused. "Johnson was up at the organ fixing something—that the way you figure it? He was caught before he had time to defend himself . . . No, wait a minute. That won't work. The girl was there, too, wasn't she? What was she doing while Johnson was getting his?"

"She could have been out in the office," I suggested. "She keeps her music out there. And if Oscar was fixing something in the organ, she couldn't be playing it."

"That'd fit," Ran agreed. He half shut his eyes, appeared to visualize the scene as it must have happened. "It's a sort of split-second thing, but it would work. If she was in your office and heard a noise, she'd have to come clear through the chancel door before she'd see anything and the—the murderer'd only have to take a step to block the door. There'd be nothing for her to do but run."

"But why down here?" Elrod argued. "This is a cul-de-sac if there ever was one. Why didn't she try for outside? She might have gotten clear away."

"If he were right behind her and this door was open," I said slowly, "she might have dashed in and slammed the door thinking she'd be safe."

"Well, why wasn't she safe?" Elrod demanded. "If she could get the door shut, she could have locked it with the touch of a finger. Unless of course there wasn't time *to* shut it—"

I stopped him. "Don't," I said. "It wouldn't have made any difference—whether she got the door shut or not. He could have gone back for Oscar's keys . . ."

"Oh, God!" Ran said. Abruptly he sat down on the kitchen stool and stared at his feet. "I think you've got it. I'm afraid we've been going at this backwards—looking for a motive in Carol's death. It's too—too incidental. But if she had come out into the chancel and glimpsed the murderer standing over his victim, there'd been sense to it. He'd have to kill her too. And he'd have to work fast. But once she was safely holed up in here, he could go back and dispose of his victim—which had to be done quickly, too, since the choir would be arriving—and then silence her at his leisure. He'd only to obtain Oscar's keys . . ."

"There's a flight of stairs just outside this door. What was to prevent her ducking out once he'd gone away?"

I answered that, out of a depth of horror I'd never before experienced. It wasn't a nice picture we'd evolved, the girl trapped, helpless, waiting and listening while Death, sure and pitiless, prowled without the supposedly impregnable door. "If he'd taken off his shoes, she wouldn't have heard him. She wouldn't know whether he were still outside or not, and she'd be afraid to go out . . ."

They gave me a moment's respectful silence. Then Ran moved abruptly. "We missed something there. There wasn't a sign of blood on anyone's shoes but Smedley's and he'd stood in the stuff. But maybe if we'd checked on their socks . . ."

"She couldn't even call anyone," I said very soberly. "There's no telephone in here. It's just outside the door."

"She might have climbed out," Ran said, surveying the high basement windows, "but I don't think she had time. Or she could have tried to barricade the door. She didn't do anything apparently, poor kid—probably thought she was safe."

"I suppose there weren't any fingerprints?" I felt apologetic, introducing this hackneyed issue, but Ran only shook his head. "None where they'd count."

"Nothing to go on," Elrod grunted disgustedly. "Either this murderer was smart—or he was darn lucky. Not that he mayn't slip yet, of course. And, in the meantime, we've got these." He gestured with the hand that held bank books and a legal-looking envelope. "For what they're worth."

It seemed to me they might be worth a good deal. "If Carol did die last, who'd get the money?" I wanted to know. "Who are her heirs?"

Elrod shrugged. "Her husband—her family. I don't suppose she left a will. At twenty death's a long way into the future."

"Blair Thurston!" I said scornfully. "*He* doesn't need money. But the Tollivers . . ." I faltered a little. "Do you suppose she—they—knew about it?"

"About Johnson's will? I wonder. I could bear to know, too, if Johnson was in the habit of making wills or if this was the first he made and why he made it."

"Talk to Grayson," Elrod suggested. "Perhaps he can tell you. Incidentally, I've got a key here. It was sealed up in an envelope. It looks like a safety deposit key. Maybe, when we get the deposit box open, we'll know more where we're at."

Ran laughed shortly. "I doubt it. Come and see what we found in the kitchen. If any safety deposit box can top this loot . . ."

We were still hovering over it when Alec appeared and the story had to be told again. Alec sighed. "I'm afraid we took Oscar too much for granted," he said. "Some of this, of course, can be returned to the rightful owners. It must be. Mrs. Gregory's purse—Miss Erickson's set of teeth—"

"No!" I said and pounced on them. "Don't be silly, Alec. Miss Erickson's teeth were *not* in this drawer. None of you ever saw them. You never even *knew* about them. I was the only one who did. Let well enough alone. She got new ones. Why, she'd die of embarrassment if she thought anyone—especially you, Alec—ever dreamed her teeth were false. Believe me, I know. She'd a lot rather lose them than to have that happen!"

"Have it your own way," Alec gestured helplessly. "But why would he keep them in the first place? You can't make me believe Oscar wanted this stuff for its value—then, why?"

"Oscar was mean and vindictive," I said. "He was— you needn't look at me like that. I've been remembering. Things he said and did. He had a row with that Mrs. Carlson who lives near the church. He always cut across her lawn on his way to the grocery. Then last spring she had the lawn dug up and re-seeded and she told him he'd have to stop. He told me about it. He said he told her that it was in the Bible, that the earth was the Lord's and that God never put up trespassing signs. He thought that was smart. I know he didn't like the Gregorys—he was always holding them up as horrible examples of the decadent rich, and he hated Miss. Erickson because she bossed him and because she never sat down anywhere in the church without first rubbing her hand around to see if she could find any dust.

He'd *like* having something of hers that she needed and knowing she couldn't get it back unless he gave it to her. I imagine it was like scoring a victory over an enemy. It was a very little victory and maybe the enemy didn't know about it, but he did, and because he did it made him top dog for a little while. Do you see?"

"Oh, yes, we see," Alec said wearily. "I'll even admit you're very likely right. Only, in that case, why leave his money to Carol Tolliver of all people?"

Ran stood up with a grunt. "Can't tell you that now. Perhaps, after I've talked to Brannigan, I'll know more about it."

"I know Brannigan," Elrod said darkly. "He's a slippery fish. You'll know no more and no less than he chooses to tell you and, mark my words, that won't be much."

We separated then, Ran and Elrod to go down town, Alec and I home—to his house—for lunch.

It was better out of doors. The snow had stopped and the wind was dying. However the temperature was lowering momently and the cold thrust against our faces with numbing intensity. It was easier walking though. Someone had shoveled the long stretch between the church and the house. Alec and I could walk side by side.

Ruth was waiting with coffee, soup and an insatiable curiosity. While we ate, we did our best to bring her up to date. Oddly enough, she took the tale of Oscar's "lost-and-found" cache with calm.

"I left my purse over there once—that petit point thing I got in Paris. It was at a Guild meeting and it had about four dollars in it and my ration books. Next day I asked Oscar about it and he brought it right to me. Do you think that means he loved me?"

"He didn't leave *you* any money," I pointed out nastily.

"No," Ruth sighed. "I wish he had. It would have come in useful twenty years from now to educate the twins. I want Sandy to be a doctor and you know how a medical career costs."

"Perhaps Oscar didn't like twins," I suggested.

"I wouldn't be surprised," Ruth said. "I'm not sure I do myself. They're nothing but duplicating machines. Two bumps instead of one, two bottles to wash and fill, two little panties to change—"

Alec looked at her vaguely and pushed back his coffee cup. "Let's get going, Tess. We've a lot to do."

He was right. My desk was still a hurrah's nest I scrabbled into coat and galoshes, was ready first.

Ruth had followed us to the hall. "Come back for dinner, darling?"

I shook my head. "I don't think so. It's time I acquired some new clothes. Thanks just the same."

"Oh, do," Ruth said, ending it. "Ran's coming. He can take you home afterwards if you insist."

Ran was powerful bait. I agreed.

Georgia Brastock was the first person I saw when I'd toiled up the stairs. She was perched on the edge of a chair, gazing at our resident policeman with fascinated curiosity. She wore an ancient Hudson seal coat and a red peasant cap that came down over her ears. The cap didn't go with her sallow lined skin. Neither did it match the blue-red of her nose.

She jumped up when she saw me. She said, "Oh, Miss King, I'm so glad you've come! It's horrible out, isn't it? So cold. I took a taxi over. Frederick insisted."

Nice of Frederick, I thought, as I stood on one foot to remove an overshoe. But, on the other hand, why come at all? Curiosity or an urge to learn, first-hand, what went on?

She seemed to read my thoughts. "It's the music. For Carol's funeral. Frederick thinks there *should* be music and

I agree. She loved music so. Frederick will sing. *The Lord's
Prayer,* by Malotte."

I thought, oh, yes, *The Lord's Prayer* by Malotte. Everyone takes a whack at it sooner or later.

"Where will the funeral take place? From the church?"

"From the mortuary," Alec said, speaking for the first
time.

"Oh, yes. Dear Dean MacDonald, what a tragedy this
all is! And how painful the necessity for making such
plans! Frederick thought a quartet perhaps, to sing for ten
minutes preceding the service. Mr. Dennison is so very
unsatisfactory on the organ, don't you think? Frederick
thought a few favorite hymns . . ."

Alec, queried, didn't know Carol's favorite hymns but
he agreed to find out what they were. While he made entry, in an overcrowded notebook, she twittered thanks and
prepared to depart.

It was at the door and well behind Alec's back that she
beckoned to me. I followed her out, not without misgiv-
ings. What now?

I found out at once. In the entry way, she faced me
firmly. "Miss King, there is something I feel that you—
that someone—should know. And at once. Frederick does
not agree with me. He feels that I am overwrought, perhaps prejudiced. Believe me, that is not true. I should be
the last—the very last—to cast aspersions upon a fellow
creature . . ."

"Just what," I interrupted impatiently, "are you talking
about?"

She went on as though she hadn't heard. "But when
there is a distinct discrepancy in a man's testimony. I was
the only one to notice—in fact, I was the only one who
was in a position *to* notice—"

"Will you stop talking in riddles?" I asked through
gritted teeth. "Whose testimony?"

"Charles Dennison's. Miss King, he was *not* at the organ when we came in last night, Frederick and I. I know that's what he told Mr. Garrison, but it wasn't true. It was a little after seven when we arrived and there was no one in the choir room. I went to the chancel doors and looked out into the body of the church—I always do; it's a habit. The lights were on at the organ but there was no one there. I didn't see Charles Dennison *at all!*"

I said, "But—but are you sure? The organ lights aren't very bright—he might have been there. Yon could have missed seeing him."

"I didn't. He wasn't there. And then, while I was standing there, I heard a door slam. Downstairs." She looked at me triumphantly, as though she had clinched a point.

When I said, nothing—how could I? my head was whirling—she resumed, "I didn't think anything about it—then I went back and took off my wraps. Frederick wanted to sort out some quartets and I helped him. We were just started when Charles Dennison appeared at the chancel door and began to scold about Carol using the organ. Miss King, he must have been downstairs. *Do you think he's the murderer?*"

I said of course I didn't. I soothed and petted her and sent her away, promising to tell Ran what she'd said at the first opportunity.

I'd said I didn't believe, but I wasn't sure it wasn't true. I was—wondering. There was the will. If Dennison had known about that . . . And certainly he'd had a queer sort of foreknowledge of Carol's death . . .

When I got back to the office, Alec had vanished. He hadn't gone past me so I presumed that he was somewhere in the body of the church or the basement. I asked the somnolent policeman if he knew where Ran was. He didn't, so after a futile call to the station, I decided to write letters.

I had written three when Alec stalked through the office again. I tried to stop him but he said he was in a hurry and unless it was very important . . .

I let him go. I wrote four more letters. It was three o'clock. I tried another call for Ran. He was still incommunicado. I checked over a list of new residents. At half past three, "Red" Brannigan walked in.

I say "walked in" but it wasn't quite that easy. Hanson was still playing bodyguard but apparently Brannigan had the right answers for he was permitted to come in. He settled himself in a chair near my desk and looked around the office with open curiosity. He was a big, red-faced man whose fringe of graying hair still gave sufficient explanation for his nickname. He wore work clothes and a leather jacket.

His survey of the office ended, he looked at me. "You the boss here? Where's Garrison?"

I said I didn't know and he slumped down comfortably and folded his arms across his chest. "Figured there wasn't so danged much hurry when he said to be here at three sharp."

It was on the tip of my tongue to announce that it was half-past three now but I didn't. All the psychology books insisted that you got farther with people by being nice to them. I put down my pencil and said sweetly, "It's too bad you were inconvenienced, Mr. Brannigan. I know what it's like to be taken off a job—"

He cut me off. "I wasn't working. You know how cold it is outside? Naw, it was just that I don't like taking orders from nobody, see? Especially the police!"

I never got a chance to answer that for Ran came running up the stairs and took over. He dismissed Hanson with a nod and the policeman struggled into his overcoat muttering something about getting a "cuppa cawfee." I hesitated, wondering if I, too, should make graceful exit, but Ran jerked his head at me. "Mind helping out, Tess? We're short-handed as all get out at the station—the draft's taken all the younger men and none of the older ones are stenographers."

"Red" Brannigan shot up out of his chair. "Naw, you don't. Nobody ain't going to take down what I say because I ain't saying nothing, see? This's a free country. You ain't got no right—"

"Sit down, Mr. Brannigan," Ran said smoothly, "We have no intention of infringing upon any of your rights. The situation is simply this. Oscar Johnson has been murdered. We know very little about him. You were one of his friends. We hoped that you might be able to help us."

Brannigan sat down again with caution. "Yeah, well, maybe," he said dubiously. "What's it you want to know?"

He either didn't know anything or he wasn't telling it, I decided as my pencil raced. Oh, he appeared frank enough—yeah, he'd known Oscar. Oh, a long time—say twenty years or more. Yeah, he saw Oscar often—dropped in once or twice a week for coffee. They liked to chin a lot. Politics and—well, you know, politics. Yeah, he guessed Oscar had some relatives somewhere—everybody did. In the old country, maybe. Oscar was sorta closemouthed about himself. Friends—well, that was something else. He mentioned two or three names. Naw, there wasn't nobody else there yesterday when he saw Oscar. How long'd he stay? Not long—maybe an hour, maybe less—how'd he know? He wasn't watching no clock. He knew it was after five when he came back down town and it was fixing to storm so he got him something to eat and went home and played the radio. Where'd he live? He barked a laugh. He had a room at the Regal Hotel—he guessed the police knew where *that* was all right, all right.

Ran said, "Yes," and then was quiet for a moment. "Know anything about Johnson's financial affairs?"

Even I could feel the tension in the room. Brannigan's very eyebrows were wary. "Not much."

"You knew he had money though?"

"I knew he musta had *some*. Oscar never spent nothing if he could help it."

"It was more than 'some,'" Ran told him quietly. "It was close to thirty thousand dollars."

Brannigan said nothing with eloquence.

"Had he ever said anything to you about the disposal of that money if he should die?"

Some of the tension died. Brannigan said, "Maybe . . ." with caution.

"He left a will, you see," Ran said softly. "He left all that money—thirty thousand dollars—to the little Tolliver girl, the one who was murdered here last night."

Brannigan said, "Yeah . . ." again. He sounded bored.

"Any idea why he left it to her?"

For the first time "Red" Brannigan relaxed, became completely natural. "Yeah, I know that. He told me. It was because she was always nice to him. You know, a job like this one here ain't no siney-cure. All the old hens in the church come picking around criticizing and giving orders and calling him 'Johnson' and 'Oscar' and never a decent word of thanks nor nothing. He said the Tolliver kid was different. She always called him 'Mr. Johnson' and if she asked him to do something for her she thanked him. He said she always acted glad to see him and she always talked pleasant and chatted when he came upstairs. Oscar liked music and he had a lot of swell records and sometimes she'd come down and listen to them. He said she was a swell kid who was having a tough time and he wished to God she was his daughter because then he could help her out. He'd offered to give her the money but she wouldn't take it—proud, I guess—so he said he was going to fix things so she'd get it anyway. Sometime."

As simple as that. I had an instant's flicker of shame myself. I'd been one of those who said "Oscar" and who'd given orders. Had I always thanked him on completion of those orders? I couldn't remember.

Ran was speaking again. "If it can be established that Johnson died first, the money will now go to Carol Tolliver's heirs. But in case she predeceased him, there was another provision in that will. In that case, Mr. Brannigan, suppose that I told you the money comes to you!"

I don't think Ran expected the reaction he got. I know I certainly hadn't. The man jumped to his feet and there was surprise and horror—no, more than horror—actual loathing upon his face.

"No!" he said. "No! He can't do that to me—not that money— Oh, God, no! I don't want it—I won't take it—"

His voice died into a strangled gurgle. He turned and stumbled to the door, was out before either Ran or I could stop him.

We remained, staring blankly and guiltily at one another.

10

I had dinner with Ruth and Alec—as I had promised—but Ran never came—as *they* had promised. By nine o'clock, we had yawned ourselves out of conversation and, over their protests, I called a taxi and went to the apartment that I name home.

But not without promising to come back next day. Alec and Ruth were insistent about it. Alec had to be away a lot evenings and that would leave Ruth alone, since the latest incumbent of the maid's room was quitting—as of right now. She'd never been "mixed up in any murders" and she was sure that her mother wouldn't want her to be now. I agreed to move over, bag and baggage, until the excitement had died down or until the murders were solved.

Just the same, it was nice to be back among my own possessions even though I did feel the necessity of searching closets and looking under the bed to be sure the place held no tenant other than myself. That done, I had a long hot bath and collapsed into bed, after setting the alarm that would rouse me in plenty of time for the inquests.

To me the inquests, in contrast to the taut drama I'd witnessed at the church, were unbelievably dull. They were held in a large room at the courthouse. In spite of the cold, the room was jammed to its doors with thrill seekers who got little for their money. Or so I thought. The coroner spoke in a mumble scarcely to be heard beyond the first four rows. Only a few witnesses were called—Ran, Alec, Dr. Morton, the Brastocks, Philip Smedley, myself, and the young Irish policeman who'd discovered Carol's body. Such questions as we were called upon to answer were cut to the bone. We were given no opportunity for speculation or the introduction of the irrelevant. The verdicts were the old familiar ones—death at the hands of a person or persons unknown.

I told Ruth about it at noon. We were alone, Alec having gone to be with the Tollivers until the actual time of the funeral. Ruth, spooning apple sauce and carrots into her offspring, listened without comment.

"Oh, well, inquests!" she said when I was done. "They're silly things at best. I think Ran was lucky. What if the whole thing had run away from him?"

"What do you mean?" Fascinated, I watched a blob of apple sauce trickle to the jut of Frances' chin, hover there.

Ruth wiped it off with firmness. "Dribble puss!" she said fondly. "Why, I mean just what you think I do, Tess. There were a lot of things that didn't come out, weren't there? Suppose someone—the coroner or the jury—had asked awkward questions? They do sometimes."

I shrugged. Although the ways of inquests were strange to me, this one had had all the qualities of the rehearsed . . .

I elected to stay home with the twins and let Ruth go to the funeral. I knew that few would notice whether Tess King was there or not, whereas if the dean's wife stayed away . . . When I pointed this out to Ruth, she gave in at once. Staving off criticism is one of the heavy duties of a minister's wife.

I'd anticipated a peaceful afternoon but I didn't get it. Between the telephone and the babies, my hands were full. From three o'clock on, after the post-luncheon nap, until their six o'clock bath and supper, was the twin's "play time." It was a hectic interval with both ready to battle royally for whatever treasure the other chanced to hold.

I was refereeing a hair-pulling match when the doorbell rang. I shook my own hair out of my eyes—it had suffered in the general mêlée—and went to answer. It was Ran. I suppose I looked surprised because his own eyebrows went up. "What's, the matter?"

"Nothing," I said. "I thought you'd be at the funeral. Leave your coat over there—that's what the chair's for."

He obeyed and then followed me into the living room. Temporarily at least, it presented a peaceful picture with lamplight and firelight and the twins standing side by side in their play pen, the tears dried on their cheeks, their latest brawl forgotten in mutual curiosity.

Ran looked around, sighed comfortably and sat. "Nice domestic atmosphere," he remarked.

"Lovely," I agreed grimly. "Don't think it's like this all the time—this is just an interlude. By the way, where were you last night?"

He didn't answer right away. He was looking around. "Ruth and Alec at the funeral, I suppose. When'll they be back?"

"Almost any time," I said soberly. "There's just the service, you know. Interment will have to wait until—until the weather warms up. But you haven't told me—"

"Ghastly the tricks our climate plays. Last night, Miss King? Last night I was meeting the nine o'clock bus to be certain young Thurston came in on it. He did."

"That doesn't mean anything," I said scornfully. "He could have been here Thursday night and then gone to some little town and recaught the bus. *If* he wanted an alibi."

"Thanks. We have ideas like that ourselves. But did you ever try to check with a bus driver or a conductor about a sailor? If all cats look alike after dark, so do all males

once they put on a uniform. A sailor, yes—they might remember—but a particular set of features on a particular
sailor, no."

"You sound remarkably indifferent."

"I am. I don't think the Thurston angle amounts to a
damn."

"Please," I said. "The young fry have ears. Also tongues."

He looked at them unbelieving. "You don't mean those
things can *talk?*"

"And how," I said. I beamed at Frances. "Say something
for the gentleman, darling."

Sandy said promptly, "Daddy come—no, no—go by-
by—moo cow!" while Frances added a wistful postscript.
"Coo-kie?"

Vindicated, I said, "You see! All right, pet—you shall
have your 'coo-kie' in a minute. But first I want to hear
what the nice man has to say."

"Flattery yet!" Ran said, his eyes crinkling. "The nice
man has nothing to say." I suppose my face fell visibly
for he went on, "Oh, well. I suppose you're entitled to
a crumb or two. I only meant that the farther I get into
this thing the more I'm convinced that the girl's death was
incidental and that Oscar's the one with which we should
be concerned."

"Oh, I hope so!" I said, so fervently that he smiled
again, faintly. "Has—has anything new happened?"

"Yes." He was bent far forward now, hands swinging
between his knees. "We opened Oscar's deposit box this
noon—after considerable red tape. It was full of money."

"More money!" I repeated stupidly. "Where on earth
did he get it? How much?"

"A little better than two thousand dollars. Most of it
in small bills."

I sat down heavily. "Ran, it doesn't make sense. That's—
why, that's more than thirty thousand dollars all together!

How could he have that much money? Where did he get
it? He couldn't possibly have saved it—not on his salary."

"No. Of course, there are ways in which money may be
obtained without earning it. Inheritance, for one. However, so far as we know, Oscar had no relatives in this
country and there are no records of an estate coming to
him. Besides, inheritances are not commonly paid in bills
of small denomination."

"It could have come to him in some other form and
then been liquidated," I argued.

"Certainly. Only I don't think it was. Moreover, according to bank records, Oscar was in the habit of visiting his
deposit box at least once a week which would argue that
the two thousand was deposited in small sums at more or
less regular intervals."

"It sounds like business profits," I said dubiously. "I
suppose he could have been part owner of a gas station. He
might have had outside interests, mightn't he?"

"Gas stations being so very profitable in these days of
A and B ration cards. Of course, there's black market gas
but that has to come from somewhere and . . . No, if
Oscar were engaged in any legitimate business, why keep
it secret?"

"He might have been afraid he'd lose his job here," I
suggested. "Although I don't see the fascination in sixty
dollars per when . . ." A thought struck me. "You said
'legitimate'—what did you mean by that?"

"Because I've a hunch that his business wasn't legitimate. Now, wait a minute. We were talking about the ways
in which a man could obtain money. In the light of this,
have you any ideas?"

"By inheriting it, by earning it or by stealing it," I
murmured. "Or, I suppose he could have found it. If St.
Thomas' were an old English cathedral and it had a hidden
treasure—"

"Come back to earth. St. Thomas' is not an old English cathedral—it was built in eighteen-ninety—and God knows there was no treasure hidden in it."

"Robbery, then," I said, vaguely disappointed. "But that doesn't make sense either."

"Hardly. There've been no unsolved big robberies around here and darn few small ones. No, I think we can wash out robbery. Well, let's see what's left. This is war time and our enemies do have agents over here. Oscar had relatives in the old country—it's possible the Nazis might have had a hold over him in that way. But just what good Oscar could do them here . . ."

But I liked that idea, was ready to battle for it. "There's the stockyards," I pointed out. "They're huge. And the bomber base. The machine works, the packing plants—oh, I can think of lots of things."

"Not thirty thousand dollars' worth. The Nazis don't pay that well. One of the disillusioning things about this subversive stuff is the pittance for which a man is willing to sell his soul. I'm not saying we haven't had some spy activity around here. We have but the F.B.I. takes care of it handily. And Oscar isn't on their lists. We checked it."

"I've another idea," I said. "It just came to me. If this were a long time ago, I'd say that Oscar'd been bootlegging. But—what about gambling?"

"In one form or another," Ran murmured. "Ever hear of the numbers racket?"

"I think so," I said. "I mean, I know I have. But I don't understand it very well and I've always thought of it as something that belonged to bigger places than Dorchester."

"Dorchester's about a hundred thousand now and the game, in spite of our efforts, flourishes here, thank you."

"It's something like betting, isn't it?"

"Betting under cover." He spoke absently as though he only half way attended to me. "All very hush-hush but the lower east side is honeycombed with it. The west side, too, for that matter. Mostly small sums but, even so, the take must be enormous. And someone's got to head the thing."

I thought of the brilliantly lighted bars that lined lower sixth and seventh. I thought of the furtive down-at-the-heels gentry you glimpsed upon the sidewalks before them. I thought of their plushier counterparts in the respectable down town area. I shook my head. "Not Oscar. He was neither fish nor fowl. He wouldn't fit."

"Perhaps not. Ever hear of Black Jack Bailey?"

"No. Should I have? Who is he?"

"Night life character. Gambler, vice—er—lord, if rumor tells the truth."

"Ran!" I sat bolt upright now. "You're not connecting a—a vice lord with St. Thomas' are you?"

His face was impenetrable. "I'm canvassing possibilities, that's all. There are still a few you—we—haven't mentioned."

"I know I've thought of one or two more myself. There's counterfeiting." His snort of disgust hurried me on. "Oh, all right, then! What about dope running—well, people do do that!—or the stock market? He could have played that."

"He could but he didn't. Look, Tess, I don't know whether your sense of delicacy forbids or not, but so far you've skipped the one way by which Oscar could have made money that adds up with the rest of this mess. Blackmail."

I felt cold clear to my toe tips. "Thirty thousand dollars' worth?"

"That would depend upon the number of his—er—clients, wouldn't it?"

I was silent and he leaned forward to emphasize the earnestness of his words with a tapping forefinger upon my unresponsive knee. "Listen, darling. Oscar was a pretty queer duck—we've proven that. He disliked most people

and to those he disliked he was vindictive. Remember Miss
Erickson's teeth, Mrs. Gregory's purse. Those were little
ineffectual hurts, granted. But how do you think he would
have acted if he'd gotten hold of something really big—
something perhaps definitely criminal, prosecutable by
law—that involved one or more of the people he disliked?"

"I don't know." I didn't either. I didn't think anyone
did. Or ever would, now that Oscar was dead. "But so
much money . . ."

"I'm not suggesting that it all came from one person.
I'm not even insisting it *was* blackmail. I'm only saying it's
a possibility."

I made a dissenting gesture. "Not in Dorchester. Not
at St. Thomas'."

He spoke gravely. "My dear, forget St. Thomas'. You're
not talking to Alec now. St. Thomas' is not responsible
for Oscar. What I'm trying to get across to you is that we
human beings are poor weak creatures at best and there
are few of us who have not at one time or another invited
blackmail. One slip, a single false step, and he who learns
of it becomes possessed of a weapon that, revealed, may
destroy happiness, a home, or the most promising of business careers. And, under threat of such destruction, who of
us is strong enough to risk the loss of all he loved or possessed? Who wouldn't pay—and then pay again? Wouldn't you?"

I walked over to the window and stood there looking
out. But I was blind to that which spread before me. I
turned back. I met his eyes honestly. "Yes," I said. "I'm
afraid I'd pay."

He pounced on that. "But you haven't?"

I thought I was insulted. "Certainly not!" I snapped.
"What do you think I am?"

"A poor weak human like the rest of us," he told me
soberly. "And one, moreover, who was rather consistently
under Oscar's eye. No navy blue spots in your past, Tess?"

"None that I know of." I spoke absently, to his back because he'd gone into the hall and was taking up his coat. "Aren't you staying for tea?"

He glanced at his wrist watch. "Sorry. I've stayed too long as it is." He picked up his hat. "Good-by. If anything turns up, you know where you can get me."

"Wait!" I ignored the howl the twins put up, came into the hall myself. "I've just thought of something. That Brannigan seemed to know a lot about Oscar's money. Couldn't you ask him?"

"I could." Ran's mouth was wry. "And I would. Gladly. Not only that—I'd like to tell him he's in no danger of getting Oscar's money. The difficulty is he's no longer available. Sometime during the night he got away from the man I had watching him."

"Got away! You mean he's left town?"

Rah shrugged. "I doubt it. There are plenty of places to hide out in Dorchester if you have the right contacts. I think Brannigan had."

My brain was perking on all six. "Then if he disappeared like that, it must have been because he knew you'd try to find out more about the money and he didn't want to tell you. And if he didn't want to tell you, it must have been because you're right and there is something wrong about the money."

His hand was on the door. "Oh, yes. I think we can safely go that far. There's something decidedly wrong about the money." He sounded amused.

I wasn't. I was beginning to smolder. "You don't need to be so smart about it," I said. "I don't know why you came here this afternoon—it certainly wasn't to pick my brains. You didn't need to. I think you know a lot that you haven't told me—"

He interrupted me. "I came here because I was tired and I needed a rest for a little while. And I wasn't trying to pick your brains—God knows I never meant to talk about this thing at all. Especially not with you. It's too nasty. But—well, I had to talk to someone and Alec's no good. His point of view isn't mine—we're traveling on parallel lines that never can meet. And you're right about the rest of it. I do know a few things you don't and, so help me, this time I'm keeping them to myself. That's the real reason I'm getting out now. You're too disarming, my dear. Before I know it, I'll have told you everything."

In spite of myself, I was flattered. Disarming, was I? All right—I'd disarm some more. "Don't go," I coaxed. I even dared a hand on his arm. "I won't ask questions—I promise you. Please stay to dinner—Ruth would want you to."

"Thanks, no." He eyed my hand as though it were going to bite him and I snatched it away. He frowned at that but he opened the door, held it half way. "I've work to do."

I didn't say anything and, after a second, he shut the door again and stood leaning against it. The scar that made a line above his right eyebrow showed lividly. "Tess, I swore I wouldn't ask this of you but apparently I'll have to. I've got to have someone and Alec isn't disposed to be helpful. If I show you a list of names, can you check them over and tell me offhand how many are connected in any way with St. Thomas'?"

"I think so," I said. "Now?"

For answer he took a folded slip of paper from his pocket, handed it to me. I walked back into the living room, sat in the lamplighted circle of a big chair, and reached for one of the pencils Ruth keeps scattered around for Alec's benefit. Ran followed me in, stood against the mantel, watching me.

There were approximately thirty names on the list which was written in ink in a shambling unformed hand. Two of the names had lines drawn through them. Some of them were unfamiliar but there were a number I knew only too well. I double-checked for safety and then looked up at Ran. He stood unmoving. "How many?"

"Seven," I said slowly. "Seven who are communicants or attendants at St. Thomas'."

He let out his breath in a slow whistle. "And of these seven, how many were present the other night?"

I got angry again. "You know that as well as I. Six." I counted the names aloud. "Miss Erickson, Philip Smedley, Georgia Brastock, Charles Dennison, Mary Collins, Bill Carter."

"And the other one? The one who wasn't there?"

"You know that too." My tongue tripped. "Blair Thurston."

"Thanks," he said and reached out a hand. "I wanted to hear you say them."

"Because of the beauty of my pronunciation? Ran— what is this? Where did you get this list?"

He looked at me soberly. "It was in Oscar Johnson's deposit box. The only thing that *was* there beside the money."

11

Again he was on his way to the door. Again I stopped him. "You can't go now," I said. "Please. I want to know about this."

"Sorry. I really meant it when I said I had things to do. And about this." He was restoring the folded paper to an inside pocket. "That's all I know. It's just a list of names and it was in Oscar's box."

"And what a list!" I said scornfully. "Seven people who attend St. Thomas'. Six who were at the church the night he was killed. But, Ran—not one of those people has ever done a thing for which he could be blackmailed."

"How do you know?"

It fell as coldly as a stone. I said, "Why—why, of course I don't know but . . ."

"Look, Tess," he said. "There are thirty names there. Twenty-three have no connection with St Thomas'. You say so and you should know. Seven have. It would take the hell of a long time to run down the twenty-three. No addresses and only initials. Nice common names, too, aren't they? Smith and Nelson and Brown. So let's skip Messrs. Smith, Nelson and Brown for the present and concentrate on the other seven. They *do* have a connection with St. Thomas' and thereby with Oscar. Six of the seven, as you have so succinctly stated, were present the night he died.

Let's play it smart. If the six fizzle out, we've still got one more and, if he does too, we've still twenty-three others."

I jabbed the pencil into the chair arm and thought. Miss Erickson, a school teacher. Georgia Brastock, wife of a successful musician but a comparatively poor man. Charles Dennison, an ancient, poverty-stricken organist. Philip Smedley, under-clerk in a clothing store. Mary Collins, cashier in a chain grocery. Bill Carter, manager of a local loan company. "None of them," I said at last with conviction, "could pay blackmail."

"It might not have been blackmail," Ran said slowly. I looked at him in disgust. "But you said—"

"I said it was a possibility. It may have been something else."

"What?"

"I don't know—yet. I'd have to talk to these people first."

"You won't find out anything," I told him. "They're all scared to death. The one who killed him and the ones who didn't—if it was any of them." It sounded very complicated but there seemed no point in attempting clarification.

"No," Ran said on a sigh, "I don't suppose I will. But I'll have a try at it."

"And if not—what then?"

"I don't know."

He really did go then and I returned to the babies who sat in opposite corners of the play pen howling their heads off. A guilty look at the clock told me they had reason for their grief. Five-thirty was the scheduled bath time and it was already perilously toward six.

I got them bathed and powdered and sleepered. I sat them in their high chairs—the blue one for Sandy, the pink for Frances. I crisped bacon and cut toast into finger lengths. All this before I heard Ruth and Alec in the hall.

"I'm in the kitchen," I called. "Come on out."

They came, Alec scolding because I'd forgotten to lock the front door and Ruth with a critical eye on my labors. "Nice going," she approved. "Oh, keep quiet, Alec—everybody forgets something sometime! Darling, when are you going to give up your caree-ah for love and a couple like this?"

I laughed as I washed Sandy's buttery paws. "Any time Mr. Right comes along. But one of these at a time will do, thanks. There's no double trouble on my family tree."

Alec cut in on Ruth's speculations about Ran's family with a martyred, "Girls, I hate to mention it, but I'd like dinner as soon as possible. I've work to do this evening."

"He has, too," Ruth told me when we were tucking the twins away. "His sermon for tomorrow. Why do you suppose ministers always leave them to the last minute?"

"Lack of inspiration," I guessed. "Or maybe it's the same principle we worked on when we attended English 8. If we waited long enough, the professor might die or the building burn down, and then we wouldn't have to turn in our themes."

"Well, St. Thomas' isn't going to burn down and he will have to preach a sermon." Ruth led the way down the backstairs to the kitchen. "It's going to be bad, too, tomorrow—the service, I mean. It'll be worse than Christmas or Easter. Wait and see. Everyone and his pet cat will be there. They'll probably put chairs in at the back and even then there won't be enough."

"It's too bad the Guild can't conduct a sightseeing tour and charge for it," I grumbled as I gathered plates and cups together. "They'd pay for the new carpet in half no time."

"Shh!" Ruth warned. "Don't let Alec hear you say anything like that—he'd be furious. At that, I bet people would go, right enough. Did you hear anything from Ran?"

I leaned against the door frame and told her about it, even the list of names. It was all right. Ran hadn't said not to tell.

Ruth listened, slicing potatoes with a steady hand. "I suppose that list's what they call a clue," she said scornfully. "Well, I don't think much of it. Lists! Everybody makes lists one time or another."

"They don't usually keep them in safety deposit boxes," I pointed out.

"No-o." Ruth slammed the frying pan on the stove and turned up the gas. "Twenty minutes for the steak," she murmured. "I can't hurry it any faster. Poor Alec! I'm afraid dinner will be late after all. Are you going to tell him?"

"Alec? I suppose so. Why not?"

"No reason at all, only—well, Alec has a sort of guilt complex about Oscar. He says it's disgraceful that any man should work the length of time Oscar did for a church and the church know no more about him. And the worst of it is," said Ruth, opening her eyes very wider, "it's true. We don't know what he did away from the church nor how he spent his evenings nor who his friends were. Alec blames himself."

"He needn't," I said. "Oscar wanted it that way. The rest he can charge up to the non-existent caste system of the American people. And so far as his activities are concerned, I've learned enough about them, thank you."

"Now, you're being silly," Ruth said.

I didn't answer. I knew it.

Ruth creamed carrots. I made salad, conveyed it to the dining room. We fashioned a dessert of preserved figs, crackers and cheese. Coffee began to bubble in the percolator.

Ruth slid the steak to its hot platter and faced me. "Honestly, Tess, I can't get those people—the ones on that list—out of my mind. And I think Ran Garrison's gone completely out of *his!* Can you see Charlie Dennison or Leota Erickson murdering anybody?"

"No," I said. "I can't."

"And as for blackmail—phooey!" She began to sound more cheerful. "How could you blackmail Leota Erickson? And for what? If it were the other way around now . . ."

"Ran said it mightn't be blackmail." I was trying to be fair.

"Then what on earth could it be?" Ruth asked inconsistently. "The only thing those people have in common is that they sing in the choir. And they're all as poor as church mice!"

Alec ate his dinner in a bemused silence and vanished. Ruth and I did the dishes and then sat by the living room fire. We didn't talk. We were past conversation. She knitted and I tried to read. Subconsciously, I think we were both waiting for the phone to ring. It didn't. When, at eleven o'clock, we decided on bed, Alec's light still burned in the study.

On the stair landing, Ruth paused to pull aside the curtain, and peer out at the star-spangled sky. "I wish it would snow tomorrow," she said bitterly. "I wish it would blizzard. Then perhaps we wouldn't have such a Roman circus at the church."

She didn't get her wish. Sunday dawned with snow sparkling under a winter-bright sun. The sky was and blue and cold. Perfect winter weather.

Everything moved in double time that morning. When the first bell rang for church school, I discovered, rather to my surprise, that I was dressed and ready. I went downstairs. Alec had long since disappeared but Ruth was in the living room, somberly regarding the twins as they staggered about their play pen. I said tentatively, "If you'd like to go . . ."

She shook her head. "I wouldn't. I wish there didn't have to be any service. It'll only be a mockery. I told Alec so and he was shocked. But I don't care—that's the way I feel."

I teetered uncertainly from one foot to the other. "Well, I guess I'll go over," I said at last when it was evident that she didn't want to talk. "I'll tell you everything that happens."

"I don't think I want you to," she said soberly. "Sometimes you're happier if you don't know. I wish I were Alec. I think his way's best."

And just what was Alec's way, I wondered as I let myself out of the front door. I was pretty certain I knew. Alec, I thought, had made his decision. It was the age-old conflict between church and state. The murders, even though they had occurred on church property, belonged properly to the province of the state. Let the state take over. Alec would neither help nor hinder.

Stragglers were being shooed into the church as I came around the corner. The echoes of the last bell were dying. Even so early as this, cars lined the street. I thought sadly that Ruth was right. This day the church would be crammed to its doors.

I was seldom so early. Church school begins at nine-thirty and lasts until ten-thirty. The regular morning service begins promptly at eleven o'clock. There is little for me to do beyond filling a seat in the choir and taking charge of the collection.

When I came into the choir room, I saw, with a little shiver of nerves, that the bishop was there. That shiver didn't mean that I don't like the bishop, I do. He's a saint. But saints are not necessarily easy to get along with.

Bishop Walters is a tall old man with a fine-carved profile that belongs on an antique coin. He is very thin, almost emaciated. Ruth, who adores him, insists that the food he is persuaded to ingest nourishes the flame of his spirit rather than that of his body. Beside him, Alec

resembles a schoolboy. But there is a basic likeness between them, none the less. Even as I shook hands and murmured appropriate nothings, I was reflecting sadly that,
given another twenty years, the likeness would grow indisputable. For the present, the older man's flame but burned
the brighter, that was all.

Alec and the bishop vanished and I made for the telephone to warn Ruth there'd be a guest for dinner. Not that
it was really necessary—a dean's household is geared for
unexpected guests.

I had just replaced the hand set when Charles Dennison came shuffling up the stairs. He wore his usual blue
serge, frayed and shiny—and an ancient mustard-colored
overcoat. He was sucking candy—peppermint this time.

I caught its acrid bitter odor.

He headed straight my way, his light little eyes avid.
"They find out anything—the police? Know yet who killed
Oscar and the girl?"

I shook my head. I'd determined that the one thing I
was not going to do this morning was to talk about the
murders. Let Ran do that, if talking was needed.

But Charles Dennison wasn't satisfied. "They gave this
place a going over, didn't they? They must of found fingerprints or something!"

"I'm not sure but I don't think there were any prints,"
I said carefully.

"You could find out, couldn't you?" His tone wheedled.
"You're thick with the dean and that police fellow. They'd
tell you and think nothing of it."

I shrugged. "If you really want to know, why don't you
ask Mr. Garrison yourself? He'll probably be here this
morning."

He jumped backwards as though he'd been stabbed with
a pin. "Me? Want to know? Great gollies, it doesn't matter
one way nor another to me! Fellow can't help wondering

though. It doesn't seem right. Two murders happen almost under my nose and I don't know any more about them than the people who read the papers. How'd I know they haven't been finding my fingerprints—they must be all over—and fixing to put it on me? Fellow can be pardoned for a little natural curiosity in those circumstances, can't he?"

"Curiosity's natural enough," I said slowly. A little devil of experiment was prodding me. Charles Dennison's name had been on that list, hadn't it? I could drop an innocuous bombshell. "There's one thing I do know. It—surprised me, rather. Did you know that Oscar died a wealthy man?"

"That so?" His eyes were wary now. "I don't know that that's what you'd call exclusive news. It's all over town. Likewise that the Tolliver kid gets it now. Or her family."

I was wondering who'd let that out—the Tollivers, perhaps—wondering, too, if he could possibly know that he, too, was concerned in the provisions of that will—when other footsteps stamped on the stairs. Charles Dennison scuttled for his robe as the Brastocks walked in.

Because that list was heavy on my mind and because Georgia Brastock's name had been on it, I studied her with new interest Something beyond interest—surprise. For, almost overnight, Georgia Brastock had changed. Gone were her nervous flutterings and fidgets. She looked serene, happy. Even the lines had smoothed out of her face. She looked ten years younger.

I turned from her to her husband. So far as I could tell, Frederick Brastock appeared much as usual. A little less aggressive, perhaps, but that was all. Briskly businesslike, he discarded his overcoat and began to insert the anthems for the day into their stiff black covers.

The Brastocks were but the vanguard of the rest of the choir. The wall clock showed fifteen minutes of eleven. People began to mill about the wardrobe where the vestments hung, about the long mirrors between the windows.

Charles Dennison had gone out to the organ. The throb of music came faintly to us.

The bishop and Alec stood robed and ready. It was time for me to dress.

I found my robe without difficulty—each has its wearer's name sewed into it—and the space about the wardrobe had cleared. I was one of the last to dress. As I stood before the mirror to adjust the tassel on my mortarboard, Ran's face swam for a second above my shoulder. I drew a breath of gladness. Thank heaven, he was here! But, when I turned to speak to him, I found he no longer stood behind me. He had crossed to the opposite side of the room where Alec was introducing him to the bishop.

The processional was forming. Hymn books were opening. I glanced at mine, saw the hymn was familiar: *Jesus, King of Glory.* I noted that Len Tolliver, who was our crucifer, was not present and that Frederick Brastock had the substitute cornered and was giving instructions, no less emphatic because they were last minute.

Beside me, Leota Erickson stood in pious readiness. I gave her an exasperated glance. I had never wasted liking on Leota. No matter what Oscar's death had meant to the rest of us, she had not altered by a hair's breadth. Her mortarboard, skewered to her gray braids, sat unwobbling. Her tassel swung in rigid correctness. Her hands clasped hymn book, anthem and the prayer book she knew by heart. Later on, during the service, she would, I knew, be swiftest to her knees. Her voice would be the loudest in the responses, her head the longest bowed. I hated her.

Scarcely a Christian attitude, I thought wryly as I turned resolutely away. Well, that made three out of the six upon whom I'd cast my eagle eye to discover exactly nothing. Was it possible I was not a good discoverer? Or was it simply that there was nothing to discover? I didn't know.

Bill Carter, another of those tantalizing names, stood over by the windows, laughing and talking with one of the high-school sopranos. He seemed as usual. How in the world could he be implicated, I wondered. He'd only been in town a short while.

Mary Collins wasn't there, nor was I surprised. Mary prided herself on being of finer clay than the rest of us, a circumstance which made understandable her faint of the other night. She claimed to be more sensitive, more nervous and more highly strung than the average. Knowing that, I hadn't really expected her.

Of the six, that left only Philip Smedley and he, too, was absent. Nor was *his* absence surprising. If Ruth's contention was right and he had been in love with Carol . . .

He wasn't absent. He was clattering up the stairs, flinging off coat and hat as he came. Alec's eyes gave reproof but the bishop seemed completely oblivious to the sudden turmoil.

His suit coat was tossed upon a chair. He was at the wardrobe. Hangers rattled along the central rail. "I can't find my robe," he said shrilly. "Somebody's wearing it— I know they are! It was right here. I always leave it right here . . ."

The hands of the clock were moving irresistibly toward eleven. Frederick Brastock spoke in tight-lipped exasperation. "Take someone else's then. And hurry up!"

I crossed to the wardrobe. "Let me look," I said. I knew well how helpless men were when it came to finding things. "Probably it's just been pushed along." I touched the robe farthest back, started to pull it forward.

Instinctively my hands recoiled. They dropped to my sides. I was suddenly cold all over, conscious that I was going to scream. Then, blessedly, I knew that I wasn't. I set my teeth.

"Here!" I said. I snatched at a robe, any robe. "Put this on. And here—take my hymnal—and anthem—"

His head was coming through the cotta neck. Thank goodness, he'd noticed nothing. "But you—what'll you do?"

"I'll get another."

But I knew I wouldn't, I couldn't. Frederick Brastock was gesturing toward the table where there were extra anthems and hymnals. Dumbly I shook my head. There was a chair against the wall and I sank into it. I wondered how my voice would sound if I tried to speak to Ran. For Alec's sake there must be no panic . . .

Ran had seen. He had stepped out of line, shoved Smedley into his vacant place. Charles Dennison had reduced the organ to whispering softness. Solemnly the final strokes of the bell sounded. I heard Alec's voice, clipped and clean, and then the organ swelled into the processional hymn.

Frederick Brastock stood by the door. He was counting softly. "One—two—three—four. One—two—three—now!" He raised his not inconsiderable tenon. "Jesus, King of Glory, Throned above the Sky . . ."

The door was open, the first soprano and alto embarked upon their swaying journey.

The door was closed. Ran had closed it. He was standing over me. He said, "What was it? What did you find?"

I was feeling sick again. I got up and walked toward the window. "Yes," I said, "I found something. The last robe to your right. I touched it. It felt stiff . . ."

Again hangers rattled along the pole. When I turned, he was holding the robe. I said, "It's blood, isn't it? Nothing else would make it feel so—so thick and queer . . ."

"It's blood all right."

I watched him fumble for the name tag. My throat felt tight. "Whose is it?"

"Whose?" He looked at me out of eyes in which consternation and disbelief struggled for mastery. "Good lord, it can't be—but it is! It's Charles Dennison's!"

12

I said, "Cover that thing, will you? It's making me sick to look at it." Then, as Ran stood irresolutely, "Put it back where you got it, why don't you? You can stay right here. Nobody can take it."

I heard his low whistle as he obeyed. When he came back to me, his mouth was grimmer than usual.

"It's blood, all right. There are stains on the side wall, on the floor. That thing must have been put away dripping. No wonder we found no blood on anyone's clothes."

"It could have been." I knew an insane impulse toward laughter. "We never use vestments at choir practice. There'd have been plenty of time for it to—dry."

But Ran wasn't listening. He said bitterly, "I told those lunkheads to go over this place and I meant it! If it wasn't war time and men so hard to get, I'd have their badges for this. The double-distilled idiots—the—"

"Wait!" I hurried it because his tone, if not his words, was becoming highly unsuitable for utterance in a church. "They didn't search the wardrobe because they couldn't get it open. It has a combination lock. I opened it for Hanson myself. He just shoved the robes around a little. It's probably all my fault. I knew about the robes—I should have realized that the murderer could have worn one of them and—and kept completely covered."

"Why should you? You've not been plotting or planning a murder—I hope."

I said, "Ran!" and he laughed. It wasn't a nice laugh. "Never mind, darling—finding that thing's got me down. Here I had it all figured out it was one of those spur of the moment affairs. A quarrel, possibly, in Oscar's sanctum, a weapon handy, Oscar summoned upstairs to the organ, the murderer following . . ." He moved his hand in a quick gesture. "Now, what have I got? Premeditation if I ever saw it. We've got a murderer who enters the church, goes to the wardrobe and takes a choir robe—for a definite purpose—goes downstairs to Oscar's apartment for a weapon, returns in full regalia and cuts Oscar's throat, goes back downstairs and kills Carol, reclimbs the stairs, tucks Oscar's body tidily away, replaces the church keys in their accustomed place, and rehangs the robe in the wardrobe. What kind of a maniac have I got hold of?"

"You haven't," I said. "Got hold of him, I mean. And about the robe being Charlie Dennison's—that doesn't mean a thing. I can explain that. It just happened. It could have been anyone's robe. I don't think it was taken even to throw suspicion on Charlie—"

"As if anyone needed to throw suspicion on Charlie," Ran murmured.

It exasperated me. "Oh, Ran, try to make sense! I suppose you're thinking about that money. But how could Charlie Dennison kill Oscar? Oscar was younger than he is—I know that—and a whole lot stronger. Why, even, Carol . . . It just couldn't be possible!"

"It could so," Ran said but his tone lacked conviction. "Perhaps I forgot to tell you that Oscar was clunked over the head before he was—er—eased out of existence. And so far as Carol goes, she was a little thing. Any one of our suspects could have handled her. Then, too, Morton says those chest wounds were inflicted before her throat was cut. They would have made a difference. By the way, can they hear us out there?"

"How could they? We can scarcely hear the organ." Hysterical laughter overcame me. "Oh, Ran, what they must be thinking! You and I staying behind together—there'll be a wonderful choir scandal!"

"Never mind that now. You were going to tell me something about the robe—Dennison's robe."

"Oh, yes." The knowledge sobered me. "You know, members of the choir are supposed to hang up their own robes when service is over. Well, Charles Dennison never does. If he condescends to get it as far as this room, he just tosses it over a chair and leaves it for whosoever will to put away. The times I've hung it up myself! And often he doesn't even bring it this far. Half the time he leaves it on the organ bench or in the choir stalls while he hikes out the front door. And I was just thinking—he might have left it downstairs some time. Oscar could have found it. He and Dennison didn't get along very well—"

Ran said, "Oh!" and I hurried on. "Oscar could have kept it, hidden it, even, for meanness."

"It makes more sense that way," Ran admitted slowly. "It puts it back downstairs where I'd prefer it to be. If the murderer found not only a weapon to his hand but a means to protect himself from bloodstains . . ." His voice trailed off.

"What are you going to do?"

"Do? I think for the present we'll play this robe close to our chests. I'll take it down to the station, send it away for analysis, although I don't think there's a question as to the nature of the stains. For the rest, we'll keep quiet—let whoever hung it away stew in his own juice for a while."

I was disappointed. "Aren't you going to talk to Dennison?"

"Dennison?" he repeated vaguely. "Oh, yes, Dennison. Certainly we'll talk to him."

Delighted, I accused him. "You said 'we.' Is that me too?"

Ran smothered what he pretended was a yawn. "Why not? You've been knee-deep in this so far. Why shut you out now?"

The policy of keeping silent made it imperative we talk to Charles Dennison after the others had gone. As soon as the first notes of the recessional sounded, Ran put on his coat and went around to the church entrance. "To prevent any unexpected getaway" as he phrased it. I remained sitting quietly where I was. None of the returning choir members seemed surprised to see me there. My post as secretary had given me a status somewhat akin to that of any other piece of church equipment. One or two asked me if I were ill. I pleaded headache and the statement went unchallenged. They were all too anxious to get away to the delights of a good Sunday dinner and an afternoon of leisure to want to quibble.

The big room emptied slowly but presently it was empty. Even Alec and the. bishop had gone when Ran finally appeared, driving a sputtering Dennison before him.

The organist was angry. I could hear his high querulous voice before he came in sight. "Talk to me," he was saying. "What about—that's what I want to know—what about? Do you think I've got time to sit around Sundays and talk? Can't it wait until tomorrow? Here it is the day of rest, so-called, and I've already put in two good hours of hard work and I want my dinner and you say sit around and talk! What do you want to talk about, hey?"

He had been stripping off cotta and cassock as he spoke. Now he tossed them over a chair back. Ran picked up the cassock.

"I won't keep you long," he said mildly. "This yours?"

The organist glared at him. "No, it isn't!" he snapped. "I don't know whose it is and I don't care. All this business of wearing the same robe every Sunday's nothing but nonsense. First come, first served, I say. I get here early so I can get first choice. If the rest of them don't like it, they can lump it."

"The name in it says Smedley," Ran observed. He laid the robe over the chair back again and looked at Dennison. "Where's yours?"

"I don't know and I don't care." The organist tossed his head angrily. "I haven't seen it for a couple of weeks." Suddenly he seemed to suspect a purpose behind the question and he eyed Ran warily. "Why? What difference does it make?"

Ran was moving toward the wardrobe. "Would you like to see it now?"

"What I like or don't like doesn't seem to matter," Dennison grumbled. "I don't know's I care—one way or the other."

Ran swung around then and the organist's voice rose in a sudden high cackle. "What's that on it? What're those marks? All down the front! That's not my robe—you can't prove it is—"

"Your name's in it," Ran said dispassionately. "And the stains are blood. Whoever killed Johnson and Carol wore this robe."

Before our eyes, Charles Dennison seemed to wilt. Sweat pricked out along the high expanse of his forehead, "You can't prove it was me," he said and his voice wavered. "You can't prove it was me wore that robe. I never killed them—I never killed anybody! What are you trying to do—put it on me? Just because I'm an old man and I haven't any friends to help me and you know it—" Cunning leaped suddenly to his eyes. "I want a lawyer! I'm not going to answer one more question unless I get a lawyer!"

"You don't need a lawyer," Ran said patiently. "I'm not accusing you of anything. I simply want to know about this robe—when you wore it last. You can answer that without a lawyer, can't you?"

"Oh, it's that way, is it?" Dennison smoothed a trembling hand over his face. "You've got your eyes on somebody else, have you? Well, I guess maybe I can answer that. How long ago? Let's see. It was two weeks ago this Sunday as I recollect and I wore my own robe because that Mrs. Brastock gave it to me. Somebody'd been complaining I'd worn theirs, I suppose, for when I came in that morning she was here and she handed it to me. 'Here's your robe, Mr. Dennison,' she says. 'I got it out for you!' So there was nothing to do but take it and put it on. That was the last time I saw it."

"How was that?"

"How do I know? That danged Oscar maybe. The way it is—someone's always yap-yapping about us hanging up our robes as soon as we take them off. Say it makes less work for Oscar. She," he pointed to me, "is one of the worst. Well, I can't always be doing that. Sometimes I have to go downstairs first. You understand." He looked at Ran and then at me with a sort of defiant delicacy. "I'm getting older and my kidneys aren't so good. That Sunday the service was longer than usual and as soon as my postlude was done I had to go. Didn't even stop to take off my robe until I got downstairs and then I left it. I remember hanging it in the men's room. Oscar probably found it and hid it out of meanness. Anyway he didn't bring it upstairs again. I know that, for next Sunday Mrs. Brastock was there first again. 'Oh, Mr. Dennison,' she says, 'I couldn't find your robe this morning.' And I says, 'Well, what of it? I can wear someone else's, can't I?' And I did." He chuckled a little. "Today I was dressed when the lady got here so there wasn't anything she could do." He shuffled his feet suggestively. "Well, now that I've told you and if that's all you want to know . . ."

"Just another question or two," Ran said. He wasn't even looking at Dennison now. "You said Johnson might have hidden your robe out of meanness. Why would he do that?"

"It was the way he was. Poison mean. You ask anybody."

"I'm asking you. Had you known him long?"

Charles, Dennison snorted. "I've been playing this organ at St. Thomas' for more than thirty years. Oscar came soon after I did. I guess maybe you could say I knew him a while."

"Ever have any trouble with him?"

"Not lately. I used to long ago. Then I did him a favor and he's been pretty decent since, except if you're going to take it he was the one who hid my robe on me."

"What sort of a favor did you do him?"

"What difference does that make? Besides, it was a long time ago—twelve—fifteen years."

"What did you mean by saying you used to have trouble with him? What kind of trouble?"

Dennison must have given up hope of ever achieving dinner. He sighed and sat down again. "Look here, Garrison, you're new to Dorchester and this church. You didn't know Oscar nor how he was. He never went in for big trouble—little meannesses were big enough for him. Things that could pin prick you and yet weren't hardly worth making a fuss about. Like shutting off the organ power. You see, the motor that runs the organ is down in a little room off the kitchen. There's a switch there that shuts it off. Well, Oscar used to throw that switch and then lock the kitchen door and go off, especially on the nights he thought I'd want to be over practicing. When I'd get here, the organ would be dead and the kitchen locked and there'd be nothing I could do about it. That happened

five—six times and then I went to the dean. Old Dean
Morrison, that was. He gave me a key to the kitchen and
that fixed that. Next thing it was my music. There's a cabinet out here I'm supposed to keep it in but sometimes I'd
forget and leave it on the organ bench. When I did, it disappeared. Lots of Sundays when I got here, I couldn't find
the music I'd been meaning to play, I'd ask Oscar and he'd
not know anything about it. So I went to the dean again
and after that I didn't have any more difficulty that way.
But there were other things—nothing to mention—just
pin pricks. That was Oscar's way."

"And that lasted until you—oh—did him this favor?"

"More or less. Why? It wasn't important—just pin
pricks. Nothing to do but consider the source. That's what
I did."

"Ever have any business dealings with him?"

"Business dealings—what do you mean? We both
worked for St. Thomas'. Maybe you'd call that business
dealings, I don't know. Are you trying to tell me Oscar had
some business outside?"

"I'm not trying to tell you anything," Ran said. "I'm
asking you. Did you?"

"You tell me what sort of business you think maybe
Oscar was in and then maybe I can tell you," Dennison
said cunningly.

Two pair of eyes met in a long stare. Then Ran stood up
with a shrug. "All right—thanks," he said. "Sorry I kept
you so long from your dinner. By the way, I'm sending
that robe off for analysis. Until we're sure those stains are
blood, I'm going to ask you not to mention them to anyone.
Miss King won't talk. Neither will I. If it gets out . . ."

"It won't from me," Dennison promised. He was already halfway into his coat. "It's likely I'd talk, isn't it?—
when the first one that'd hear it would say it was me did it

on account of knowing how I felt about that Tolliver girl. No, sir! I'll keep my mouth shut. You can bank on that!"

Ran waited until the door slammed and then raised a shoulder at me. "Nice people. Well, did we get any 'forrader,' do you think, or not?"

Something was bothering me. "You didn't say one word about the will," I accused. "Why not? Shouldn't he know?"

"He'll find out soon enough," Ran said grimly. "Besides—it's just possible he *does* know—Oscar may have told him—and is hoping and praying we don't. If he does, he'll keep quiet—no danger of his introducing such a lovely motive for murder. Think of it—all he had to do, to get the money, was to kill Oscar and Carol, being careful, of course, to kill Carol first . . ."

"But to get the money he'd have to prove he died first and how could he . . . Ran! You're making fun of me! You don't think he had a thing to do with it, do you?"

"No, I don't," Ran said soberly. "And the reason I didn't tell the old fellow was because I didn't want to raise any false hopes. Now come on or we'll both be late to dinner."

I felt a little guilty, being so late, but no one seemed to have noticed. Alec and the bishop were talking comfortably before the fire. I gave Ran a push in their direction and headed for the kitchen. I pushed the swing door open, looked in. "Need any help?"

"And how!" Ruth said tragically: "Come in and shut that door! Tess, he's going to stay here—he said so! Until the whole mess is solved."

"He may be here quite a while then. I don't suppose you can exactly throw him out. Of course—" I stopped for a minute, struck. "I'll go, Ruth. You won't need me. If he's going to be here, you won't be alone."

"Oh, yes, I'll need you," Ruth said grimly. "You'll have to manage the bishop. I can do pretty well with Alec but—

don't you see? Alec doesn't approve of any of this—this murder investigation—and with the bishop to support him . . . Poor Ran! Alec's bad enough but you wait until the bishop gets started throwing monkey wrenches."

But dinner passed peaceably enough. It was true that Alec was unwontedly silent, but that might have been because of the subjects chosen for conversation. Ran talked carefully about the murders and his subsequent investigation. Bishop Walters was interested. He asked questions.

It was while Ruth was pouring coffee that Ran said he thought he'd go over to the church again. "I've an idea we may have missed something in Oscar's apartment. I thought the search a trifle cursory at the time but it didn't seem of any particular importance then. I suppose Tess has keys?"

Alec lifted heavy eyes. "We both have."

Ran looked thoughtfully at his ice cream. "How many sets of keys are there out?"

Alec didn't offer to reply and I said hastily that there were quite a few.

"Who has them?"

But that I couldn't say. "Alec and I, of course. And Charles Dennison. Carol had one. So does Frederick Brastock. Oh, and there was Oscar's. . . And the superintendent of the church school and Mrs. Forde—she's president of one of the guilds. Miss Erickson had one but I think she turned it in. I've the complete list at the office. Of course there may be others who've had keys and never turned them in. But the lists will tell that."

"Even so, there are too many keys out." Ran looked directly at Alec. "I think those locks should be changed. It would be a pity if there were something to find in Oscar's rooms and the killer found it before we did."

"I agree," said the bishop surprisingly and Alec, following so obvious a lead, said, very well, he'd see about it in the morning. The first thing.

That was all until, our ice cream eaten, our coffee drunk, we arose from the table. It was then that the bishop cast his first monkey wrench.

"I believe," he said breaking what had been rather a long silence, "that, when you go to the church this afternoon, I will accompany you."

I saw Ran's start of surprise, Alec's incredulity. Ruth's eyes met mine in agonized appeal. But there was nothing I could do. You don't say no to a bishop.

He came with us.

13

Alec didn't. He explained that he had the Young People's Fellowship at five o'clock and that he needed the time to get ready. The Y.P.F. was coming to the house since the vestry had decided it was unwise to hold any meetings—especially of young people—at the church for the present.

Already Ruth was getting out cups and counting doughnuts. I offered to stay and help but she refused. "Ran may need you," she said. "And anyway someone's got to keep an eye on that man! (That man being the bishop.) Goodness knows what he'll be up to!"

I raised my eyebrows at her. I didn't quite see how I could stop the bishop and, in the end, it was just as well that I didn't try.

We went in at the side door. I think I've said before that the church only had three doors—the back one that led directly to the basement, the front door that could be unlocked only from inside, and the door that led to my office.

I had been shivering on our brief walk from house to church. The sky, which had been so brilliantly blue in the morning, had long since turned to leaden gray. The air was clammy with the chill that presages snow.

At no time is St. Thomas' a cheerful church. Cheerfulness was not the object of the builders. There is much paneling in the darkest of oak. The pews are massive and solid and not even the most optimistic could call the choir screen delicate or graceful. Even the memorial windows, although the most beautiful in Dorchester, are of somber, dark-toned glass. The great Crusader window at the rear is the one exception, but today there was no sun to fire its crimson splendors. The light that filtered through arch and pillar was gray and cheerless and eerily dim.

My fingers itched for the light switches but Ran said no; there was no use in calling attention to activity within the church. When we got to Oscar's apartment, which was not visible from the street, I could turn on all the lamps I wanted. In the meantime we'd make do with his pocket flashlight.

The flashlight interested the bishop and provoked a complete new train of thought. He stopped where he was, under the Good Shepherd window. "Mr. Garrison," he asked, "are you armed?"

Ran assured him that he wasn't. "This is a peaceful expedition," he said. The bishop moved forward again, satisfied. I wasn't quite so satisfied. I had heard the two words that had followed that assurance. They were: "I hope."

It was cold in the basement. With no further services scheduled for the day, the temporary janitor was allowing the fires to die. The old man was very deaf and to give him instructions it was necessary to write on a little pad of paper. I wondered if that was the reason he showed no apprehension at taking over Oscar's duties. It was certain that he could hear nothing and, presumably, so long as he saw nothing . . .

The apartment was as undisturbed as we had left it. I thought Ran looked slightly disappointed as he stood looking about. Perhaps he thought that no indication of attempted search meant that there was nothing to search for.

The bishop was delighted with the whole proceeding which he appeared to consider in the light of unprecedented adventure. "A nice little apartment," he pronounced it, "comfortable and convenient. I quite envy Oscar."

It was definitely not the thing to say and the bishop, realizing it, quickly plunged ahead.

"Music and flowers—what more can man desire—unless it be communion with great minds and he had that as well. There are books here."

"Rather peculiar books," Ran said grimly. "Oscar was a man of parts—as you'll realize if you take the trouble s to look over those shelves."

"Indeed." The bishop approached the shelves cautiously; so might a cat walk on wet pavements. "Dear me, I fancy you are right. What have we here? Darwin and Huxley—ah, yes, the scientific approach. Who would have suspected that a janitor . . . It only goes to show how little we understand our fellow men. *The Evolution of Man—Trend of the Race. Mendel's Principles of Heredity* by Bateson—do you know, this quite takes me back to my college days. *Genetics and Eugenics*—Bateson again. Rather ponderous reading—wouldn't you think?—for the layman. De Vries in two volumes—*The Mutation Theory*. An expensive hobby—such books—but, from what you've told me, doubtless Oscar could afford them." He sighed, ran a finger along the backs of the remaining books. "Castle—Davenport—Guyer. Havelock Ellis—hmm."

I think Ran was amused. He said, "You are a student, sir. What do you make of it?"

"'The proper study,'" quoted the bishop sententiously, "of mankind is man.' I should be the last to dispute it. These books have been read."

"So I noticed," Ran said dryly. "Not only read—annotated."

"Indeed?" Bishop Walters reached out a hand and removed a book or two at random. "Well thumbed—ah, yes, I see what you mean. Here, for instance, I find a sentence which has been underscored." He adjusted his glasses and read it aloud. "'And finally, if both parents be blue-eyed and possess none of the brown pigmentation, then none of their germ cells will have the determiner and all children will be blue-eyed.' It would have been interesting to know what impelled Oscar to mark that passage."

He closed the book and beamed at us. "You understand to what it refers? A facet of the Mendelian Law. What a wise fellow old Mendel was, to be sure, and how remarkable to lay down pronouncements that later men find it difficult to disprove! Brown eyes—blue eyes—whichever is given to us we accept without cavil, but the chances are, the blue-eyed maiden who marries a blue-eyed boy will sigh in vain for brown-eyed children. But, my young friends, do not rush too hastily to the conclusion that the corollary—that brown-eyed parents must likewise have only brown-eyed children—is true for you would be wrong. Brown eyes are simply blue eyes plus a certain brown pigment known as *melanin*. Blue eyes are without such pigment. *But* a man and wife, one of whom is blue-eyed and the other brown, will have a proportion of blue-eyed children and the brown-eyed children of such a marriage may also transmit, in proportion, blue eyes to a certain number of *their* children. It is only the blue-eyed who possess none of the brown pigment, who may not transmit it. Do I make myself clear? Dear me, I fear I have been lecturing again. It is most unwise, you know, to offer a clergyman the opportunity to speak. Nevertheless, young man, be warned. You have blue eyes, I note. If you desire brown eyes for your children, you must provide them with a brown-eyed mother."

"I am afraid," said Ran gravely and looked at me, "that it is too late and I must resign myself to blue."

My eyes are blue. To my horror, I felt the slow upward creep of a blush. I tried to stare Ran down and failed. The last thing I saw, before I gave up and looked away, was Ran—laughing.

What the bishop noticed or thought, I do not know. He talked on blithely. "Fascinating—the problems of heredity, the traits that come down to us out of the mists of the past. The shape of a thumb, the curve of a nose . . ." Abruptly he stopped, looked aghast. "My dear Mr. Garrison, why have you not stopped me? Time passes—ah, yes, time passes but I chatter on. I can only offer my apologies and promise to amend my ways for a little while at least." His eyes twinkled at us.

"No apologies are necessary," Ran said mendaciously. "It's been very interesting and instructive. But, as you say, time moves on and perhaps we'd better get going. I think I'll take the bedroom to pieces. What do you want to tackle, Tess?"

Not very enthusiastically I said I'd take the kitchen. The bishop, deprecating his powers as a sleuth, decided that his part would be that of observer and critic. "Music critic," he said with a smile. "I see some interesting records. Would it disturb your—er—detections if I should play a few?"

It was obvious that he was trying to be playful even though his style did appear labored. Ran told him to go ahead and started for the bedroom. I caught at his sleeve.

"Ran, for the love of Mike, tell me what we're looking for?"

"You know," he said. He was impatient to be gone. "Papers, notebooks—anything that will establish a connection between Johnson and the names of that list. If you

don't remember them, or if you find a name—any name—
ask me and we'll check. Don't skip a thing. If it's here, it
may be well hidden so don't take any chances."

I didn't. I lifted papers, poked into cans, opened the
oven, removed ice box trays, shook out the piles of neatly
folded dish towels. But I found nothing.

As I passed through the living room on my way to report, I saw that the bishop was sunk in a big chair, his
eyes closed and one finger beating intermittent time while
strains of Beethoven's *Fifth Symphony* filled the air.

Ran seemed neither surprised nor disappointed. He was
doing a very thorough job. At the moment he had the bed
torn apart and was poking at the mattress. He lifted an
eyebrow in my direction.

"Start on the desk then," he said. "But don't miss anything there. Not that Elrod didn't look it over pretty carefully, but we weren't looking for names then."

The desk was the old-fashioned roll-top type. It had
seven good-sized drawers and innumerable cubby-holes. It
was rampant with papers. A whole week's work, I thought,
disgruntled, if I'm to do it half justice. A few minutes
later I revised that opinion. It would take at least a year.

I began on the bigger drawers because they held the
least. The top one on the left was crammed with miscellanea. An ancient clothes brush. Pipe cleaners. An emery
stone. Two empty wallets. An old rag, ink-spattered. A
notebook. A pair of well-worn leather gloves. Nothing
under the papers that lined the drawer. Nothing in the
notebook. Disgusted, I slammed the drawer shut. The second drawer held only an automatic in a leather holster.
I called Ran and he removed the clip, dropping it in his
pocket. He laid gun, holster and all, on the table.

I stared at it. "If he had a loaded gun," I began, "I don't
quite see—"

"Oscar was killed upstairs—remember? By the way, where's the bishop?"

I said crossly, now made aware of the silence about me, that I didn't know; I'd been too busy to miss him. Ran went to the door and I heard him call. Presently Bishop Walters answered. He was right here, he was just looking around a little. Had Mr. Garrison any objection? Since it was his church rather than ours, Ran said that he hadn't, but please not to go too far away, and if he heard anyone coming to return to us at once.

Like myself, the bishop was a quibbler. He came to the door. "But the church is locked . . ."

"And uncounted numbers have keys," Ran said shortly.

"Keys—ah, yes. You made that point at dinner. Yes, certainly the locks should be changed."

He wandered off.

I attacked the third drawer. It held typewriter paper, envelopes, a spare typewriter ribbon, blotters. Nothing else.

The lower drawer was filled with bank statements. They were in order and covered a period of seven years. The books of check stubs were with them. I looked at one or two but they weren't helpful. All of the checks, signed O. Johnson in an execrable hand, were for varying amounts and made out to cash.

I sat back and looked at them. If Ran thought I was going through that mess alone, he had another think coming. I went out to the kitchen and got some string. I tied the yellow folds of paper together and laid them beside the automatic. That was that.

I got a surprise when I pulled at the drawers on the other side. They were the usual shams, constructed to conceal a typewriter, in this case a late model Remington. I shut those drawers too. And that was *that*.

Now I was free to begin on the upper part of the desk and for a time it was the same old story. The small drawers, of which there were four, held only further hodgepodge. Paper clips, steel pens, a knife with a broken blade, one of those red-glass affairs to sharpen razorblades, two empty spectacle cases. Search of the central shelves revealed two blank notebooks, a stamp pad and a pocket dictionary from which, although I scrutinized it scrupulously, page by page, I gained no more than the definition for "enervate," a word whose meaning has always eluded me. The sections at the sides held blotters, the trays ink-rusted pens and a pencil of tarnished silver.

The bishop came wandering by just then and asked for the key to the kitchen. Not seeing what harm he could do there—or good either—I gave him mine and he went out again.

I began on the pigeonholes. The first ones held the usual miscellanea—envelopes and ration books and a file of garage receipts for work done on his ancient car. They were all two years old because Oscar had sold the car when gas rationing came in.

That was all until I reached the last two, the first of which was jammed with copies of *The Recorder,* a mimeographed sheet gotten out weekly for business firms and listing property mortgages, mortgages taken by finance firms on household goods, cars, etc., as well as complete lists of sales made on "time" by dealers.

There wasn't a complete file. I thumbed through them rapidly. Some dated back as far as ten years. There was a May, a June and a December of the past year, a January of the present. I ran hastily through them. I found a name I recognized. Mary Collins had placed a mortgage on her household goods with the Lyon Credit Company for the amount of $215.00.

My hands were shaking a little now. I gathered all of the *Recorders* together, snapped a rubber around them, and attacked the remaining drawer. There were two things in it. A bunch of clippings taken from other *Recorders*—the print was the same—and a cheap leather notebook. I opened that to the first page. It had been written on. I gazed at a list of figures. Bald, unrevealing figures. Tens and fives and fifteens and twenties. One thirty. A twelve-fifty and a seventeen-fifty. That was all. There was nothing to tell for what they stood; nothing to show to what they referred. There were no dollar signs before them, only the decimal point that marked the fifties away from the twelve and seventeen. There was a bracketed "1" at the top of the page, nothing more.

I turned hastily to the second page. Here again was the bracket with a "2" in it this time, the same uncompromising list of figures. With one difference—two of the figures halfway down had been crossed out and question marks lightly penciled alongside.

There was nothing at all on the third page, nothing in the rest of the book. I turned to the front again and re-studied the first page.

There was that "1" at the top. A page number, obviously. Still "1" could stand for January as well, "2" for February. This was February. Could it be . . . Hastily I counted the numbers. There were thirty of them. I made a quick calculation.

They added up to three hundred and fifteen and I sat back trembling. Three hundred and fifteen—dollars, presumably; else why the decimals? And the District Attorney had said that Oscar's bank books showed he'd been depositing more than three hundred dollars a month Then these figures meant something. They had to.

I called Ran who was now engaged in taking the living room to pieces. I showed him the *Recorders,* the clippings, the notebook. I babbled incoherently. "It's just figures," I said, "but there's thirty of them and that's the same as the list of names, and they add up to more than three hundred. Oh, Ran, do you think it's what we're looking for?"

"Maybe," Ran said. But he was interested. Excitement mounted in him like mercury in a thermometer tube. But he wouldn't admit it. He bent over me, touched my hands. "Darling, you're all shot. Shivering. This place is getting cold. I'll tell you—I'll just finish this—I'm nearly done—and then we'll bundle up all your loot and take it over to the house. We can figure it out there."

"Alec won't like it," I said, out of a sure knowledge of Alec. "Not tonight."

"Blast—" He bit that off. "Oh, well, then—bother Alec! All right, we'll go to your place—or that station. Either one will do. The bishop can come along as chaperon if he insists."

I giggled. "I wondered about that. Do you think that's why—?"

Ran shrugged. "I suspect so. Ask him, why don't you? He's coming now."

Footsteps clicked across the hall and the bishop appeared, smiling with a sort of shy pleasure.

"I wonder," he said diffidently, "if I've discovered something that will help. I am not at all certain, you understand; I simply suggest that it is possible. I have been making a tour of the basement, the kitchen included. That was the reason I—ah—requested the keys. The church is in excellent condition—excellent. I was surprised, pleasantly so. And the kitchen—the ladies of St. Thomas' may well be proud of their kitchen. Really this man Johnson—whatever else his faults—gave the church splendid service. I am sure St. Thomas' will miss him."

"Possibly," Ran said gravely. "But what did you discover, sir?"

The bishop searched his pockets without result. "I fear I've left it in the kitchen," he confessed. "It was a—ah—note addressed to—ah—Oscar. If you will come with me—yes, perhaps it is just as well I did leave it in the kitchen. I—ah—have a little surprise for you. I am afraid I've been taking liberties with the stores of the good ladies of the parish. I trust a little refreshment will not come amiss? Some time ago I set the kettle to boil. My wife is good enough to say that I make excellent tea . . ."

We followed him across the hall. Ran's face was a study in withheld emotion. I wanted to laugh but I didn't. Bishop Walters was too delighted with his little treat for me to dream of spoiling his pleasure.

There were three cups on the white enamel table, three plates, accompanying knives and spoons. There was an opened jar of strawberry jam, a dish high-piled with soda cracker. A green glass sugar bowl held some of the Guild's precious sugar cubes. An open package of tea stood beside a brown pottery teapot.

"Why, how nice!" I said, impelled to speech. "Tea is just what we needed, isn't it, Ran? And don't worry about the ladies, Bishop Walters. I'm sure they'd be delighted to have you take anything you want."

"You think so? Well, that is very kind of you, my dear. Now, the kettle is boiling. I will just rinse the pot and then three teaspoons, I think, for the three of us. There—now, as soon as the tea has steeped, we shall have our little feast. No butter, of course, but in these days of rationing that is not unprecedented. Ah, I believe we are ready. Miss King, will you pour?"

It had a nightmarish quality, this macabre tea party, but by this time we were completely cowed. It wasn't until I was pouring second cups of tea that Ran recovered enough to ask about the note. The bishop rose at once.

"Ah, yes, the note. I have it here . . . Dear me, I did have it. Now, where did I put it? Ah, I remember. Under the coffee can."

The note, which I read over Ran's shoulder, was scrawled on paper torn from the scratch pad that always hung beside the telephone. It said: "Dear Mr. Johnson. The screw is working loose from the swell pedal again. Could you please look at it? I'll be back at half past six. Thanks." It was signed "Carol." Carol Tolliver.

There was a pin prick hole in one corner. Ran indicated it. "What do you make of that?"

"It's been pinned to something," I said slowly. "The door, I suppose. But if it was pinned to the door that would mean that Oscar wasn't in his apartment when she left. Unless it's an old note . . ."

"Let's skip that possibility for the present. Let's assume that Oscar *was* out. You knew Oscar. If he came in and found that note, what would he do?"

"He'd fix the organ," I said with certainty. "But I can't see how that helps."

"It makes all the difference in the world," Ran said. His shoulders were back; suddenly he looked like a different man. "Don't you see? Take it this way. Suppose Oscar didn't come in alone. Suppose our—our murderer was with him."

I saw it. "And they were quarreling over—well, whatever there was to quarrel about. And then Oscar saw Carol's note. He'd unlock the apartment and put away his overcoat and hat and then he'd get his screw driver and go upstairs."

"Leaving the other in possession. It fits, Tess—it fits!"

"And then," I said slowly, "there the murderer'd be alone—with Alec's knives on the table. He'd take one and follow Oscar."

"You're forgetting the robe," Ran said.

"Oh, well, the robe could be there—of course it would! It was Charles Dennison's and Oscar didn't like him. If he put it anywhere else, Dennison could have found it, but not here—locked in the apartment."

"If I read Dennison right, I don't think it would make any difference to him whether he got his robe back or not—so long as he could swipe some other one. All right—we've got the murderer upstairs and Oscar dead and his body hidden away. Then what?"

"Then," I said soberly, "he'd come back downstairs and look for—well, whatever it is we've been looking for. And while he was looking, Carol came in the back door and saw the apartment lit—perhaps in his excitement he'd forgotten to shut the door—and she walked in and there he was with the robe and bloody knife . . ."

"Or," Ran said thoughtfully, "she could have been in the apartment when he came back, knife, bloody robe and all. I like that better, Tess. And either way he'd have to kill her."

The bishop's glance on us was benign. "Is that what you call deductive reasoning?" he wanted to know.

Ran smiled wryly. "I'm afraid I'd call it imaginative reconstruction, sir. All impressions to the contrary, you do have to use your imagination in police work. Oh, I'll grant you a lot of it's plain routine. Checking and rechecking, hard spade work that gets undeniable results. But once in a while you come across a case where you've nothing to check. Then you go beyond routine. We've just been treating you to a sample. Of course, I'm not saying that our reconstruction was correct, but it makes a lot more sense than the hide-and-seek chase through the church that we've been considering."

"Then the note helped," Bishop Walters said in a tone of satisfaction. "I am gratified. And now what do we do?"

Ran didn't bat an eye. "We call it a day, I think. Tess is tired and it's getting late. I've only to roll up a rug or two and I'll be done. By the way, sir, you never did tell us where you found that note."

"It was in the wastebasket in the kitchen, the only piece of paper in it. It was all crumpled together. I smoothed it out and read it. It seemed to me to have bearing on the crime."

"Quite," Ran said. "We are very grateful. But where in Liberia was it when my men searched the church? Or did they search the church . . . Wait for me. I'll be right back."

He vanished, muttering, and the bishop looked pained. I attempted reassurance. "Oscar might have crumpled it up and tossed it away. It wasn't very big. Perhaps the police missed it entirely. Probably the new janitor found it and threw it in that wastebasket. He wouldn't know that it was important."

"No doubt," said the bishop, "it was so."

Minutes later, with our *Recorders* and bank statements and clippings, we walked back to the house where a half a dozen cars and a line of overshoes upon the porch indicated that the Young People's Fellowship was still in residence.

Dubiously I looked at the others. I was weary and grimy and there was a streak of dust across Ran's nose. "I think we'd better sneak in," I said. "Let's go around to the back. If we call and Ruth hears our voices, she'll let us in."

But the bishop declined to sneak. "I am afraid," he said with melancholy amusement, "my dignity demands a frontal approach. My young friends, I shall see you later."

"Much later," Ran said in my ear.

We stood and waited until the door had dosed behind him. We looked at one another. Then, suddenly, we laughed and caught hands and ran. Away from the house. Down to the corner drugstore where we could call a cab.

14

Up in my apartment, we spread our finds on the dining room table and got to work. I had made coffee and offered something more substantial, but Ran said no, that when we were through, we'd go somewhere for dinner. We took the bank statements and worked through them year by year, and, when we were done, we knew nothing more than that, during the seven years so represented, Oscar had written occasional checks for amounts ranging from fifty dollars to two hundred and fifty and that the checks were all made out to "Self." Deposits during those years ranged from one hundred and fifty dollars in January of 1937 to three hundred and fifteen dollars in January of the present year.

Three hundred and fifteen dollars! I caught my breath. I snatched at the little leather notebook. "Look!" I said. "These figures—I added them. That's what they amount to. And there are thirty of them. Do you suppose . . . ?"

"I'd be a fool if I didn't," Ran said promptly. "Let me see that. Thirty, eh? And the list of names could be the key—if the numbers were always written down in the same order."

"It could be. Let's try it that way—see how we come out."

Sets of figures are not very interesting and there's no good in putting it all down, but when we'd done placing names against number, we had this. It was rather startling.

Philip Smedley	20
Georgia Brastock	10
William Carter	15
Blair Thurston	30
Charles Dennison	12.50
Mary Collins	20
Leota Erickson	25

Two of the names—those of Blair Thurston and William Carter—had lines drawn through them. The clinching point that we were on the right track was the fact that it was the corresponding numbers in the notebook that had been crossed off and question marks penciled in beside them.

I shoved the paper from me. "What on earth does it mean?"

Ran was lighting a cigarette. One eyebrow quirked at me but, when he spoke, it was seriously enough. "On the face of it, these people were paying Oscar regular monthly sums. Why, I wonder. So far as we know he was selling nothing, certainly nothing that could have an equal appeal to such opposite types as Miss Erickson and—well, Blair Thurston. So let's consider something different." He was speaking more slowly now. "What if Oscar had loaned them money—we know he had it to loan—and these were return payments. Suppose that was the explanation for his unexplained fortune. A nice little usury business—small loans to small people at God knows what rate of interest. It's happened before. Only—what sort of a loan business could you run with no more visible data than we've been able to find? He must have had some hold over these people—a note—or something. Damn it! It must be there. Somewhere along the line we've fumbled badly!"

I sighed. I was cold no longer but I *was* getting hungry. "Why can't we try the *Recorders?* Perhaps we'll find it there."

But all our combing of that wavering print produced only two items of information. The mortgaging of Mary Collins' furniture and the fact that, three years before, Philip Smedley had purchased an automobile from the Walton Buick Agency, refinanced by the Lyon Credit Company.

Ran tapped his finger on that last. "How old is Smedley now? About twenty-four? Three years ago he'd be twenty-one. Umm. How long has he worked at the clothing store?"

"Ever since he left high school, I think," I said dubiously. "He started in as a sort of errand boy and he worked as a clerk on Fridays and Saturdays, during the busiest times. Then pretty soon someone else was running the errands and Phil was clerking steadily. I imagine they thought he helped business. He's popular with the younger crowd."

"A Buick's an expensive car for a youngster," Ran observed. "Has he still got it?"

"I think so. He offered to take Miss Erickson home the other night."

"True. How much of a family has he? Any responsibilities?"

"His mother's a widow and he's the only child. I don't imagine the father left them anything—he was a salesman for a coffee line. I think Phil is her main support."

Ran said nothing. Suddenly he slapped his hand down—hard—on the paper with the list of seven names and the numbers marked against them. "Which of these do you think would crack easiest?"

I didn't know. "Not Charles Dennison," I said, "nor Mrs. Brastock—she slithers so. Not Bill Carter. Phil

Smedley—I wouldn't know. Certainly not Miss Erickson." He smiled a little at that. "Perhaps Mary Collins. Or Blair Thurston."

Again he sat in silence. "All right," he said at last. "We'll see. Come on—let's get this stuff together. We can dump it at the station before we eat."

Somehow I had expected that once we were over the hump of Sunday, we might attain a measure of peace. Or at least the opportunity to catch our breaths. I was wrong. Monday came in with a hurrah, boys, and continued at the same mad pace.

The first thing that happened was that Ruth slipped on the stairs and cracked a bone in her ankle, a circumstance that automatically ended any idea I might have had of resuming my work at the church. I was sorry for her, of course, but not sorry to be kept from the office. For the present, the church held no appeal for me.

It was a hectic morning. The doctor came and went. The twins, forgotten, howled in their play pen. While I worked with hot and cold compresses, Alec was telephoning frantic appeals to various help agencies. The bishop washed the breakfast dishes.

By noon we were fairly well organized. The doctor had sent over a wheel chair. The twins were bathed and comforted. Alec and I had made up the couch in his study and the bishop and I had contrived a luncheon of sorts out of the Sunday leftovers.

It was while he was serving the creamed chicken that Alec told us Oscar's funeral would be held that afternoon.

I laid down my fork. "But nobody knows about it!"

"No reason why they shouldn't," Alec said virtuously. "I announced it at church and it was in the Sunday papers."

I hadn't been in church and I didn't read the Sunday papers so I couldn't argue. "I meant to send flowers," I began.

"You *did* send flowers," Alec told me crossly. "We all did. I saw to it. Don't fuss so, Tess. Flowers or no flowers, relatives or no relatives, we can't keep the poor man above ground forever!"

I might have argued that but for the bishop. "Who has the service?" I asked, taking up my fork again.

"We do. Oscar attended none of the churches in Dorchester. We feel we have at least a claim . . .""

I thought furiously. As soon as lunch was over, I went to the telephone and called Ran. After I'd told him about Ruth's mishap, I said, "Alec says Oscar's funeral is this afternoon. Would you like me to go?"

He had expressed proper sympathy for Ruth. Now his voice floated to me, calm but infuriating. "Why?"

"Why not?" I snapped. "I thought possibly I might recognize some of the people who came to see him."

"You might," Ran said agreeably. "But then again you mightn't. Anyway, haven't you your hands pretty full where you are?"

"Full!" I said. "They're running over! But if you thought I could help . . ."

"I don't know," he said frankly. "Even if you did recognize anyone, you couldn't necessarily know who he was. And we've tried to provide for that by reviving an old custom—a funeral register book."

I said, "Ran, do you think 'Red' Brannigan will come? Have you had any word of him?"

He answered only my last question. I suppose the other was too silly to merit consideration. "None. We're still working on it, of course."

And all at once, through the medium of those half a dozen words, I gained an entirely new aspect of the thing. Of course the police were working on it—not just Ran but behind him and under him the individual units of the police organization. Fingerprint men, detectives, radio car

operators, investigators, the very policemen on the beats—
they all had their parts to play. They were broadcasting
descriptions, receiving reports, collecting evidence, col-
lating all the varied bits into an attempt to make a perfect whole. The fact that I was not actually seeing them
do it meant nothing. Neither did the fact that Ran had
occasionally asked my help. Just because I'd been able to
answer a question or two to his satisfaction was no evidence that he expected me to solve the murders nor that
he couldn't have gained the same information from other
sources if I hadn't happened to have been there at hand.

I felt unwontedly humble. I said, "Ran, I didn't mean
that I thought it was up to me. I only wanted to help."

"I know," he cut in. "And you *can* help. Only just now—
well, sit tight, will you? And, Tess, promise me something.
I won't be here to compel you but—stay away from the
church. And that goes for the others as well. Alec, too.
Tell them, will you?"

"Why, of course," I said. "But, Ran, are you— What are
you going to do? Where—"

There was no answer. He had hung up.

I frowned over it a good part of the afternoon. The
house seemed quiet after the turmoil of the morning. Alec
and the bishop had gone to the funeral. The twins were
asleep. Ruth, too, slept—the doctor had given her a seda-
tive. Momentarily there was nothing for me to do. I could
rest and try to figure out what we'd have for dinner. Ration
books and a trip to the grocery were indicated. I couldn't
expect the bishop to plan all the meals.

Rest nothing! There were beds to make. Reluctantly I
dragged myself up out of comfort and to the stairs.

A perfunctory glance from the landing window showed
activity at the church. A police car, conspicuous in its cream
and green, was drawing to the curb. As I watched, several
men got out and headed purposely for the side door.

In spite of my good resolutions, I felt cheated, left out. They must be intending to search the church again, but why hadn't Ran told me? Surely telling me wouldn't have hurt and I'd be feeling better. Common sense came to my rescue. Well, why should he? I wasn't part of the police organization—hadn't I got that through my thick head *yet?*

Still—the church was more or less my property. If curiosity had me too hard, I could go over there. I could invent an errand. Surely with the police in residence it would be safe enough.

Whoa, there! I pulled myself up sharply. Ran had asked me to stay away, made a point of it. All right, I would.

By the time I'd straightened the bedrooms and freshened up myself, the twins were awake. I came down the stairs, crab-fashion, one twin clutched under each arm. They were in boisterous good spirits but inclined to be suspicious of me. Once in their play pen their "Ma-ma—ma-ma" resounded plaintively through the house.

I went into Alec's study. Ruth was awake. When I offered to bring the twins to her, she said no, that her foot wasn't so very sore; if I'd help her into the wheel chair, she thought she'd like to come out by the fire.

"We can have tea when Alec comes back—that is, if you won't mind making it, Tess? Oh, I feel like such an idiot—falling downstairs at a time like this! But the 'Y' has promised Alec that tomorrow they'll send someone. It'll just be day help but that's better than nothing. So if you can manage until then . . ." She looked at me anxiously.

I laughed. "Haven't I got the bishop?" I asked as I rolled her into the living room.

She laughed too but sobered quickly. "He's a darling. I wish I had a picture of him in his blue apron washing dishes, of all things! But that's the way he is—if he sees any way he can help, he does. It would never occur to

Alec. But then, of course, Bishop Walters is older—he's got more sense."

"Alec's got sense enough," I said grimly. "But he doesn't help—he hinders."

Ruth rushed to his defense. "Oh, Tess, don't say that. I don't think he does it consciously. It's just that—well, I don't think he realizes these murders have really happened. And not in St. Thomas'. It's like a bad dream and one he hopes he'll wake from."

"Well, the sooner he wakes up the better," I said. "That's where the bishop scores. He knows they happened and he accepts them. And Alec had jolly well better do the same!"

"Poor Alec!" Ruth said. There were tears in her eyes.

The twins were delighted to see their mother again, even more enchanted with the wheel chair and its potentialities. They, said "Wide!" so firmly and so often that at last I dumped them both in Ruth's lap and rolled all three off on a tour of the downstairs. They were shrieking hilariously when Alec and the bishop came in, cold, hungry and tired.

The water was boiling by this time. Alec made the tea because he has ideas about tea-making and who was I to challenge them? Instead I sat on the hearth and stuck bread slices on a long fork and toasted them over the coals. There was a pot of apricot jam. We all ate largely, even the twins. It was all very pleasant and relaxing. I wished Ran were there.

So much so, that when the doorbell rang I leaped to answer it, on the somewhat unsound theory that perhaps I was wrong and that Ran had never told me he was going away.

It wasn't Ran. It was the Thurstons, father and son, and they asked for Alec.

I ushered them into an atmosphere of peace and they disrupted it. At once Ruth, the bishop and I began to make polite noises of withdrawal. Only the twins were natural. They simply stood and stared at the newcomers.

The Thurstons were polite too. They refused to countenance our going. It was not necessary. Harvey Thurston said, with a sad smile, "We have no secrets any more."

We offered tea and it was refused with the result that the rest of us shamefacedly gobbled what we had on our plates and then pushed them aside.

Harvey Thurston began by clearing his throat and announcing that they had been at the funeral. "We had hoped to see Mr. Garrison. Unaccountably he was not there. Neither is he in his office." Apparently he couldn't bring himself to say "police station." "You are, to some extent, in his confidence, Dean MacDonald. Can you tell me my son's status in this investigation? Does Garrison suspect him?"

"Why?"

It was said so flatly that Thurston père, taken unaware, could only gape. He was a big heavy man of the type known as forceful. His hair was scant, his eyes cold. Both he and his wife had eyes of the same watered-out shade of blue, whereas Blair's, fixed now upon Alec, were as meltingly brown as a puppy's. Rumor had it that Thurston's money had been made on the stock market in the pre-1929 days. Fifteen years ago he had bought into the Dorchester National Bank and was now its president.

He recovered. "No reason, of course, no reason at all. However the unfortunate chance of his presence here—his position as Carol's husband . . . His furlough will soon be ending. Frankly, we are worried. His mother . . ."

"I know nothing of what or whom Garrison suspects," Alec said tiredly. "He has not confided in me. I should imagine that if Blair knows himself innocent, he need have no fear of the police."

Blair, who'd been twisting his hands nervously together, now swallowed audibly. The Navy had certainly done things for him—he stood better, had lost his pimples and even gained a little weight—but there was still room for improvement.

"Carol and I were all washed up," he said in a high uncertain voice. "I guess it was a fool sort of thing to do—get married like we did—and when I heard she'd been trying to put the bee on Dad, I was through. I wrote and told her so. She knew the way I felt, all right!" He nodded, as though pleased with what he'd said.

"The settlement was to have been made, of course," his father said smoothly. "It was arranged. We were to move for an annulment during Blair's furlough. The girl understood that. It could have been done. It was not as though it were the ordinary marriage . . ."

Alec moved uncomfortably. The topics of annulment and divorce are not agreeable subjects for discussion in an Episcopal minister's home. "So I understood," he said coldly. "I am sorry. My best advice is for you to see Mr. Garrison as soon as possible. He can advise you better than I."

There was a moment's silence and then Alec began to speak firmly of church affairs. He had called a meeting of the vestry. Would Mr. Thurston be there? I wanted to shake him—Alec. This was his chance. Why didn't he take advantage of it? My hands, as I gathered up cups and plates, were shaking.

Alec looked at me as though I were a disturbing insect and suggested removal to the study. The bishop, invited, merely shook his head and settled deeper into his chair. As I took his plate, his eyes met mine. His lips moved soundlessly. "The boy. Talk to the boy." I was halfway to the kitchen before I realized that the bishop, the old sport, had given me carte blanche. When I came back, my mind was made up.

Ruth was making polite conversation about Blair's boot training experiences. I interrupted without conscience. I said, "You know, Blair, if it hadn't been that your furlough began later, I'd have sworn it was you who telephoned the church and asked for Carol the night she was killed."

He glanced quickly at me, quickly at the closed study door. "It was," he said in a hoarse half-whisper. "But don't you tell anybody. Even my folks don't know. You see, Carol and I weren't nearly so much washed up as I've been letting on. I mean, I was crazy about her. I didn't believe what Dad wrote me—that all she wanted out of us was money. So I thought if I could talk to her without anyone else around . . ." His voice trailed off.

"But you didn't?" I asked sympathetically.

"No. I came up on the train. I'd just got in when I called. And when you said she wasn't there I didn't know what to do. So I came up near the church and just hung around outside, waiting, in case she came out. Nobody saw me—it was snowing and I had to keep walking up and down to keep from freezing. Then the police cars came and I knew something was wrong. But I was scared to come in and I didn't want them to see me and so I walked around a couple of blocks and then came back. There was a policeman standing by the side door and I went up to him and asked him what was going on. He said, 'What's it to you?' first and then he kind of relented, I guess. He told me I'd better beat it, that there was a couple of nasty murders inside and it didn't pay outsiders to stick their noses in. So I asked who'd been murdered—anybody would—and he said the janitor and a kid organist. So then I knew and—well, I did what he told me to. I beat it. I didn't know what else to do—I didn't want to get mixed up in it—the folks and all . . . And I knew there was a train going back to the Hills so I hopped it. Nobody saw me—there wasn't anybody on the train I knew and I kept out of sight as much as I could. Next day I came in on the bus the way I was supposed to." His eyes searched ours plaintively. "Have I got to tell Garrison that?"

"I think I should, my boy," the bishop said judicially. "The police already know of the phone call. They've been trying to check on it. Your admission would write off its importance."

"It was a pay phone," Blair Thurston said irrelevantly. "From the depot. Oh, gosh—I suppose it'll all have to come out. Who—who killed her, sir? Who'd want to? She—she wasn't the way they said . . . I know she wasn't." His lips were trembling.

The bishop rose, clearing his throat. "No—no, my boy. She wasn't. I believe that firmly. You must believe it too. Think of her as she was when you knew her—young and sweet, with all of her life before her. Never forget that."

"I won't. She—she was sweet, all right. Sure she liked money—who doesn't? And she needed it—gosh, all that family! But nobody'd kill her just for that . . ."

"I'm afraid," said the bishop sadly, "that her death was a useless sacrifice." It was evident that Blair didn't understand and the bishop went on, "We believe that she saw Oscar's murderer and so had to die."

"Well, but who'd kill Oscar either?" Blair exploded. "Oh, he was an old crab but he liked Carol. He was swell to her. I ought to know."

The bishop didn't pick that up so I did. "How do you mean—swell?"

He turned to me. "Well, we got engaged in October, sort of, and she said I could get her a ring. So I wanted to give her something smashing and I got a chance to buy her a one-carat stone, only the guy wanted four hundred for it—it was worth eight—but all I could raise was a hundred or so and I couldn't go to my folks. So— Well, Oscar heard about it somewhere and offered to lend me the money."

Was this it? I could hardly breathe. "Oscar lent *you* money?"

"Sure. He said he had it and I was welcome. I was to pay him back so much a month. Thirty dollars."

"And—and no interest?" My throat was dry now.

"Well, it was this way. He lent me three hundred dollars and. I was to pay it back thirty dollars a month for eleven months. That made three hundred and thirty dollars I paid back, but I didn't care. Ten per cent—it was cheap at the price."

Yes, I thought, but it doesn't help us any. A profit of thirty dollars over a period of eleven months—you didn't accumulate tens of thousands of dollars that way. I asked, "Did you sign a note or anything?"

"No." There was a touch of arrogance in his tone. "He knew I was good for it. He just handed it over."

Another headache. No note—was it like that with the rest of them? If so, that would mean that the men at the church were wasting their time—there was nothing to look for.

"Then you still owe him money?" This was Ruth. For my part, I was out of questions.

"Not any more," Blair said firmly. "I sold my old bus when I knew I was called up and I paid off most of it then. I sent the rest two weeks ago."

I knew when I was licked. As a detective I was getting nowhere fast. I dropped detection for speculation. "I wonder where the ring is now? Have you got it?"

"Have I got it? Don't be a dope! How'd I get it? *She* had it—"

"She never wore it," I said. "I'd have noticed—a diamond that size."

"Sure you would—that's the way she figured it. She wore it around her neck on a ribbon, see? She didn't want folks talking. We were supposed to be keeping it secret . . ." He stopped suddenly, swallowed hard. "Wasn't it on her when—when she was killed?"

"I didn't know. I said, "It's queer. No one has mentioned it—they should have found it . . ."

"Sure they should!" He was on his feet now, glaring suspicion. "Where is it then—you tell me that? Who the hell's got it now?"

I couldn't tell him. It was without my province. I doubted if even Ran, within whose province it certainly was, could tell him.

It was just another mystery. As though there weren't enough already . . .

15

By the time the Thurstons decided to go, it was too late for trips to grocery stores. While I put the twins out of circulation, the bishop, after a hasty inventory of our stores, talked knowledgeably about an omelet. It was a good thing he knew how to cook. Alec did a sketchy setting of the table and Ruth insisted upon being wheeled out to the kitchen where she concocted a salad. We pieced out the rest by opening cans.

It was as we reached dessert—salad fruits, crackers and cheese—that I asked Alec if he'd remembered to have the locks changed at the church.

He snapped his fingers. "I did not! I meant to see about it the first thing this morning. Where were my wits?"

Ruth said promptly that they were woolgathering as usual, and I frowned. I said, "Well, I don't suppose it matters so much. The police were at the church all afternoon."

"They were!" Alec's spoon clicked down. "And what were they doing there, may I ask?"

I held on to patience with both hands. "Alec, why don't you get your head out of the sand and face it? Oscar was conducting some sort of illicit business from the church. The police were looking for evidence."

Alec sighed. "Oh, yes, that wretched money. Where would he get it? Does Ran know yet?"

"He thought it was blackmail at first," I said with a shrug. "Now, I think he believes Oscar was making loans to people who needed money desperately and charging them exorbitant rates of interest."

"Has he proof of that?" Alec asked sternly.

"You sound like the Spanish inquisition," I said. "No, not proof yet—unless they found some this afternoon. Just indications."

"I wish it was over and done with," Alec muttered. For the first time I noted the shadows beneath his eyes, the tautness with which the skin pulled across his cheek bones. "The whole thing is ghastly—ghastly. I'd give my right arm . . ." He lapsed into distasteful thought.

The evening began quietly enough. Alec went to a "Y" board meeting. Bishop Walters rummaged happily among the book shelves. Ruth declined bed in spite of the fact that her foot was giving her pain; she'd wait for Alec, she said stubbornly. I knit and answered the telephone.

There was the usual round of calls. Alec was to get in touch with Dr. Gleason, the Methodist minister, as soon as possible. The Calhoun P.T.A. needed a speaker for their April meeting. Would Dean MacDonald be available? Should St. Mary's Chapter hold their regular bimonthly meeting or were all church activities suspended for the present? A young lieutenant, who would be home on furlough, wanted to arrange—via his mother—to be married next week. Would Dean MacDonald perform the ceremony? Mrs. Bates, very agitated, wanted to report that her sister had been taken to the Rosewood Hospital for an emergency appendectomy. If Dean MacDonald could find time to call on her . . . Just an ordinary evening.

Until the doorbell rang at ten minutes past eight.

It was Miss Erickson, I saw, when I'd switched on the porch light. She asked for Alec and, when I told her he wasn't at home, refused to come in. "No," she said. "Oh, no. It was the dean I wanted to see. If he's away, I won't bother Mrs. MacDonald."

"Oh, but do," I said. The air from the opened door struck coldly through the hall. "I don't mean 'bother Ruth,' but please do come in. You've had a long walk. Come and catch your breath."

She agreed, without enthusiasm, and I ushered her into the living room, making casual talk of Ruth's accident. Ruth looked surprised, but she rose nobly to the occasion, and the bishop put down his book, saying indeed, yes, he remembered Miss Erickson. It was a pleasure to meet her again.

It was evident that it was no pleasure to Miss Erickson. She sat primly on the edge of a chair and refused to loosen her coat. She must not stay. Her mother was alone and not—well. She was having furnace difficulties. The last coal she had been able to obtain was not very satisfactory. It did not catch fire at all well and there were so many ashes . . .

I thought, but, good grief, she didn't come here to talk to Alec about her coal, did she? I looked at her more closely. She hadn't changed a great deal from the Miss Erickson I'd had in eighth-grade English and yet there was something intangibly different. She was older, of course, but then so was I. No dictate of fashion had ever made her alter the mat of tight gray braids she spread across the back of her head. Her hat was still utilitarian, her shoes flat-heeled for comfort. Her seal coat was a little shabbier . . .

I drew in my breath suddenly. That was it—the way she'd changed. Her clothes had always fitted into the category of serviceable but good. Now they were definitely shabby. The shoes were resoled, the hat retrimmed. There were bare patches on the once luxuriant fur of her coat, mended spots on the gloves that gripped the ancient purse so tightly.

I felt a queer half-wave of guilt, as though in some way the fault was mine. When had it happened and why hadn't I noticed before? She'd been smart enough once—well, perhaps not *smart*—but well-dressed. School teachers' salaries, while admittedly not of the highest, were adequate. Of course she had her mother to look after, but still . . .

Was it possible that Oscar, Oscar and his loan activity, had brought her to this pass? She was down on that list Ran had found. I tried to remember what the amount after her name had been, and failed. Twenty or thirty dollars, I thought. Not so much and yet a sizable hunk out of a salary of—what? A hundred and sixty-five dollars or so—surely, after all her years in the school system, she was making that much.

The very intensity of my thoughts must have penetrated to her. Without realizing it, I had been staring. Suddenly her eyes, meeting mine, were stricken. The unimportant words she'd been saying died in her throat. She sat rigidly, her mouth a little open.

"Miss Erickson!" Ruth was leaning forward. "What is it? Are you ill? Tess—"

But the bishop was before me. "You are in trouble?" he asked gently. "You wanted to see Dean. MacDonald but unfortunately he's not here. Will you let us, instead, try to help you?"

She wanted to, you could tell that, but she held herself rigidly against the impulse. She said, "I don't know—I don't know," but her eyes were miserable, her hands fumbling with the handle of her purse.

"Is it something that has to do with the murders in St. Thomas'?" the bishop probed gently. "In that event, it might be better if you saw Mr. Garrison."

The words came then in sudden spate. "I tried to see him—he isn't at the police station. I—I couldn't talk to a strange policeman—I don't even know Mr. Garrison very well. And I had to talk to someone. I thought of the dean . . ."

The bishop said, "Yes?" encouragingly.

Perhaps it was something in his tone for she seemed all at once to make decision. "Perhaps it is nothing, perhaps I distress myself unnecessarily! It is the murders, of course. Not that the police are not fully competent—I'm sure they are. But I had Carol in school. She was a very clever, bright little girl. No one regrets more than I . . . But Oscar—" here she leaned forward and spoke with earnestness. "I know that one should not speak ill of the dead but, Bishop Walters, Oscar was an evil man. His god was money and he didn't care whom he sacrificed to it so long as he obtained what he wanted. I—I should know . . ." She was silent.

"You had business dealings with him?" the bishop asked at last.

"Yes," she said. "Yes. I had—business dealings."

"What was his business, Miss Erickson?"

Her reaction to that was instant and a little terrified. "You don't know? But I thought that the police . . . Then I needn't have . . . I . . ."

The bishop looked at her sadly. "We know. At least we have suspected. The money changer in the temple—phaugh!" He turned away abruptly and stood looking out of the window, his hands clasped behind him. When he swung around again, his voice had lost its bitterness. "You borrowed money from Oscar?"

"I had to," she said dully. "There wasn't anyone else. I'd tried. The banks—I'd no security. And our house is mortgaged. And the doctor said Mama had to have that operation. It's cancer. Only, there've been other operations and nurses and doctor bills and medicines. And there's no one to do things for her but me. Papa died when I was a little girl and then my sister . . . You remember my sister, Bishop Walters? If Essie had lived . . .”

Bishop Walters cleared his throat and assured her that he did indeed remember Essie. I tried to remember, too, and failed. Only ragtags of story remained. Essie—Esther Erickson—had been her only sister. She'd died somewhere in the east—away at college, I thought. But that had been years ago surely. More than twenty years ago . . .

She was continuing, her voice dreary, without hope. “And I couldn't get the money anywhere. I was nearly crazy.”

“How long ago was this, Miss Erickson?”

“How long? I don't know exactly—I can't seem to think. Four or five years ago, it must have been. There's been another operation since but there won't be any more. Dr. Bliss says that they can't operate now. It wouldn't do any good. It was that way from the first, and I knew it, only, you can't stop—you can't just let people die. You have to try . . . That was why I had to get the money somewhere. I went to the banks but they said they were sorry, that banks couldn't just lend money without some sort of security to show and I had none. Everything was gone. And nobody else would lend me any—people always think school teachers have plenty of money, but they don't. They only have salaries, and you have to keep up and take special courses, and then when there's sickness . . .”

Again the bishop cleared his throat. “How did it happen that Oscar lent you the money?”

“It was the day I'd been everywhere and it was Thursday, choir practice night. I didn't want to go but Mrs. Holley, next door, said she'd sit with Mama and for me to go, that it would do me good. So I went. I was early and no one was there but Oscar. He was straightening the chairs or something and he asked me about Mama, he said he'd heard she was sick. He seemed nice and sorry and I found myself telling him all about it. Even the money and

how hard I'd tried to get it. That was when he said *he'd*
lend it to me. He asked me how much I wanted and I told
him two hundred dollars and he said I could have it right
away and pay him back so much a month. I signed a note."

"A note, eh?" the bishop mused. "At what rate of interest?"

"I don't know. I'm afraid I wasn't very business-like,
but I was so glad to get the money and he seemed so nice
about it, so really glad to help."

"Yes," the bishop said dryly. "But it didn't work out?"

"It did at first. I paid him each month and he kept
telling me he was glad to accommodate me and if I needed more . . . So when I did, I went back to him and he
let me have it. There was another note that I signed . . .
But I kept getting behind. Mama kept needing more and
more things—extras—and my money just wouldn't reach.
A school teacher's salary sounds large but it isn't—it isn't.
Not when you've mortgage interest to meet and taxes and
coal and a new roof and three months in the summer when
you don't get paid at all . . . I just couldn't do it. So twice
more I had to borrow and I still was behind and Mama
wasn't getting any better. This fall I just seemed to reach
the end so I went to Oscar and told him I couldn't make
any payments for a few months. It was then he got ugly.
He said I'd have to—that he'd sue me. He said he'd go
to the Board of Education and garnishee my salary and,
Bishop Walters, I couldn't have that. The Board wouldn't
understand. They might refuse to renew my contract and I
must keep on teaching—I must! It's all I've got."

"You paid him?"

"I had to. I let some other things go. But it was only
a stop gap. I couldn't go on much longer. That was why I
was afraid if the police found it out they'd think perhaps
that I'd killed him."

The bishop ignored that. "How much did you borrow
in all?"

"Two hundred dollars at first and then one hundred. Then later on I borrowed fifty dollars twice."

"Four hundred in all. And you've been paying it back at so much a month?"

"Twenty-five dollars a month," she said drearily. "It doesn't sound like a lot, but it is—it is! It meant that I couldn't have any new clothes and a teacher has to look well—she mustn't go shabby. The others talk . . ."

"But, my dear Miss Erickson!" The bishop's voice was soft with shock. "Four hundred dollars—do you realize that over a period of four years you have paid back more than double what you borrowed?"

"I know," she said. "But what could I do? I had no way of proving it. He—he never gave me any receipts and he wouldn't take my check. What I paid had to be in cash. He'd mark it down in a little book and I kept track too and I thought it would be all right. I trusted him . . ."

The bishop was on his feet now, walking back and forth in agitation. "But, this is dreadful! It goes beyond my comprehension! A minister is not supposed to be particularly business-like but I should have imagined that a school teacher . . ."

"You don't think of business when you need money. And I thought it would be all right."

But Bishop Walters was remembering something else. "You say that you signed new notes for each additional amount you borrowed. In what amounts were they?"

"The first note was for two hundred dollars and then, when I needed the next hundred dollars, he said we'd make out a new note for three hundred. He said it was the simplest way as long as I hadn't paid back any of the principal. That wasn't true—I knew it—but what could I do? Then the next one was for three hundred and fifty and the last for four hundred. He said he'd destroy the old notes.

I thought he should have given them back to me but he said they were in the bank and that he'd tear them up . . . What is it?" She was on her feet. "Why do you look at me like that?"

The bishop, indeed, was staring at her with undisguised horror. "I would not have believed it—I would not have believed it!" he muttered. He took another turn about the room. "My good woman, do you realize that in all probability Oscar did *not* destroy those notes and that even now they are hidden away somewhere among his possessions to provide evidence that you had borrowed, not four hundred dollars from him, but twelve hundred and fifty?"

At that she gave him one wild look and then went off into shrieking hysterics. We had a lovely time calming her down, which we did eventually by commandeering some of Alec's brandy and almost literally pouring it down her throat. Then, when she was quiet enough and after the bishop had given her his word that he'd talk to Ran and that there'd be no scandal at which the school board could cavil, we called a taxi and sent her home.

We didn't talk after she'd gone. I think we all felt the thing had gotten beyond words. The bishop sat grimly silent in his big chair. Ruth looked frightened. As for me— well, in spite of myself, reaction had set in. I'd had a busy day and I was just plain sleepy. I began to yawn.

After the fourth yawn, which I stifled with difficulty, I got resolutely to my feet. I offered to help Ruth to bed but she said she'd wait for Alec. The bishop said nothing so, after promising to look in at the twins, I dragged myself up the stairs.

I was trying to poke Francie's starfish legs and arms back through the bars of her crib without breaking them when I heard the front door open and shut. "Alec," I thought as I crossed over to where Sandy sprawled on top of his blankets.

It wasn't Alec. Almost at once I heard Ruth calling. "Tess—oh, Tess! Come down here quick! The bishop . . ."

I made the top step in one jump. "What is it? What about the bishop?"

"He's gone!" Ruth half-sobbed.

"Gone!" I repeated stupidly. "Where?"

"I don't know. He was looking out of the window in here and then, all of a sudden, he shot out into the hall. I heard him get his coat out of the closet but before I could call to him he was gone!"

I had an idea. "What window?"

"The north one—the one you can see the church from," Ruth called back ungrammatically.

My idea was right. I knew it. I ran into the bedroom—mine—which also overlooked the church. There was a dim light in Oscar's apartment. Then, even as I watched, it flickered out.

I snatched my coat from the bed and flung it around my shoulders. I grabbed my keys from the chest. Then I practically fell down the stairs.

"Get out of my way!" I gasped. "I know where he went! There was a light in Oscar's rooms—he must have seen it. I'm going too—"

"You can't!" Ruth wailed.

"Yes, I can. You call the police—call the fire department—anyone else you can think of! Tell them to get up here quick! I'll leave the side door unlocked . . ."

I slammed the door on her "But, Tess, if it's the murderer—!" and fled. There wasn't time to talk about murderers. Besides it wasn't a subject I cared to discuss. Not then.

I've never been quite certain just how I managed to get over to that side door. I was too busy thinking of the bishop, rushing alone and unarmed into heaven only knew what danger, to make plans or consider routes. I must have gone through the hedge for afterwards I discovered my stockings were torn and my face and hands red-lined with scratches. I know that I ploughed through snow drifts and that, in places, the cold whiteness struck well above my knees.

The side door was unlocked but I didn't take time to figure who unlocked it nor why. It might have been the bishop or it might have been—someone else. I took the door knob in both hands as a precaution against squeaks and slowly pulled the door open. Then I eased it shut again.

I stood in blackness at the foot of the stairs. No sound came from above. No lights although I strained my eyes against the dark.

I could not stand there indefinitely. Presumably the bishop had taken this way before me. But—where had he gone? And why hadn't he switched on the lights? Only a few minutes had elapsed between his leaving the house and mine. What had happened to him in that brief space? Had he found the prowler or—impossible to contemplate—had the prowler found him?

I could not stand here thinking. Thought only served to clog action and the bishop might be in danger. I was wearing soft-soled moccasins but I stepped out of these. The bare polished boards felt cold to my stockinged feet. The enclosed stairway was narrow and, as I edged upward, I stayed close to the wall in the hope of minimizing any betraying creaks the ancient stair might give forth.

It took me forever. A dozen times a day, since I'd been church secretary, I'd run up and down those stairs without regard to their length. Now as I stepped, halted, balanced, they seemed to stretch upward without end.

The darkness of that narrow enclosure sat smotheringly upon my chest. My heart was pounding a drumbeat in my ears. My hands, as I felt along the wall, were slippery with sweat.

I was at the top—my questing foot found nothing more tangible than air. Three steps now and from the shelter of the doorway I could reach around to the electric button.

I reached it, pushed it inward. There was a faint click but that was all. No answering lights. I thought that the master switch must have been cut and then at once remembered that it couldn't have been. There'd been lights in Oscar's apartment only minutes ago. Perhaps it was just the switch for this room that had been pulled. If that was so and I could feel my way over to the board, could I locate the proper switches solely by memory and the sense of touch? It would be a risky business and I might let myself in for a nasty shock, but it would be worth it. If I could light the church like a beacon . . .

It was then, as I still hesitated, that I heard the sound. Not so much a sound either as a sensing of movement within the choir room.

It wasn't as dark within the choir room as it had been in the enclosed stair. Light from the living night outside seeped in through the long, uncurtained windows to make gray twilight against the high ceiling and leave only the lower half of the room in blackness. Now, as I watched, unbelievingly, a portion of that blackness seemed to detach itself and rear upward in silent deadly menace.

It caught me off guard. My breath drew inward in a sharp sibilance as betraying as the futile click of the light button had been. The hovering darkness before me poised as though listening, gathered itself together, began to move forward in horrible slow advance.

And, as it advanced, I retreated. Not very far—one step, two. There was no place to go. I dared not attempt the stairs—before I was halfway down, I knew, I would be caught. My shoulders touched the wall. I leaned back against it, my arms wide-flung. I waited.

The thing was almost upon me. Even through the blood that pounded in my ears I could hear the careful pad of footsteps, a sound of breathing other than my own. I closed my eyes. The breathing was very near now. It seemed almost that I could feel the first impact of questing finger tips . . .

And then, suddenly, they were gone. There was only that other thing. The distant wail of sirens coming closer—ever closer . . .

The other heard too and at once the very air appeared to explode into motion. Something rushed past me, unseen, felt only in the wide-flung rush of its garments. I caught at it, knew in a moment the rough nubbiness of cloth. It tore through my hands. Then there was only the clatter of feet upon the stair below me, the slam of the outside door. Whoever—whatever it had been—was gone.

Weakly, bereft of strength, I leaned against the wall. I was still there when the cacophony of sirens rose to ear-splitting clamor, the door was flung open and powerful flashlights sprang upward. There were noisy footsteps behind the lights and the rasp of voices. "What's going on here?"

I couldn't see the speaker but I flung out my hands toward him. "I don't know," I said inanely. "I'm so glad you've come. Someone was here and the lights—the lights didn't work. And I'm afraid for the bishop . . ."

He came up in great leaping bounds, three steps at a time until he stood beside me. I saw the dull gleam of brass buttons, my clutching hands felt the smoothness of leather belt and holster. He fended off my hands, grunting, "Here! You take it easy. What's this about a bishop?"

As he spoke he swung his flashlight in a great circle. Light picked out the chairs, a table, the triangular curve of the grand piano. Something else, too. A huddle of clothes upon the floor, a head whose silver was streaked obscenely with scarlet.

I heard the man's expletive, unbecoming to a church, as I shoved past him. The light's circle focused, held, while I touched frantic fingers to wrist and heart.

I looked up then. "It's all right," I said. "I mean—he's alive. The lights are over there. Will you turn them all on, please? This—this is the bishop!"

16

While the officer—he told me he was Sergeant White—telephoned for a doctor, I got water from the little ante-room where flowers for the church are made ready and bathed the bishop's head and wrists. I was afraid to attempt much more, but even my inexperience could see that the cut was only superficial. As a matter of fact, before Dr. Morton arrived, he had stirred uneasily and tried to sit up.

I said, "No—no, you mustn't. Lie still—the doctor's coming."

He obeyed. His eyes perplexed, blinked at me. "Ah, it's you, Miss King. I'm afraid I've bumped my head . . ."

It was such an anticlimax that I giggled. I couldn't help it.

The giggle brought him back to full consciousness. His gaze steadied. "Ah, yes. I remember now. He tripped me. Is that a police officer I see? Did they intercept him?"

I said no, that unfortunately he'd gotten away but that the police were here. Then, as Sergeant White, intrigued, came over, I told the story as I knew it. "Whoever it was must have turned out the lights and started upstairs before Bishop Walters got here. Then, if he heard the bishop—" I asked the question direct. "Did you make any noise when you came in?"

Not even the purple bruise upon his temple nor his recumbent position could rob the bishop of his angry dignity. "Certainly I made no attempt at concealment. Why should I? I was not the intruder."

"Sure—sure," the Sergeant soothed. "We get you. Only them that's careful lives the longest. Look at Hitler."

The bishop's expression made it plain that he didn't want to look at Hitler or anyone else and Sergeant White went on. "Down in Johnson's apartment, was he?" He made a gesture to the faces that peered from the doorway. "Okay, boys—you know what to do. Get going."

They tiptoed past—a couple of them—with hats off and with respectful side glances for the bishop—and three or four more clattered back down the stairs up which they'd just come. After these last, the sergeant gazed thoughtfully.

"Got to take a look around," he told us. "Not that it'll do a damn—beg pardon, Bishop—a bit of good. *He* won't be hanging around, that's a cinch, and you can't go insulting passersby on the streets unless you got a reason."

The men came back upstairs to report. Nobody was in the basement, nothing appeared to have been disturbed and Oscar's apartment was dark. It was also locked. They were sent back to the police station to get the keys Ran had impounded so that further search might be made.

The doctor arrived and pronounced the bishop convalescent. They had been schoolboys together, and, as the doctor's clever fingers dabbed at the inch-long cut, he twitted his old friend. "Little old, aren't you, John, to be playing cops and robbers? Next time you'd better leave it to them that know how."

"I'd have copped and robbered him if I'd caught him," Bishop Walters said grimly. He was sitting in a chair now. "Unfortunately he didn't give me the opportunity."

Here the sergeant cleared his throat noisily. There were questions he'd like to ask . . .

The bishop wasn't able to help him much. Entirely by accident, he'd seen the light in Oscar's rooms where no light should be. He'd taken the church key, from Alec's desk and his own overcoat. He it was who'd left the church door unlocked. "For reinforcements. I knew I could count on Mrs. MacDonald," he said with a twinkle. Like myself he had climbed the stairs, tried the lights. He, too, had thought of the switchboard and had been on his way toward it when he was tripped, but of course it was quite possible he had been mistaken as to that. "I saw no one. There was an obstruction of some sort. I went down. I remember falling. My head struck something. After that . . ." He shook the head in question. "Could it have been that I imagined all this? That I simply became involved with a chair—that chair." He pointed to one conveniently placed. "And stumbled."

But I could refute that. Hastily I told my story—the darkness that had reared up before me, the rush of movement past. "Whoever it was must have been down on the floor beside you when I clicked that light button. So then he came after me. And if it hadn't been for the sirens . . ."

"I wonder if he contemplated killing me?" The bishop shivered a little. "You make it seem very sinister, my dear. Kneeling beside . . . I don't like the idea and yet—why else—"

"More likely he was feeling around for this." The sergeant made a dive under a table and came up with a large flashlight which he held gingerly by its ring. He swung it back and forth, weighting it. "Not heavy enough to kill but plenty heavy to cause damage. Well, Bishop, I guess you got conked all right."

"I think I did." The bishop put a careful hand to his decoration of plaster and gauze. "Miss King, I am very grateful for your timely appearance . . ."

"Wait a minute!" Sergeant White interrupted. "You sure this was a man we're talking about?"

The bishop said why, no, he wasn't sure at all. He had neither seen, heard, nor touched the intruder. The sergeant grunted and looked at me.

I shrugged. "I suppose anyone rising up suddenly out of darkness would look tall. As for touching—I did touch some clothing but I didn't hang on. It felt rough—I thought of a man's coat but I suppose it could have been a woman's. I wouldn't know."

The sergeant grunted again. This time in disgust.

It was getting cold in the church—or rather, since the fires were indifferent, we were beginning to notice the chill. Dr. Morton finished winding a rakish turban about the bishop's bludgeoned head and stepped back with a chuckle. "What the well-dressed man wears for the hospital—oh, yes, you're going to the hospital, John. For tonight anyway and until I get some X-rays. Don't be a fool, man! You can't take a busted head next door. Who's going to look after you tonight? Mrs. Mac is laid up and I've an idea Tess has her hands full with the rest of them."

The bishop subsided—how well he knew the way things were at the MacDonalds!—and with a satisfied little jerk of his head Dr. Morton went to call the ambulance.

The sergeant's men came back with the keys and were sent downstairs. The ambulance officials arrived and departed with the bishop. I knew I should be getting back to the house and Ruth but still I lingered—so obviously that the sergeant began to view me with a jaundiced eye.

"You want me to send one of the boys over home with you?" he asked pointedly.

I said no, that I wasn't afraid. But the consciousness that I was about to be thrown out on my ear emboldened me. "You were here at the church this afternoon—I saw you. Did you find anything?"

Sergeant White looked affronted. Then something—perhaps doubt as to my exact status in the affair, perhaps the fear that I was indeed his chief's "girl"—modified his expression. "Nope. Not yet."

"Are you going to keep on looking?"

"Depends on the chief. But what else can we do? This guy in here again tonight looks like there's got to be something."

"Maybe there was. But what if he got what he was looking for tonight?"

"Don't think he did. Don't look like it." He was shying off again. "Sure you don't want me to send a man over with you?"

"Sure," I said, and laughed. "I know you want to get rid of me, Sergeant, and I'm really going. Only first—I've been doing some thinking. About where it could be. I think that if Oscar really had something he wanted to hide, he wouldn't leave it in his apartment That would be the first place anyone'd look. He had a safety deposit box—we know that. I suppose he could have had others but if he had the police would have found them."

The sergeant said, "Yeah," and watched me very cautiously.

"There are lots of places in a church where you can hide things," I went on. "But a church is open to lots of people. Anyone might stumble on a hiding place. But there is one place that, so far as I know, only two people have ever been—Oscar and the organ tuner."

"Huh?" Sergeant White looked chagrined, unbelieving, excited, all at once. "Say that again."

"The organ chambers are always kept locked," I said. "An organ is a valuable piece of property. If children or someone who was just curious should get in and poke around, they might do a lot of damage. So—Oscar was the only one who could get in, outside of Mr. Parker, the tuner. Oscar would have known it was safe to hide something there for Mr. Parker only comes four times a year unless we telephone him. Don't you think—?"

"Yeah." There was actual admiration in the sergeant's eyes. "Come on—who's got the keys? We'll take a look right now—"

"No, we won't," I said firmly. "It's not as simple as all that. You and your men can't just blunder around in those chambers. You might break something. Those pipes are sensitive. Just a touch will throw some of them off pitch."

"Huh!" said the sergeant. "Okay, what's your idea?"

"Call Mr. Parker and let him do the searching for you. He's not connected with the church in any other way—he's Methodist—and he's perfectly trustworthy."

Sergeant White made a lunge at the phone. "What's his number?"

I gave it to him, listened to the one-sided conversation. Apparently Walter Parker was nursing a cold and he refused to leave his bed for anyone, including the police. The sergeant fumed without result and then made an appointment for the following morning. Early. Eight o'clock . . .

That done, he slammed the receiver down and beamed at me. "All set. He'll be here at eight. I guess I better leave a man here overnight—make sure nobody gets into them chambers."

"Don't get too hopeful," I warned. "I could be wrong. There may be nothing *to* be found."

"Don't give me that," Sergeant White said jocosely. "I gotta hunch everything's going to be okay."

His "hunch" was still buoying him up when he insisted upon seeing me back to the house. I got the impression that I was now considered a precious thing. When I thanked him, he responded with a pat on the shoulder and a gallant, "Nix—it was a pleasure."

Reaction was getting me. When I plodded wearily into the house, I found Ruth's wheel chair drawn up against the windows that overlooked the church. When I said I was sorry I hadn't called her sooner, she waved away apologies.

"I heard the sirens and I saw the lights. I thought if anything *had* happened, I'd have heard."

"Enough did," I sighed, as I began the saga of the bishop. Halfway through, Alec came in and I had to begin all over again. After that I answered Ruth's questions and listened to Alec's hymn of horror—he seemed to consider the attack on the bishop more a breach of hospitality than a forward step in the pursuit of a killer. When my eyes failed to respond to my will and began to fall shut in the midst of sentences, I went to bed.

I was awake early. Definitely before eight. All the time I was dressing, I kept looking out of the window for signs of activity around the church. I tried to think of some plausible excuse that would take me over. Why shouldn't I go? It had been my idea, hadn't it? Perhaps if I enlisted Alec's aid . . .

But Alec had gone by the time I'd collected the twins and wobbled down the stairs. The "Y" had been as good as its word. There were good smells from the kitchen. Ruth was having breakfast. She waved a piece of toast at me.

"Hello, angels. Dump them in the kitchen, Tess, and I'll pour your coffee. Mrs. Morse will feed them. She says she just loves children. Rather a break, if true."

My breakfast was tasteless. I kept waiting for the telephone to ring. If didn't.

By half past nine, I'd given up. The twins were safe in their play pen. Alec had dashed in with the news that Bishop Walters had had a restful night and might be allowed to come back to us by evening. He'd then dashed out again without informing us of his destination. Ruth was placid, sewing buttons on a tiny pair of rompers.

I decided to do some work myself. So far I hadn't touched the Sunday offering. St. Thomas' used envelopes and they made for an elaborate system of bookkeeping.

Each envelope had to be opened and its contents credited against the proper number and name. There was loose collection to count. A full morning's work.

I got my books and spread them on the dining room table. I sorted the envelopes by numbers into four little piles. I shoved the loose collection and some miscellaneous envelopes—Sunday School ones, a few blanks—to one side and got to work. I was nearly done when Ran walked in.

He came straight to the dining room. I don't know whether it was Ruth or instinct that guided him. I finished an entry: Mrs. Harold English, $5.00—Envelope Number 286, before I looked up.

He was standing very close to the table. He looked cross. I smiled, said a polite "Good morning!"

My only answer was a grunt as he slapped an ancient box file down upon the table. He said, "I thought I told you to stay away from the church."

"Oh, you told *me,*" I said meekly. "You forgot to tell the bishop."

"So you rushed off to the rescue," he scoffed. "Who'd you think you were—Superman?" But his eyes were kind. They encouraged me to say, "Ran, I wasn't super-anything. I was scared stiff."

He took it calmly. "You had reason to be. Our friend doesn't play for tiddly-winks. Next time—"

"There won't be a next time," I assured him hastily. "But I'm not sorry—really I'm not. Not if it got you that." I pointed to the box file.

He stared at it with disfavor. "Thanks for nothing. I'm not sure it's such a prize."

I said, "What do you mean? Have you looked at it?"

"Only superficially."

"And it doesn't tell you anything?"

"It told me that Johnson was running a modest loan business but I knew that before. Oh, there's plenty more."

He slapped his hand down on the box. "Names and addresses and amounts. Paid high for what they got, too, most of
them, poor devils! As much as five or six hundred per cent."

I was horrified. "But, Ran, that's usury—"

He cut me off.

"All right—so it's usury. The man's dead—there's nothing to be done about him now."

"What about his victims?" I asked bitterly. "There's
Miss Erickson—"

"Yes," he said evenly. "There's Miss Erickson."

It woke me up. "What do *you* know about Miss Erickson?"

"We talked to the bishop."

I said, "Oh. Then you know about Blair Thurston too"

"I had a full report, thank you." His mouth twitched
with a hidden smile.

I looked at the box file and hated it. "Are her—Miss
Erickson's—notes in there? Was it the way she said?"

"They are and it is. Twelve hundred and fifty dollars
worth. She'd never have gotten out of his clutches, I'm
afraid."

Unless he died—unless he died. The words came unbid-
den to my lips. I bit them back. "How about the others?
Was it the same way with them?"

"We'll know more about that after we've checked the
file over carefully. That still has to be done. But the thing's
out of the mythical now. We've something to go on."

"Won't it be an awful job?"

"Not so bad. Johnson's clientele seems to have been
small. Thirty or thirty-five. Probably all he could handle.
We may know more about that end of it if we ever catch
up with Brannigan."

I said, "But I don't see . . ."

He shrugged. "Guessing. That's all I've done so far in
this case. I've an idea Brannigan was the one who provided
Johnson with clients."

"And of course that's why he didn't want any of the money! But if he—disapproved, why did he keep on supplying clients?"

"Perhaps he didn't. Most of the accounts I've looked at go over a period of years. Once he got them, he kept them."

I said, "I can't help it—it seems to me silly. It can't be that hard to borrow money that you'd have to go to a man like Oscar Johnson!"

Ran shrugged. "Not for you, perhaps. Sure there are plenty of banks and legitimate loan offices. But the loan offices make a regular monthly salary a qualification and the banks ask financial statements and character references and security of one kind or another. If you need money desperately and if you haven't any property or any salary or any friends, someone like Oscar is about your only solution."

"But Oscar'd want security," I said scornfully. "You can't tell me he wouldn't."

"I'm not trying to tell you he didn't. He has something on all of them. In Miss Erickson's case, it's the notes. As nearly as I can tell you, it's the same deal with Mary Collins. In the Brastock file there's an envelope which contains a diamond ring. Probably her engagement ring. Carter's and Thurston's are empty save for a record of payment that's marked paid and initialed. They look perfectly straight transactions—I doubt if we find any monkey business in either. Smedley now—that's something queer. On the face of things it looks as though Oscar owned that Buick car and was simply renting it to Smedley—by the month. The title is in Johnson's name; so's the record of the license."

"What about Charles Dennison?"

"Another funny one. There's the record of an old loan for about four hundred dollars. Then, about ten years ago, it's written off as paid. Didn't Dennison say something about having done Johnson a favor some ten or fifteen years back? There's a more recent loan—made about three years ago—on which payments have been made occasionally. No apparent security was taken nor are there any notes in the file."

I didn't like the way that last was said. "I believe you think, deep down in your heart, that the murderer is really Charles Dennison," I accused.

He shook his head. "No, I've an open mind on the subject. But Dennison's got some explaining to do."

"So have the others," I said stubbornly.

"Granted. They'll get their chance."

"When? What are you going to do?"

He raised an eyebrow at me. "Well, first I'm turning over all but those seven names to a couple of my men. They'll check the stories on them. The seven, I'm reserving for myself."

"You're going to check those?"

"I personally. Want to help?"

I was so surprised I fairly stuttered. "Me? You want *me* to help?"

"I could use you. I told you we were short of men on the force. Besides you know these people better than I. You may be able to pry loose the information we must have."

"You're the police," I said doubtfully. "I should think they'd have to talk to you."

"Oh, you would!" he mocked. "You'd be surprised at how little people are moved to communicate to authority unless they feel so inclined. Of course, if you'd rather not—"

"Oh, no," I said. "I'll help. Of course I'll help. I want this thing cleared up. I want to be able to go over to the church again and feel safe."

Something like a shadow crossed Ran's face. "I think I can promise you it'll be cleared up. About the rest of it—well, it's not wise to take too many chances even in a church. It may be sacred ground to you but there are others who don't regard it in the same light. These are not the first crimes that have been committed in a church. They probably won't be the last."

"I suppose not," I said soberly. "All right—I'll be careful—I promise." I looked down at the littered table. "This stuff—I really ought to finish it," I murmured. "They'll be needing the table for lunch."

Ran laughed. "There's no awful rush. Go ahead and finish. I've got to go down to the station, sort over the stuff in the file and set my men to work. There's not much to be done until late afternoon. Suppose I call you . . ."

But I wasn't going to be shunted off that way. "If you'd just wait a minute," I pleaded. "I'm about done. Then I have to go down to the bank with this money. You could drive me down and then I could—I could—" I stopped, not quite sure what it was I could do.

Ran laughed again and pulled out an opposite chair. "All right—you win. I'll wait. What are you doing anyway? Entering the pay roll? Why don't I help?"

It went ever so fast after that. Ran opened the envelopes, read off number and amount enclosed, and I entered them in the treasurer's book.

We finished the regular envelopes and began on the others. There were only about a dozen, belonging mostly to people who'd lost or mislaid their regular collection envelopes and were making do with whatever came to hand. All but one had name or number inscribed upon the outside. That one, the last, was an ordinary, cheap letter-size, the sort of envelope you buy packaged at the dime store. Ran weighted it thoughtfully.

"Something in here," he murmured, "but it doesn't feel like money. I wonder . . ."

Quickly he ripped up the flap and shook out the contents. Something dropped with a little click upon the polished wood of the table, something that flashed rainbowed red and green and purple under the lights of the overhead chandelier. It was a ring, a large square diamond set in raw red gold.

Even as I still gasped with shock, Ran was poking at it with a cautious forefinger. "Know what it is, of course?"

"Of course," I echoed. "It's Carol's diamond—it must be. The one Blair Thurston gave her—the one no one knew about. But—how on earth did it get into the church collection?"

"If we knew that," Ran said grimly, "I suspect our work would be over. We'd have our murderer."

17

My mind felt blank. I reached out and in my turn touched the ring. "It's so beautiful. How could anyone—even a murderer—bear to give it up?"

"He wouldn't have much choice," Ran told me. "It was this—or hide it. He couldn't have sold it, not a stone that size. Sooner or later we'd have gotten on its track and then—blooey. No, this was smart."

"But not so smart to put it in the collection plate," I argued. "I mean—doesn't this definitely narrow things down?"

"It does—on the face of it anyway. To the same seven people. How many were in church yesterday?"

"Six of them," I said firmly. "You ought to know. You were there. Mary Collins wasn't."

"They don't pass collection plates to the choir," Ran mused. "How many of these people have envelopes—make regular contributions?"

"All but Philip Smedley. Oh, and of course, Georgia Brastock. The Brastocks don't belong at St. Thomas'— they're Presbyterians or something."

Ran's eyes were narrowing. "Then neither Smedley nor Mrs. Brastock would have church envelopes in their possession?"

I looked at him with scorn. "Don't let that get you excited. You can't tell me that anyone in his right mind would seal that ring into an envelope that could be traced directly back to him."

Ran was imperturbable. "If you'll confine yourself to answering questions, young lady, we'll get further faster. Now—how many of the people on our list—omitting Mrs. Brastock and Smedley—are represented by their regular collection envelopes?"

I knew but I rechecked just to be sure. "Four—Mary Collins wasn't there."

"Four," he repeated. "Miss Erickson, Carter, Blair Thurston and Dennison. Three of them in the choir where no plates are passed. How do they manage to get their envelopes in?"

"Well, not the way you do," I said. "You mail a check on the first of the month. But the plates are left at the altar—it's a simple matter for those in the choir to slip in and leave their envelopes."

"Very simple," Ran agreed. "Pick your own time. No one to see you or notice what sort of an envelope you slipped in."

"I don't believe it," I said wearily. "I mean, that it was one of them. If it was someone who needed money desperately—that ring was worth plenty—why toss it away like that?"

"Sometimes," Ran said, "the soundness of your reasoning startles me. Why indeed? To which I propound another question: what if it was someone who didn't need the money the ring represented? Someone who could afford to toss it away?"

"Now you're contradicting yourself," I said. "There isn't one who can afford to throw money away."

"Isn't there?" Ran asked softly. "Are you sure?"

"No," I said crossly, "I'm not. I'm not sure of anything any more. I—"

I never went on with what I was saying because there came an interruption just then. Ruth, in her wheel chair, with Harvey Thurston in tow. I wasn't too surprised. Dimly I remembered having heard a bell ring somewhere . . .

"Mr. Thurston wanted to see you, Ran," was Ruth's greeting. "I thought perhaps you wouldn't mind if I brought him right out here . . . What in the world have you two been doing so long?" she went on gaily. "I never thought that church collections were so heavy that you—"

She didn't get a chance to finish. Abruptly Harvey Thurston cut in. "I want to talk to you, Garrison, about my son. He—" He stopped. All at once he was rigid, staring down at the table. "What's that?" he asked harshly.

Ran folded his arms across his chest, took a step backwards. "Just what it appears to be, Mr. Thurston. A diamond ring."

"A ring?" Ruth repeated. She glanced uncertainly from Ran to me. You could see "engagement" in her eye. I shook my head and her "Why, how nice!" died a-borning. She said, "Whose is it? Where did it come from?"

Thurston had it. He was turning it over and over between his fingers. "It's my son's ring," he said gruffly. "It's the one he gave to his—his wife."

Ran put out his hand. "We thought it was. But—thanks for the identification."

Thurston didn't respond to the outstretched hand, instead he glared at Ran and thrust the ring into his watch pocket. "I'm keeping this."

Ran smiled. It was a lazy smile but definitely not nice. "Sorry. You can't. It's evidence—police evidence."

"My son bought it," Thurston said stubbornly. "It belongs to him."

"He gave it to Carol Tolliver. Her murderer, we believe, took it from her after she was dead. Because he became frightened, or for some other reason, he dumped it into Sunday's collection. To whom it now belongs, I have no idea. It's not for me to decide. But for the present I'm keeping it. Hand it over."

Thurston obeyed. "My son," he said in a strangled voice, "my son had nothing to do with this. He wasn't even in Dorchester. How could he commit murder from a distance?"

"It's been done," Ran murmured, "although not, I'll admit, by this method."

"Hardly." Thurston drew a long breath, seemed to expand before our eyes. "Garrison, you're a sensible man. The boy had nothing to do with this—you can see that I'd appreciate it if you'd go easy with him. He's had a shock. These boy and girl attachments—"

"I'd put it a little stronger than that," Ran remarked. "They were married."

Thurston waved an impatient hand. "The girl's idea, not his. What she wanted was money. She put her cards on the table just as soon as he was safe in camp. When Blair found out about it—" he made a quick slapping motion of one hand—"it was all over. Blair's not a complete fool, he can see what's thrust in front of his eyes."

There was a silence. I suspected Ruth, as I, was remembering the afternoon before and Blair's trembling voice, his bewilderment and anger. "Carol and I weren't near so much washed up as I've been letting on . . . She wasn't the way they said—I know she wasn't." I wondered if Ran knew that, if the bishop had told him.

No time for finding out. Ran was buttoning his overcoat; he was saying, "I'll tell you, Thurston—send the boy over to the station this afternoon. We'll have him identify the ring and if his story checks, we'll write him off. Okay?"

"We-ll," Thurston said grudgingly. "No harm in that, I suppose. After all, he wasn't *here* . . .'"

He took himself off with that. Ran made no move to follow so, for politeness' sake, I went with him to the door. Then I came back to the dining room. I leaned against the door frame. "I could bear," I said, "to know something. Just where was Moses when the lights went out?"

Abruptly Ran looked up from the glove he was drawing on, looked down again. He didn't speak.

"That's not what's bothering me," Ruth said slowly. "That's too—oh, well, obvious. Somebody must have found that out. But—" She stopped, didn't go on.

Ran was looking directly at her. "All right," he said, half under his breath. "I'm not promising to answer but I'll listen to you. What is it?"

Ruth sounded distressed. "I hate to say it only—how could Harvey Thurston make such positive identification of that ring unless—"

Ran took it away from her. "Unless he were the murderer? Well, that's one possibility, I'll admit, but there are at least two others—Blair might have shown it to him or the girl could have. Then, too, it's a large diamond with a rather unusual setting. If he'd had any sort of description . . ."

"Old fair-play Garrison!" I scoffed. "Ran, could he be the murderer?"

"Suppose I answer that first question of yours now," Ran said slowly. "Both last night and the night of the murders, Harvey Thurston worked late at the bank. His dinners were sent in."

I said, "Wha-at?" and "Then you *do* think—?" But Ran only shook his head and gathered the file under one arm. "I'll call you this afternoon, Tess," he said briefly and was gone.

"I'll call you this afternoon, Tess," I mimicked bitterly. "Thanks for nothing. Why did that old fuddy-duddy have to come over here this morning of all mornings?"

It was plain that Ruth wasn't listening. Grumpily I said, "Now what's the matter with you? Lost interest in my love life?"

"I'm thinking about Harvey Thurston," Ruth said, "I don't see how he could be the murderer, do you? He wouldn't kill Carol over a few thousand dollars—I know he wouldn't. It just doesn't make sense."

"It would if he's been robbing his bank," I said flippantly. "No Thurston would want the world to know he was broke."

But Ruth wasn't to be diverted. "He doesn't *look* like a murderer," she said stubbornly.

"None of them do," I said with a sigh. "But that's one thing you can't put a face to—murder, I mean. Murder's something that hides in the heart."

"Do you remember what Alec said about Carol?" Ruth asked with a shiver. "About her saying she was like the man who'd sowed the wind and was reaping the whirlwind?"

"Of course I remember," I said crossly. "But Carol didn't know she was going to be murdered then! Alec didn't say she was frightened—just nervous and upset."

"She might have been nervous because she knew Blair was coming and didn't want to see him," Ruth said. "But surely she wouldn't have been afraid of *him.*"

"Nobody in her right senses," I said firmly, "would be afraid of Blair Thurston. I could push him over with one finger. Oh, let's skip it, shall we? I'm busy."

But it wasn't that easy—skipping it. All the time I counted cash and wrote bank slips, it stayed in the back of my mind. Had Alec been wrong and was Carol's nervousness that night traceable to fear? Fear of something or someone? Not of something—my mind rejected the impersonal. Of whom then? Harvey Thurston? Blair? They were the most logical and yet even Ran believed Blair was out of it. Harvey Thurston? But Ruth was right there—

he wouldn't kill just to get out of paying a few thousand dollars. Besides, hadn't we decided that Oscar's, not Carol's, was the important murder? My head ached with speculation.

I tried to forget, during luncheon and on into the dreary afternoon that followed. There was sleet out of doors, a freezing drizzle that coated sidewalks and snow-smooth roads with glare ice. Cars crashed and banged fenders on the hill in front of the church. At three o'clock Alec brought the bishop home and we had a time of minor excitement getting him settled.

The bishop was subdued. In spite of the "realistic attitude" ascribed to him by Ruth, I don't think the old man had ever really believed in the murders. Now he did. Something like near-murder had happened to him and he wanted no more of it. Watching him, listening to him, I decided that we need have no further worry. Bishop Walters' days of barging into danger were over.

It was nearly half past four when Ran telephoned. He said, "Tess? I'll be around for you in five minutes. Bring a notebook and pencils." He hung up before I could say anything.

I was furious but I managed to parry Ruth's questions and get into my coat. When the horn sounded, I made my way down the ash-strewn walk and, still sizzling, got into the police car.

Ran raised an eyebrow at me. "Hi!"

I said, "Hello," and then shut my eyes as the car jerked forward and then slid sideways around a truck. When I opened them again, Ran was looking at me. Through clenched teeth I said, "Will you please attend to your driving? I don't know where we're going but I'd like to arrive there all in one piece."

"Oh, you would, would you?" He turned the wheel and we skidded around a corner, narrowly missing a parked car. "All right—I ought to have chains on, damn it!—but I haven't. So what?"

I refused to answer and after a second, he said coaxingly, "What's the matter with you anyway? You admit you don't know our destination and yet you have no curiosity. It's not like you."

With entire truth, I said, "I'm mad."

The eyebrow quirked up again. "Now that is a pity. May I ask why?"

"I don't like being shunted in and out of this thing. Either I'm in it or I'm not. You seem to think you can pick me up when you need me and put me down when you don't. I don't like it."

The car slackened pace for a moment, and Ran said, seriously, "Let me tell you something, my girl—you'd better make the most of what you're getting. You shouldn't be mixed up in this thing at all. Murder's nasty and God knows, if I could help it, you wouldn't get any closer to it than reading the newspapers. So, if you're getting any idea this is going to work into a permanent partnership, forget it. I have no intention of letting my wife mix into murder."

My anger was gone. I sat there, looking straight before me, my hands quiet in my lap. So it had come at last, as I'd known all along that sometime it would come, but not in the manner I'd envisioned. Somehow I'd thought of a quiet room and soft lights and the two of us alone before an open fire . . . Well, we were alone, all right, but there was no quiet room, no open fire. Instead, we were sliding down a slippery street in a battered police car and, queerly enough, the change in scene didn't seem to matter in the least . . .

I thought, well, if it's the casual approach you want, the casual approach it shall be. I said, "I beg your pardon. Could you, by any chance, be referring to me?"

Ran's lips twitched. "Well, I thought probably you'd get that idea."

"A very nice idea," I said carefully, "so far as it goes. Perhaps—if you cared to enlarge on it . . ."

I didn't go on because, just then, the car bumped the curb and stopped. The sudden cessation of motion threw me sidewards—into Ran's arms. "Well, I must say that's wonderful driving," I began and then didn't go on. I couldn't. Ran was saying things into my near ear—things like "darling" and "sweetheart" and "my heart"—all the silly, inconsequential things I'd been wanting to hear from him.

We were both a trifle breathless when we finally drew apart. "Merely the precis," Ran said. "Development can come later. But just at this moment—" He reached past me to open the car door. "We've work to do."

Work—well, after what had gone before, work was definitely an anti-climax. I said, "What do you mean? Where are we going?"

"We're not going," Ran told me. "We're here."

"Here" appeared to be an ancient four-apartment dwelling. Paint peeled from the splintering pillars of its porch. I followed up steps that needed mending into a shabby hall, watched Ran press a bell labeled "Collins."

Mary Collins's crippled sister opened the door. She wasn't old but she'd had a stroke and now she dragged one foot and her left hand was a useless claw. She led us into the living room where Mary, covered with an Afghan, lay on the davenport.

Mary wasn't glad to see us. She half sat up, spoke querulously. "What do you want? I told you everything I knew the other night. Why are you bothering me again?"

I think Ran decided there'd be no good in half measures. He waded right in. "Not quite all. I don't remember you telling me you owed Johnson money."

She shrank back against the pillows. "How—how did you know?" Her voice was a whisper.

"We have the notes."

"Notes? Notes?" Suddenly her face crumpled, she began to cry. "Then—then he lied to me! He didn't tear it up!"

Ran looked at her soberly. "I think you'd better tell us all about it."

Her story wasn't a great deal different from Miss Erickson's. She'd bought the furniture—"We'd never had anything but old things and we wanted something new!" The purchase had been financed through the Lyon Credit Company and then Oscar had heard about it—how she didn't know. (We suspected we did.) He'd told her about the terrible rates the loan companies charged. Wouldn't she rather borrow from a private individual—someone like himself—who had money he didn't need and would be apt to be more lenient than the hard-hearted finance companies? She'd fallen for it and he'd lent her the money to take up the loan and a little more. "We'd never had a radio and I got a chance to buy one second hand." But when the time for payment came along, Oscar hadn't been lenient at all. He demanded more than the finance company's payment had been. When she'd objected, he'd threatened to go to her employer, garnishee her wages. "I'm only a bookkeeper in a grocery store, you know, and I don't get so very much. Twenty dollars every month took an awful slice out of it."

She'd managed to pay the first few months and then her sister had come down with a bad cold. There were medicines to buy and doctor bills. It was Oscar who suggested he lend her enough money to bring her up to date on the payments and she'd accepted. She didn't know what else to do. He said, so far, she'd only paid the interest on her loan so he'd make out a new note for the whole amount and she could sign that. "So he did and I signed it. I knew he was lying—about me only paying the interest—I'd paid much more than that—but I couldn't prove it. He'd never given me any receipts and—he was so ugly about it. He frightened me. I—I didn't know what to do. And he did say he'd destroy the old note—" Her reddened eyes flashed hopefully toward Ran.

"He didn't," Ran said flatly. "There are two notes—one for two hundred and fifty dollars, the other for three hundred."

Mary Collins said, "Five hundred and fifty dollars!" and leaned back against her pillows. Her eyes were shut and she was so white that I thought she'd fainted. I stood up, with the vague notion of getting some water, but the sister was before me.

"You get out of here!" she said in her slurred, dragging speech. "She didn't kill him—she told you that. She couldn't have—"

"I couldn't have," Mary repeated faintly. "I was at the store that night—Friday is our busy day—and I worked right up until almost eight o'clock. All the clerks were there—we didn't even go out for supper. We just took some bread and meat and made sandwiches. Ask any of them—they'll tell you."

"I have," Ran said and stood up. "You're in the clear so far as the—murders are concerned. One more question. Last night—where were you?"

"Where do you suppose?" The sister glared at him. "Right here. In bed. She had a sort of hysterical spell—crying—and I called the doctor. He was here till after ten. It was Dr. Farrender. You ask him."

"Check!" Ran said. "All right, Miss Collins—sorry I had to bother you. One more question—do the words 'blue' and 'brown' mean anything to you? Have you ever heard Oscar use them in any conversation?"

She shook her head indifferently. She did not even open her eyes.

"Here's a date—January 15, 1922. Ever hear of that?"

"No."

Even her lips were white. I tugged at Ran's arm. "Come on—we oughtn't to bother her. She's ill . . ."

But Ran lingered to say, "I wouldn't worry too much about the notes, Miss Collins. I imagine some sort of compromise can be worked out."

The sister followed us into the hall, closing the door behind her. "Don't mind Mary," she said. "She doesn't know a thing about these murders, but they were what made her sick just the same. It was the blood—she can't stand the sight of blood. You see, our father shot himself in the bathroom when we were little girls. It was Mary who found him and ever since . . ."

We went soberly to the car. I let him close the door on me, waited until he had stepped on the starter. Then I said, "Ran, you don't need to worry—ever—about my mixing into your police business. I've seen all I want. Never—never again!"

"I thought you'd feel like that," Ran said. He sounded satisfied.

18

I said, "What do we do next?" and "What was all that about blue and brown? You never mentioned them before."

"Because I didn't know about them. I only found this thing this afternoon." He dug into a pocket, produced a crumpled piece of paper. "It was in a file pocket all by itself. May mean something—may not. Take a look."

Under the pale dashboard light, I studied it. The paper showed an upside-down triangle—the words "blue" forming the upper angles, "brown" written at the apex. To one side was the notation "possible" followed by a question mark. Below was a date—January 15, 1922—and the word "check." Still lower down was a rough circle halved by a single heavy line.

I gave it back. "It's Greek to me and it obviously didn't mean anything to Mary Collins. What chance is there it will to anyone?"

"I don't know," Ran said with a shrug. "But I've a hunch it means something and we can't risk not trying it."

I was cold and I was growing hungry. "Tonight?" I asked plaintively. "All of them?"

"No. Carter's out of it. I talked to him today. His was a straight accommodation loan—thirty days and he paid it off on the dot. Johnson didn't try any funny stuff with him. Probably saved it for his women clients."

"Bill Carter runs a loan company," I said. "Why go out-side the family to do his borrowing?"

"He's just the manager and loan companies frown on their employees going in debt. Don't worry about him—he had no reason for killing Oscar and he scarcely knew Carol. Moreover," he added significantly, "he was tied up last night in a poker game."

"Well, they're going one by one," I said. "Bill Carter, Mary Collins. Oh, well, you still have Charles Dennison and *he's* the one who gets the money."

Ran snorted—there's no other word for it. "Anyone who wants Dennison can have him as far as I'm concerned. Oh, yes, I saw him this afternoon, called him to come in as a matter of fact. I wanted a little clearer light on some of the points of his story and I also wanted to break the news about Oscar's money coming to him. I wanted to get his reaction at first hand. Only I was fool enough to break the news about the money first and I never got a sensible word out of him after that. He went higher than a kite, making all sorts of extravagant plans for spending it. I tried to get it across to him that he may not get it—that it depends on when the Tolliver child died—but I don't think he even heard me."

"Oh, well, the poor old goon," I said. "He's never had two cents to click together. I hope he gets the money. At least he wants it. Now, if it had really been going to that Brannigan . . ."

"Oh, Brannigan," Ran said. "Now there's a horse of a different color. I've had my men doing some checking on him and the consensus of opinion is that that wasn't an act he staged for our benefit the other day. It seems he's allergic to money—inherited money. He believes that all property amassed by a man during his lifetime should re-vert to the state at his death. He has said many times that the only money he wants is the money he's earned himself,

honest, fair and square. The people who know him best
say that he means it."

"I wonder where he is now," I was beginning but Ran
stopped me. "I don't know and I don't care. At present I'm
not interested."

I frowned at him. "Well, who *are* you interested in?
Blair Thurston? Did you talk to him?"

"He was in. You know," Ran went on slowly, "on the
face of it he's our best bet for the murderer. He's got the
only real motive we've unearthed so far."

"That Carol was leaving him?"

"Yes. The rest of it—what does it amount to? Admittedly Johnson was bleeding these people, but any one of
them could have stopped it if he or she'd had guts enough.
He was on the wrong side of the law. All they had to do
was stand pat, refuse to pay. Sure, he'd threatened to garnishee their wages but would he have tried it—if the thing
had come to a show-down? And even if he had, a smart
lawyer would have settled his hash in short order."

"You don't know what you're talking about," I said
scornfully. "Guts enough indeed! What good would it do?
Miss Erickson or Mary Collins wouldn't expose a crook if
they lost their jobs doing it. Of course, maybe you're right
and it wouldn't have come to anything and they wouldn't
have lost their jobs, but—don't you see? —they couldn't
take that chance. When you get as old as they are and have
responsibilities and haven't been able to save anything,
you're afraid. You don't stop to think of right or justice or
crookedness—you're just afraid."

"Not precisely the stuff of which murder is made," Ran
said thoughtfully. "I don't know—we've got to just keep
on looking into it, of course, but I'm coming to the conclusion that none of the loan stuff has a thing to do with
the murders. The murderer was interested in Oscar's treasure trove—he proved it last night. We have it but what

have we got? Not a damn thing. I'll admit I was hoping
for evidence of blackmail. I didn't get it. All right—where
does it leave us?"

"With Blair Thurston?" I asked doubtfully.

"With Blair Thurston. And the conclusion that, in spite
of all, Carol's was the first, the important murder."

I said, "Oh, but, Ran, Blair Thurston's such a drip!"

"Look at the facts. He loved the girl enough to defy
his parents and marry her. He made a secret trip back to
Dorchester for the purpose of talking her out of the marriage annulment idea. He claims he didn't get to see Carol
but he could be lying. Suppose he did see her and couldn't
talk her out of it. Suppose they quarreled. The knives Alec
had sharpened were handy on the table. He might have
picked up one and—" He took one hand from the wheel in
a quick incisive gesture.

I said slowly, "Yes. It could have been like that. Oscar
could have been upstairs fixing the organ. He might have
left them together—to talk it out. And of course he'd have
had to be killed, too, because he knew . . . But, Ran! How
could Blair have killed her? He was right about the train—
it gets in around eight. It must have been at least a quarter
after when he called."

"There's also a bus that gets in about six. Neither conductor nor bus driver can positively identify him—there
were too many other sailors on. So . . ."

"I don't think," I said, "that he could have planned it
like that—he hasn't the brains."

"It wasn't planned, Tess. Those murders were committed on the spur of the moment, with the means at hand,
and motivated by red rage or sheer panic."

"Panic of what?" I murmured. "If he loved Carol and
was losing her—yes. I can understand that. But—last
night, Ran? Where does that fit in?"

"It doesn't," Ran said hopelessly. "There wasn't a thing in that file to incriminate Blair Thurston."

"Nor anyone else," I said. "Well, what do you do now? Isn't it about time for you to announce mysteriously that you know who the murderer is, that you've known right along and that all you need now is the proof?"

"Time, and slightly overdue, I'd say," Ran told me grimly. "Unfortunately I've no talent for divination, if there's such a word. I'm just a plodder."

"I've heard them well spoken of—plodders," I said kindly. "There was the tortoise in his famous race with the— Hey! What are you stopping for?"

"We're at the Brastocks'. Come along."

Meekly I followed. We were far down town again, for the Brastocks had both studio and living quarters above Dorchester's largest music store. As we climbed the broad marble steps we heard sharp chords from a piano and the upward struggle of a soprano voice.

"Good!" Ran said. "If he's busy with a lesson, we'll be able to get her alone."

I think Georgia Brastock appreciated that fact too. She met us at the door and, finger on lip, led us down a dark and narrow hall into a warm, brightly lighted kitchen.

"I'm sorry to have to ask you out here," she said as she drew two dinette chairs forward, "but Frederick has a lesson and he must not be disturbed."

Personally, I felt that if Frederick wasn't being disturbed by his soprano, who was aiming for, and missing, a high A, he was immune to anything in the way of disturbance. However, I said nothing, and she continued composedly, "I've been expecting you. I suppose you want to know all about it."

"About what, Mrs. Brastock?" Ran asked quietly.

She widened her eyes at him. Once, perhaps, it had been a cute trick—it wasn't now. "Why, I asked Tess to tell you," she said reproachfully—the reproach was all for me. "About Charles Dennison not being at the organ—although he said he was!—last Thursday night when we got to the church."

Ran looked thoughtfully at me. "No, it wasn't that although we'll go into that later. I wanted to ask you about your loan with Oscar Johnson."

"My loan? With Oscar Johnson?" Once more her pale eyes widened. "Surely, Mr. Garrison, you are joking. You don't really imagine—?"

But Ran's patience had worn thin. "Come, Mrs. Brastock—let's not waste time fencing. I am not imagining anything. I have Oscar's loan records. I also have the ring—your engagement ring, was it?"

She stopped acting and came back to normal. "Oh, well, of course, if you already know about it," she said blandly. "Yes, it's my engagement ring. Not a very good stone, I'm afraid—my husband has always been ready to sacrifice quality for showiness—but Oscar didn't know that. I doubt if he knew much about diamonds."

"The ring was security for the loan?"

"Yes." She folded her hands in her lap, studied them for a moment. "I suppose you want the whole story. It all began when I joined the Circle Bridge Club . . ."

It wasn't an unusual story. At first the club had played for prizes. Then, when the excitement of receiving a china dish or glass vase palled, for money. Not much at first—a quarter of a cent a hundred—but they kept raising it. "You see, I was the only one who couldn't afford it and I'd been the heaviest winner so I didn't want to object. I suppose I thought I'd keep on winning. I couldn't even drop out because Frederick thought these women were good contacts—some of them had daughters he hoped to have for pupils. And then—perhaps it was the strain—I began to lose. Heavily. At first I was able to pay by borrowing from the household money, but I couldn't keep that up. And I didn't want Frederick to know because he'd be angry and—well, we just haven't the money for gambling and I should have had the sense to know it. I didn't know what to do and it kept getting worse and worse. One day I discovered that I owed the bridge club seventy-eight dollars—we settled up once a month—and the grocery money was all gone and I hadn't paid the electric light bill and I was behind two payments on Frederick's piano. I had to do something. So I borrowed from Oscar. One hundred and twenty-five dollars."

"Without your husband's knowledge?"

"Oh, yes. Oscar wanted security so I gave him the ring. I knew Frederick wouldn't notice whether I wore it or not. He never notices me any more."

Ran cleared his throat. "All this happened—when, Mrs. Brastock?"

"Last June. I dropped out of the club in July."

"Oscar charged you interest?"

"He told me there would be interest. Interest compounded on interest, I think he said—I didn't understand it very well. It seemed high, but there was nothing else for me to do."

"You made payments?"

"Ten dollars a month." She still sat primly, hands folded.

"Get any receipts?"

"Certainly." Then, as Ran's eyebrows shot skyward in surprise, she said reprovingly, "I am a business woman, Mr. Garrison. I do all of Frederick's bookkeeping."

"May I see them?"

She rose at once, opened a cupboard, removed a file of recipe cards. "I keep them here," she said. "Frederick never cooks."

Ran read the top receipt carefully, lifted his eyes to admire her. "All correct and in order. I congratulate you—

you are indeed a business woman. None of the others . . ." His finger, flicking through the thin papers, halted, "Wait a minute! I'm afraid my congratulations were offered prematurely. When he gave you the receipts, did you read them?"

"Not after the first. Why? What—?"

"Listen. This is the September one. 'Received of Georgia Brastock the promise to pay ten dollars at some future date—' Bah! This isn't worth the paper it's written on!"

Georgia Brastock had gone white. "I don't believe it . . . Let me see." Presently she lifted a stricken face. "What am I to do now? What *can* I do?"

"The question might well puzzle a lawyer," Ran murmured, "and I am not a lawyer. You're sure you didn't know that these receipts were false?"

"I did not." She was still pale but her eyes met his steadily. "If I had, I would have taken action of some sort."

"Someone did take action," Ran said grimly. "Oscar's dead."

She flinched. "It wasn't I who killed him."

"No. I didn't think it was. Still—do you mind telling me where you were last night?"

"Last night? Why? What happened last night? Who—?"

"Never mind. I'm interested in you. Where were you?"

"Right here." It was impossible not to believe her. "Frederick has been getting together a woman's quartet. To sing at banquets and things like that. Frederick has so many calls for entertainment and now, with all the men in the service . . . I played the accompaniments."

"All evening? How long were they here?"

"Mr. Garrison, you are not seriously . . . they came shortly after eight. It must have been nearly eleven when they went. I served a little lunch. Just coffee and sandwiches. I always do. It makes for good feeling."

"Your husband was here the entire evening?"

"Certainly. He directed the quartet. Mr. Garrison, won't you *please* tell me . . ."

"Someone was in Oscar's apartment at the church last night," Ran said tonelessly. "Bishop Walters saw the light and went over. He was struck on the head. Whoever did it, got away."

"Why—why, how dreadful! The poor bishop! Was he badly hurt? But of course—of course Frederick and I had nothing to do with it. You *do* see that, don't you? We were right here all evening. The girls in the quartet can tell you. I'll give you their names. If I can just find a pencil . . ."

Ran motioned to me. "I have a pencil," I said and produced it.

She recited the names of some of the best young musical talent in Dorchester and watched me anxiously as I wrote them down. "The girls are so interested," she said. "They're going to call themselves the 'Victory Belles' and wear white formals and white overseas caps. I'm not their regular accompanist, you know. Carol Tolliver is. Oh, dear!" Her face puckered distressfully. "Of course she can't be now, can she?—she's dead. I don't really know who—"

"Carol Tolliver played a great many accompaniments for your husband, didn't she?"

"She did," Georgia Brastock said primly. "Now, don't try to make anything out of *that,* Mr. Garrison. She was a very nice sweet child and we—Frederick and I—thought of her as a daughter. She was very talented and we did our best to help her. I know lots of people criticized her and thought she ought to clerk or work in an office to help out her family but genius must always be a little ruthless, don't you think? It *has* to be. Carol always said her family had managed a long time without her help and that she'd do her share of helping later on. She wanted so badly to go

away to study. That was one reason Frederick wanted her
for organist at St. Thomas' but the music committee said
that Charles Dennison—"

Ran interrupted her there. "Oh, yes, Dennison. You
were going to tell me something about him."

"I certainly am!" She sat a little straighter. "I'm surprised, Tess, that you didn't feel it of sufficient importance—"

The story was as I'd heard it before, compounded of
suspicion and pure venom. It wasn't that she'd seen him
where he shouldn't be; it was just that she had not seen
him where he should be. And there had been that door
that slammed downstairs . . .

Ran listened without expression.

"You don't care much for Dennison, do you?"

"I do not! He's a horrid old man, always sneaking
around prying into things that don't concern him. He and
Oscar—" She stopped, having caught our expressions.

"Go on," Ran said. "He and Oscar—what about them?"

"Oh, they were always off in corners, talking, and Mr.
Dennison was always going down to Oscar's rooms to see
him. I thought that he—well, it's a little hard to explain—
brought Oscar information that he could use. I mean,
about loaning money. I know there were other people
besides me who'd borrowed from Oscar, and every time
Oscar had known all about their troubles. He came and
asked them if they didn't want to borrow from him. I know
he did to me, and I always thought that it was Charles
Dennison who told him about the bridge club."

Ran looked at me. "How about it, Tess?"

I shrugged. "Could be. I wouldn't know."

He turned back to her. "How would Dennison have
known about your bridge losses?"

"He had ways. He's lived in Dorchester a long time.
(That was true.) Besides Mrs. Fred Gregory is his niece

and *she* belonged to our club. I'm not saying that she'd tell him, but she's a careless talker and if she'd even dropped a hint . . ."

"I see," Ran said. You could almost "see" him seeing it— and a lot more. He stood up. "All right, Mrs. Brastock— thanks. We'll check with your—'Victory Belles,' was it?— but apparently you're in the clear."

She preceded us, again cautioning silence, to the door. There she asked anxiously, "You won't tell Frederick?"

"I'd advise you to tell him yourself," Ran said. Then, as her eyes widened, "I'm sorry, Mrs. Brastock. But if we can establish that the motive for these killings had anything to do with Johnson's lending activities, the thing will break wide open. You'd better get your story in first."

"But I paid him back nearly all of it," she said vaguely. "It doesn't seem fair that I should have to tell *now.*"

Ran said nothing. I should have liked to have voiced my own agreement but I had not time. Ran's hand was under my arm. He hurried me down the stairs, pushed me into the car and had slammed the door and was under the wheel before I'd caught my breath.

"What's the matter with you now?" I demanded furiously. "Why the rush? You simply left that poor woman standing—"

"Because I'm in a hurry," Ran said through gritted teeth. He was having trouble. The starter whirred and groaned but there was no answering spark. "Damn it, what's the matter with the thing?"

The motor caught just then and we lurched forward. I waited until we were well embarked upon the perilous road. "Where—?" I began only to be thrown violently against the side of the car as Ran negotiated a corner. I righted myself indignantly. "Well, if you're trying to kill me too . . ."

"Oh, keep still!" Ran snapped. "No, don't. I beg your pardon, darling. It's only that I'm trying to think and—well, that woman frightened me. Now, wait—I don't mean that I think she killed Oscar or Carol either—that's ridiculous. But you heard what she said. About Oscar and Charles Dennison. Don't you see?—Brannigan's out. It's Dennison I've been looking for. He's the common link between Oscar and those others. I couldn't make it fit before but now . . . Only, if the murderer knows it too . . ."

I drew a deep breath and snatched at the door handle. We were going around another corner. "Then it's Charles Dennison we're going to see now?"

"And as fast," Ran said grimly "as we can get there!"

19

Charles Dennison lived at the old Morgan place. Once, around the turn of the century, the Morgan family had been wealthy and prominent, the house a show place. Now Miss Ella, last of the name, rented rooms and took in boarders. For ten dollars a week, Charles Dennison occupied two cramped rooms high under the turreted roof with meals and the privilege of using the piano in the downstairs front parlor for his occasional music pupils.

Miss Morgan was fat and harassed. Since I had a nodding acquaintance with her—there had been a time when I had been an inmate of the Wilson place across the street—Ran let me do the talking.

"Charlie?" She cast a speculative eye up the two long flights of stairs visible from the hall. "Well, now, I don't know. Seems like he went out. I'll tell you—if you don't mind climbing stairs—it's the first door on the right. Just knock. Or, if you want to go in and wait, I guess it'd be all right. I'd go up with you only it's our dinner hour."

Spurred by Ran's imperative nudge, I thanked her, told her not to bother, that we'd be all right. She must have believed me for we'd scarcely set foot upon the stairs before she had vanished again into those regions from which the doorbell had called her.

Save for the voices and clatter of silver from the dining room, the house was very still. Low-watt bulbs burned at the top of each flight. In the dimness we were just able to make out the cards tacked to the doors.

I knocked but I had little hope of getting an answer. No light rayed from around the loosely fitted door. Before I could knock the second time, Ran reached over my shoulder and turned the knob. The door swung open.

Ran groped for the light switch, found it. The room was revealed, a man's room, cluttered and shabby. Old leather chairs whose battered cushions sagged to long accustomed body-conformation. A mission table loaded down with old newspapers, magazines and a cracked plate on which were stale buns, an apple core, burnt match ends and a blackened pipe. Sheet music stood in piles in the corners and spilled from the deep window ledges. A combination radio and phonograph—new—stood against the east wall. There were records on the couch, under it. Over all was dust and a thin sifting of ashes.

But no one was there, neither in the room nor beyond in the curtained alcove which served as a bedroom. Ran made sure of that at once. As he flung the curtains aside, I had a glimpse of an enormous carved bed, a tipsy chest.

Somehow, with this opportunity under his hand, I'd expected Ran to search the rooms. He didn't. He simply stood in the center of the rug wrinkling his nose a little over the assorted smells. Once he moved to the table to lift a newspaper only to retreat hastily when it revealed a gnawed chunk of salami side by side with half an onion. He wiggled an eyebrow at me, crossed to the window ledge and scrutinized the top sheet of a toppling pile of music. Idly he lifted it, glanced at the next. Then suddenly he stiffened as a bird dog does at point.

I said, "What—?" but he silenced me. "Come here— have a look at this."

I looked. There, scrawled in the left hand corner of each music sheet, was the same symbol I'd seen scrawled on that other sheet that Ran had in his pocket. He took that out now, compared them. They were the same—rough circles divided down the center by a single straight line.

"C.D." Ran repeated, and there was an awed disbelief in his voice. "Charles Dennison—why the hell didn't I guess it? Well, there we are—there's the connection. Now, if I can just put my hand on Dennison—and in time—"

It was too much for me. I said, "But, Ran, how do you know you're not making too much of this? You're only guessing . . ."

"Call it a hunch," Ran said. "And, if I am, what of it? But I've an idea that we're on the right track at last. There's a secret here—someone's secret. And if they didn't want it known . . ." He was silent for a moment. When he spoke again, his words held a note of grim exultation. "And Dennison knows it—whatever it is. He hasn't told me anything yet, the old fox. But this time I'm going to be smarter than he is. When I find him, he'll talk—and talk plenty. Come on!"

I followed meekly. Half way down the stairs, he turned to ask if I thought I could dig up Mrs. Whatever-her-name-was again. I said, without enthusiasm, that I could try.

Miss Morgan was in the pantry apportioning rice pudding into dishes. She wasn't pleased at the summons but she wiped her hands on her apron and came.

But she didn't help much after all. No, Charlie didn't always eat there. There was a restaurant a couple of blocks off—the Coffee Shop—lots of his cronies forgathered there. No, she didn't know what he did with his evenings. Went to the church sometimes and played the organ, she guessed. He was an Elk and a Mason. He liked a game of cards. Once in a long while he had dinner at his niece's but he always dressed up for that. Today was Tuesday—no, it couldn't be that. Because he'd been at the Gregorys' on Sunday.

Trust Mrs. Fred Gregory, I thought. *She* wouldn't miss any bets and with practically an eye witness to murder right in the family . . .

Somehow we were out of there. Miss Morgan went back to her rice pudding and we teetered on icy steps. Ran still looked worried.

"Want to try this—what was it?—Coffee Shop? I suppose there's a chance that he may be there."

"I'd love some coffee," I said. And then, hesitantly, "Ran, you're terribly anxious to find him, aren't you? You don't think he had anything to do with the murders, do you?"

"No. But I think he knows too much for his own good. And if the murderer ever catches on that he does . . ." He made a quick slashing gesture. "Come on. We'll take a chance."

The Coffee Shop was a hole in the wall, dark, dirty and dimmed by bluish smoke. A line of backs hunched on the counter stools but none of them belonged to Charles Dennison. Booths ran along one side. They were unoccupied. Ran walked me past them all to find out.

We sat in the last, on either side of a sticky table at which a sullen counterman mopped without much result. Ran said, "Looks as though I guessed wrong. What'll you have, Tess? Better go easy—we don't want to waste too much time here."

We ordered coffee and hamburgers. The coffee was strong and hot, the hamburgers surprisingly good. I was about to express my complete approval when Ran put down his cup with a bang. "Allah is good to me," he breathed. "Look what's come in."

I looked. But it wasn't Charles Dennison hanging up his overcoat. It was Philip Smedley. Ran's call stopped him, half way to the counter. He turned and came over, blinking and suspicious.

"Eat with us," Ran said and it was an order. "I want to talk to you."

Smedley hesitated for a moment and then threw himself down beside me. "If it's about last Thursday," he said, "you're out of luck. I told you all I knew."

The counterman came over again, stood silently. "Oh—bowl of chili," Smedley flung at him. "And coffee." I said firmly that I wanted more coffee, too, and another hamburger, and Ran, after a disgusted stare, gave the order.

Philip Smedley lit a cigarette with shaking fingers. "I don't know a damn thing about those murders," he repeated. "I told you that."

"Never mind the murders," Ran said soothingly. "Just answer my questions. You were paying Johnson twenty dollars a month. What for?"

"Oh, that!" Smedley looked relieved. His hands steadied. "Nothing to that. I was losing my car—couldn't keep up the payments. Oscar found out and took over. That was all."

"Who owns the car?"

"Who do you suppose? Oscar. I just paid him rent for it."

"Twenty dollars a month?"

"Sure. It was cheap enough. I still had the car. Nobody knew it wasn't mine. Oscar didn't tell and I certainly wasn't going to. If he was satisfied, so was I."

"Altruistic old fellow—Oscar."

Smedley shot him a puzzled glance. "Well, maybe. He wasn't such a bad old guy. Liked young people. I always thought maybe he'd had a tough time himself when he was a kid. He was sure nice to me."

"Ever ask you to do anything for him?"

Smedley frowned. "What do you mean?"

"Ever talk to you about people—ask questions?"

"I don't know what you're . . . Well, yes. Sure we talked, we talked a lot." (I closed my eyes on that. Oscar the silent. Oscar the clam. Oscar who talked a lot.)

"What about?" Ran's voice was sharp.

"I don't know. Whatever you do talk about—what's going on. I thought the old fellow was lonesome. I used to go up there twice a month to pay him that twenty dollars— ten at a time. Mostly he asked me to stay and have supper. He was a swell cook."

"Did you ever tell him anything he could use?"

"Anything he could—say, what the hell are you getting at?"

"Listen, Smedley. You weren't the only one at St. Thomas' to whom Oscar lent money, and not all his transactions were as open and aboveboard as you claim yours was. Now, specifically, do you ever remember telling him about anyone whom you knew to be in financial difficulties?"

Smedley hesitated. "Well, I might have. I hear a lot of stuff at home. Mother tells me. I don't know where she gets it all. Women . . ."

He'd stopped again. Ran said, "Well?" impatiently.

Smedley looked uncomfortable. "Can't you give me some names?"

"No. If you can't suggest any yourself . . ."

"I can't."

"Ever talk to you about the Thurstons?"

"Sometimes. He didn't like the old man. He didn't like anyone with money! He never said much about Blair."

"How about Carol Tolliver?"

"He liked her. He'd have sent her to school if she'd have taken the money."

"Dennison?"

"Charlie? Oscar never talked about him but he was in and out. They squabbled a lot but I guess it didn't mean anything."

"Did he ever say anything to you about Mendel's Law?"

"Mendel's Law—what's that?"

"Heredity—the law of dominance. Color of hair or eyes. Mutations."

"Gosh, no! What—?"

"Never mind. It would take too long to explain. Ever see this before?" From his pocket, Ran produced the paper he'd shown me earlier. He flattened it out on the table.

Smedley bent over it, shook his head. "No."

"How about the date? That mean anything to you?"

"No, it . . . I don't know, though—there's something . . ." He pondered, shook his head. "Sorry. I can't remember."

"Forget it." Ran refolded the paper, thrust it back into his pocket and stood up. "All right, Tess—we'd better get going. Thanks, Smedley. If you should remember anything . . ." He left it open.

Philip Smedley slid from the booth to let me pass. His hands, on the table top, showed white at the knuckles. "Listen, Garrison, I didn't kill them. I liked Oscar and I liked Carol a—a lot. And even if I hadn't—it wouldn't have been like that. Blood—it makes me sick. The smell of it. When I was a kid in high school, I tried working summers at the packing plant. I—I couldn't stick it out."

Ran patted his shoulder.

Out in the car, I spoke. "Ran, I've been remembering what the bishop told us about Mendel's Law."

"Have you?" His tone was flat, noncommittal.

I drew a long breath, hurried on. "And I've just remembered something else—that both Mr. and Mrs. Thurston have blue eyes but Blair's are brown."

"Yes?" There was no encouragement in the cold clipped tones.

"Does—could that mean that Blair wasn't their own child—that he's adopted?"

Ran shrugged. "Perhaps."

I persisted. "If Oscar found out about it and they wanted to keep it secret—and they must because I never heard a whisper that Blair wasn't their own son—"

"Tess, please!" Ran sounded exasperated. "Now you're going too fast. I tell you we don't *know* anything yet."

I sank back, rebuffed. "That's the whole trouble. There are too darn many things we don't know."

It was Ran's turn to be angry. "What do you want me to do? Call up the Thurstons? 'I'm very sorry but I've just come across some evidence that says your son isn't your son at all'—listen, Tess, there are some things even a policeman's badge won't regularize. I may get to them eventually but just now I need Dennison—or failing him, someone else who . . . Got it!" He snapped his fingers.

"Who was it you and Alec said knew everything there was to know? Let's try her out. We'll go and see Miss Erickson!"

So we did. But first, however, we found a telephone and put in a call to the station. Charles Dennison was to be found and brought in for questioning.

"And that settles that!" Ran said. "I hope."

Miss Erickson's little cottage was next, white-painted, its windows faintly aglow. Miss Erickson herself opened the door to our ring. If she was surprised to see us, it wasn't evident from her manner. She was as neat and composed as ever.

Apparently she'd been grading papers. A card table, centered under a strong light, was littered with folded yellow themes. This table she pushed aside, seating herself after she'd motioned us to do likewise. She didn't actually say, "To what do I owe the pleasure of this visit?" but the question was there, visible almost, in the air.

Ran was making an effort to charm. He loosened his coat, beamed at her. "Miss Erickson, we are in need of help."

"Indeed?" Her voice was flat, uninflected. "I shall be only too glad . . ."

"We were sure of that." Ran hitched his chair a little nearer, fished in his pocket for that ubiquitous paper, flattened it on a corner of the card table. "This was found among Oscar Johnson's effects, Miss Erickson. Would you take a look at it, tell us if it means anything to you?" Then, as she made no move to touch it, only sat there, he went on quickly, "We hoped—because of your wide acquaintance in Dorchester . . ."

She spoke then. "I have lived in Dorchester a long time—yes." She reached out a hand, adjusted her pincenez. When she laid the paper down again, her face was inscrutable. "I'm sorry. It means nothing to me."

Ran's fingers drummed on the table. "We've unraveled a bit ourselves. That circle now—those are Dennison's initials. C. and D. written together. Charles Dennison."

"In that case, why come to me?" It seemed to me that her voice was now less rigidly under control. "Why not ask Mr. Dennison?"

"I will—gladly. Once I catch up with him."

"Mr. Dennison has—disappeared?"

"Only temporarily." Ran sounded confident, no matter what he felt. "I've a dragnet out. If we don't get him tonight, we will tomorrow. In the meantime, we must do our best without him."

She shook her head obstinately. "I'm sorry. I'm afraid I can't help you."

"I think you can." Ran's tone was grave. "I only want to ask a question or two, Miss Erickson. If you can't answer, you can't, of course, but if you'll try . . ."

She bent her head, breathed a reluctant sigh. "Very well—you may ask your questions."

"Thank you. Here is the first. Do you know if Blair Thurston is an adopted child?"

Red flushed her face, subsided. "Mr. Garrison! Why should you ask me such a question? How can you imagine such a thing? Blair Thurston adopted—the idea is preposterous!"

"Not at all. Quite sensible, really. Do you know anything about heredity, Miss Erickson—Mendel's Law—color perpetuity? No? I thought perhaps you might—residue of your University days."

"My University days were spent in a small teacher's college," Miss Erickson said dryly. "They are long behind me. Once I might have known. Now I'm afraid I have forgotten."

"It doesn't matter," Ran assured her. "The point is that both of the Thurstons are blue-eyed while Blair's eyes are a very dark brown. The probability therefore is that he is not their son. I believe it is to this fact that this paper of Johnson's refers. I believe that the date written here is Blair's birth date. I believe that Dennison unearthed this information in some manner—information which the Thurstons, for one reason or another, had endeavored to keep secret—and turned it over to Johnson to make use of as he saw fit. Don't shake your head, please. I'll admit I'm guessing but the guess is a logical one."

"You are not guessing." Miss Erickson spoke slowly as though each word were wrenched from her. "It is true. Blair is not the Thurstons' own child. Mabel's child died at birth. She could never have another. They had a chance to take this boy—his parents were dead. Only a very few people know. The Thurstons wanted to save the boy from being known as an 'adopted child.' Children, especially, can be so very cruel. That was why . . ." Her voice died away as though the effort had been too much for her.

"Who were the child's parents?"

She shook her head. "I'm sorry. That I can't tell you."

"You said that only a few people knew. How did it happen that you—"

"I used to be Mabel Thurston's best friend."

Ran was scowling now. "Did Dennison know?" he shot at her.

"I'm sure he didn't. I don't know how he could have learned it. Unless he guessed. And what he thought Oscar Johnson could do with a story like that, I haven't an idea."

"Nothing he could take hold of?"

"Nothing" she said firmly. "Blair's own father was dead, I believe. The mother died at his birth. There was only one relative to take him—an aunt or cousin as I remember. She was delighted to get him a good home. Mabel Thurston simply came out of the hospital with this child instead of her own. That's all there was to it."

"And if I went to the Thurstons," Ran said slowly, "They would tell me this same story?"

"It's all they could tell you. It is the truth. But I beg of you, Mr. Garrison," her voice took on a new earnestness, "do not go. It would be cruel. The Thurstons have had a great deal of trouble. Losing Blair—to the Navy, I mean—and now this unfortunate marriage and Carol Tolliver's death. They could really tell you little more than I and the story can in no way reflect on them."

"I can see that," Ran said, rising. "Another dead end—oh, well. Thanks very much, Miss Erickson. I'm glad I came to you."

"And I." She walked to the door with us. "I don't know that I would mention the story to Charles Dennison. Poor man, he is failing fast. If he should have forgotten . . ."

"Exactly," Ran said. As usual he was in a fever to be gone. I held him back for a second for decency's sake.

"Your mother. Miss Erickson—I meant to ask—how is she?"

"Very low." Some emotion, hooded and secret, slipped over Miss Erickson's face. "The doctor does not expect her to last through the night."

"Oh, I'm so sorry," I said. "Would you like me to send Alec—Dean MacDonald over? Or the bishop?"

"Thank you, no. There is nothing they could do. She is unconscious."

"You are not alone?" This was Ran.

She smiled faintly. "Oh, no. The nurse is upstairs. Thanks to Oscar's—generosity," there was a sardonic edge to the words, "I have been able to give her every care—while she lives. After that," she shrugged, "I do not know what will happen. I'm afraid I do not even care."

"If there's anything I can do," I offered impulsively. Again she smiled. "Thank you, my dear, you are kind. But there is nothing. There is nothing that anyone can do. Not now. It is too late."

I hated to leave her like that but Ran was urging me on. At the car, I turned to look back. But there was nothing to see. The door was closed. The cottage was as we had seen it first—neat, white-painted, serene.

20

Ran was muttering to himself as he edged away from the curb. I said, "What are you talking about?"

He turned a furious face to me. "I said," he repeated clearly, "the hell I won't go to the Thurstons!"

"But," I was beginning when he cut me off. "Why should I pay attention to Miss Erickson's notions of delicacy? Apparently I've none of my own. I could barge in on her—with a woman dying upstairs—and she could be decent about it. They can too!"

I put a hand over his. "Ran, you didn't know . . ."

"Think that helps? I'm not so sure Well, a few questions won't hurt them. I don't know that I care much for the Thurstons anyway. You think she was telling the truth?"

"Miss Erickson? Don't you?"

"I don't know. She tried to warn me off Dennison and the Thurstons—remember? And I didn't get that 'used to be Mabel Thurston's best friend.' Why 'used to be?' Why not 'am'?"

"'Used to be' is correct," I said grimly. "A little matter of refurnishing the church kitchen. The ladies didn't agree over a—an electric mixer, I think it was."

"O-oh, women!" Ran groaned. I laughed. "Men are just as bad," I said. "Bill Bradley and George Harris haven't spoken for five years because . . ."

I never went on. We were drawing up before the Thurston house. It stood far back from the street, sunk in shrubbery, a massive brick edifice. Heavily curtained windows showed only chinks of light to prove its inhabitation. It was dark, silent, forbidding.

Ran turned the ignition key. "Coming in?"

I shook my head. "They'd resent me. They'll resent you too, I'm afraid. Oh, Ran, do you really have to?"

"I have to." His lips were a thin straight line. "All right, stay here if you want to. But keep the engine running so you'll be warm. Better let that window down a little too. I think the heater's all right but I wouldn't want to come out again and find a corpse." He looked at me then and his eyes softened. "Chin up, darling. I'll only be a minute."

After he was gone, I sat there and shivered. I didn't know why. Up to now, I bad been interested and excited with the progress we were making. It had been almost as though I watched a moving picture reel unwind. I had been able to speculate pleasantly about what would happen next. Now, inexplicably, I was prey to dark forebodings. Perhaps they were engendered by the ominous silence of the house into which Ran disappeared. I had watched a door open, saw him engulfed in shadows, then nothing. Would he ever come out again?

I tried to imagine the scene that must now be taking place in the great dark living room. I had been in the Thurston home often enough. I knew the layout of the place, its heavy ugly furniture. There was a fireplace in which a gas log would flicker dimly. They would be sitting in the big chairs at either side, Mrs. Thurston's marked by a sewing table, Mr. Thurston's by his end table smoking cabinet. Somewhere a radio would whisper and the corners of the room would be deep in shadow. There were never enough lamps lighted. . . .

Where would Ran be sitting? On a straight chair, perhaps, drawn between them. He would be asking questions—would they be answered? Foolish—of course they'd have to answer. Ran represented the police. But did the police have the right to dig out secrets long kept hidden? I knew what Ran would say to that, that once murder was established there could be no secrets. Probably he was right, but just the same it was a far cry from the deaths of Oscar and Carol Tolliver to the adoption of a baby boy twenty-odd years before.

The click of the door handle aroused me from these meditations. Ran was back. He was in the car, had it in motion before I could catch my breath.

We weren't going any place. We crossed the corner intersection, stopped, and then backed around until we faced the street we'd just left. I said, "What in the world—"

Ran snapped off lights and ignition. "I've a notion someone from the Thurston place will be going somewhere fast. I'm going to follow, see where he goes."

I said, "Ran, did they answer your questions?"

In the dimness I could see him frown. "Well, yes and no. I'm afraid they put one over on me. Let's say that they confirmed my story—Miss Erickson's story. They weren't volunteering information. They were stiff and haughty—well, you know them. The insolence of a mere policeman daring to pry into their private affairs—well, you can imagine."

"Then you didn't get a thing?"

"A nugget or two. Mainly concerning Blair's parentage. Miss Erickson wasn't very specific there so I couldn't be. She lied too—Miss Erickson." Something hard crept into his voice. "The mother died all right when Blair was born but the father's still very much alive. He was a high school teacher here, married and with a family. The girl had been one of his pupils. It's the old story. The man couldn't—or wouldn't give up his family. He claimed he loved his wife. Perhaps he did—God knows. Anyway there was nothing for it but a nasty scandal or complete secrecy. They settled for that. Then the girl died. The father couldn't take the child—neither could the aunt without the whole thing coming out. Mrs. Thurston was in the hospital at the time—her baby had just died. Some way or other they heard the story and took the child. That's all there is to it."

"No names?"

"Decidedly not. They took a high line there. It was all twenty years ago—what difference did it make now?"

"You showed them that paper?"

"I did. They waved it away as if of little account. I'll admit their argument was plausible enough. Thurston said that Dennison might have stumbled over the truth but even if he had, what of it? What did he think he could do with it? The man in question was long gone from Dorchester. In any event he had only to deny the story and who could prove it? The girl was dead. I got the impression that her sister—the aunt who handed over the child—was dead too."

"Ran!" I had an idea, "What if they're both lying? Oh, not Miss Erickson because what she knows could have been just what they told her, or—well, there's a grapevine and she's a school teacher too! But what I mean is—suppose it's Mr. Thurston who's Blair's real father after all and the rest of it is just—camouflage? If Oscar wanted something on the Thurstons and Charles Dennison stumbled on *that* . . ."

"Your reasoning's a little mixed," Ran said. "If Thurston were the father, there'd be no school grapevine. Now, hush, will you? Someone's coming out."

He was right. Strong lights showed at right angles to the street. As we watched, a long black car nosed out of the Thurston driveway and swung in our direction.

"What did I tell you." Ran turned his own ignition key.

But the other car was fully a block past before Ran switched on his lights and followed.

I glued my eyes to that bobbing red light ahead. The car was going fast, too fast for the ice-covered streets. We saw it slither sideways once, make a half turn, recover. Our own car was only barely under control. When I had time to think, I said, "Oh, Ran, be careful! I don't want to end up against a tree somewhere. Do you have to follow him?"

"I want to find out where he's going," Ran said through shut teeth. "Toward town by the look of it. If . . . Oh, damn! Look at that!"

The car had swerved around a corner. The distance between us was greater now and by the time we'd negotiated the same corner, it was to see the flicker of red to green as a stop light changed and to behold three red tail-lights departing in three separate directions.

Ran pulled the car to the curb and lit a cigarette. "That's done it," he said philosophically. "Ever heard of the fellow who got on his horse and rode off in all directions? Any guess as to which was our man?"

I shook my head. "I couldn't tell. The three of them were so bunched."

"Exactly." Ran brooded, the red tip of his cigarette glowing fiercely. "After our talk I figured he'd be going one of two places—to Miss Erickson or to Dennison. Well, I want Dennison myself. That was why I hoped . . ." He, rolled down the window and tossed away his cigarette. "Well, we'll take a chance on Miss Erickson."

But the Erickson cottage was as we had seen it before, silent, dimly lighted. There was no long black car to be seen anywhere. We drove around several blocks to make sure.

Ran was grim as he headed back toward town. Once he muttered, "I don't like it! I don't like it!" I didn't either, but I wasn't quite certain what it was I didn't like. I tried to find out. I said, "Ran, you don't think it could have been Harvey Thurston after all?"

Ran shrugged. His answer was evasive. "I'd like to know where he was going and why. Of course there may have been a bank robbery, but somehow I doubt it."

"You'd have heard, wouldn't you? Isn't your radio working?"

He said, "No, it's not." And that was that. I kept silent.

Lights sprayed from the next corner. A neighborhood drugstore. Ran pulled to the curb. Through the wide window, I could see him at the telephone. When he came out, he was almost running. But his voice, as he climbed back into the car, was pleasant and natural. Too pleasant—too natural.

"No bank robbery," he said. "Had enough? I'll take you home."

I didn't like it. It had all the earmarks of a brush-off. We were going fast again, too fast, and I didn't like that. There was a tautness, a forward-thrusting of Ran's profile, seen against the light, as though, by sheer will power, he were sending the car onward. Accusingly, I spoke. "You know where Charles Dennison is, don't you?"

He didn't turn his head. "What makes you think that?"

"The way you're trying to get rid of me. But it won't work, Ran. I'll—I'll follow you!"

"Without a car?" He spared a chuckle. "Don't be silly. It's not as easy as all that. You saw what happened when we tried to follow Thurston."

"I won't be guessing," I said with meaning. "And I won't have so far to go."

"Got there, have you?" He whistled softly.

"Yes." I said it firmly. "He's at the church, isn't he? I should have guessed that's where he'd be. He often goes over evenings just to play."

Ran groaned. "How many people know that?"

"Everybody, I guess. Everyone who knows him."

"Everyone," Ran said bitterly. "Everyone but me!"

I couldn't think of anything to say but "I'm sorry." It didn't go down. Ran snorted. "Maybe you've a right to be. We've wasted a lot of evening so far. And if anything's happened to the old idiot . . ."

I tried to be soothing. "Perhaps nothing has. Besides, we could be wrong. Perhaps he didn't go into the church at all. And even if he did, how could he? The locks are different."

"He could get in all right. The locksmith couldn't get over today. Too busy. The old keys still fit."

I still persisted. "But you don't actually know that's where he is, do you? Unless someone saw him go in . . ."

"No one saw him." It came from Ran in a sort of groan. "This is my own idea. The place we haven't looked. Only it may be too late. There's been too much time lapse. Our murderer's not a fool. If he went there . . ."

I couldn't answer that. There was a shiver in my bones. We were coming down Main Avenue now. Ran had the red lights on the front of his car blinking. Other cars stopped or drew aside to let us pass.

We turned up to Ellis Avenue. We would swing around, come down the hill past the church. I said, "Ran, it's no use—I'm coming too. I've been in it too long. You can't push me out now. I'll get Alec—I'll get the bishop—"

"All right!" Ran snapped, impatiently. "You're in. Only—God help you if you get in my way!"

We were going more slowly now. I saw the lights in Ruth's living room. The church showed only darkness but that didn't mean anything. If Charles Dennison were inside, it was without permission and he wouldn't be wanting to make his presence known. Then, too, the organ lights were on an interior wall and too low to be revealed by the great windows.

Ran turned the corner and edged past the side entrance. I touched his arm. "Look! There are cars parked across the street."

He deflated me. "Doesn't mean a thing. There always are. No garages to those apartments. But, just the same, I think we'll go around the block and come back in through the alley."

That was what we did. The alley was dark and over-hung—as we neared the church—by firs and cedars. It was slippery and I held tightly to Ran's arm and prayed that I wouldn't fall. We edged up a bank and were on the cement walk that crossed the back of the church. I reached for the basement door but Ran restrained me. "Too far—we'll go in the side door. Keep into the shadow as much as you can."

The shadows were heavy on the north side of the church. Once we'd slipped inside the storm door, it gave us cover. Ran fumbled with keys and I said, "The door squeaks a little—so do the stairs."

Ran's voice was a murmur in my ears. "Take off your shoes when we get inside."

We were inside. The door was tight behind us. There'd been no squeak of betrayal. I stood on one foot and then the other, slid off overshoe and slipper. I felt a place for them against the wall. Beside me, Ran was doing the same. His overcoat came off, touched my feet for a moment.

We were climbing. Once again the stairs felt cold to my stockinged feet. "I've done this before," I thought. "Not in the madness of a recurrent dream but in actual physical fact. I've known this tightness of breath, this smothering darkness, this anguished seeking toward the feared and the unknown."

But with this difference. This time I was not alone. Now Ran was beside me, his shoulder touching mine. He pulled my head close to his, spoke in my ear. "I can't see a thing. Could be we're wrong."

I said, "I think the door at the top of the stairs is closed."

It was. My outstretched hands flattened against it. I reached for Ran, guided his fingers.

The door opened with a little sigh. Its whisper was a scream in our straining ears.

We balanced on the doorsill, waiting, listening. The great circular room was black with shadow, lightened only by the lesser dark from the unshaded windows. The grand piano made a clump of darkness to our right. There was no movement in the room. It was quiet, empty of sound. Yet sound seeped in.

The door to the chancel stood open. Just as the windows reflected grayness, so upon the polished oak, faint high-lights of warmth glimmered. It was from beyond that the voices came.

Ran touched my hand and we crept closer, slowly—slowly, careful of chairs, of the table with its toppling pile of hymnals, the menace of Frederick Brastock's unsteady music rack. And with each forward step, the voices came clearer. And now I recognized one—and then, horribly, the other. My hand jumped for Ran's hand—I clutched at it. He freed himself gently, without answering pressure, continued to move forward. There was something deadly, irrevocable, in that steady advance.

We separated, stood at either side of the chancel door. The shadows hid us, but I do not believe that even full light would have revealed us at that moment to the two we gazed upon, so engrossed they were.

Their backs were to us. Charles Dennison was twisted about on the organ bench. The white fluorescent light clamped to the music rack revealed half his profile, the glittering edge of his glasses, but the other, standing at his side and a little back, was no more than a shapeless blur, a dim and formless shadow. Yet I knew that shadow, knew it well, and I dared not disbelieve my knowledge.

Charles Dennison was speaking. His voice was high-pitched, querulous, tinged with exasperation. "But, great gollies, I told you I didn't know about Oscar's business! It didn't mean a thing to me. What makes you come around pestering me? If it's the notes that's bothering you, I told you what I'd do. Just as soon as they tell me I get the money, I'll tear them up. You won't have to pay them—they'll be gone. That ought to satisfy you!"

"I couldn't pay them anyway." The voice was low but perfectly clear. "You can't pay what you haven't got."

"You're darn right," Dennison said heartily. "That's only sense. I guess you've had it pretty tough, all right. Oscar was a funny guy and if he got a down on you, he—"

"You helped him." The words were accusation.

"What do you mean—I helped him? He was a dumb foreigner for all he'd lived in this country for forty years. He didn't know how to find out things and sometimes he asked me. That's all there was to it."

"Not all." There was a cold implacable quality in the voice that made me shudder. "You found out too much."

"You mean that hospital thing. Shucks, there was nothing to that. It was Oscar's idea—he was reading one of his scientific books and he got curious about the Thurston kid's eyes—being a different color or something. He asked me to find out what I could about the kid. I had to go clear across the state line to do it—over to Hospers which used to be Mrs. Thurston's home town. They showed me the records after I'd told them it was the Thurstons sent me. But it didn't amount to anything. The Thurston baby died all right and they took another woman's kid—her name was Benson—"

"She was my sister."

Opposite, I could sense Ran's quick convulsive move-ment, its instant repression, but Dennison's voice showed only a pleased interest. "Essie—so that was Essie! By the great gollies, you had me fooled! Oh, I knew she died around the same time but I thought it was back east—your folks coming from New York State and all."

"It was Essie. I sent her away when I—knew. I gave her *his* name. She had a right to it even if . . . The Thur-stons helped me—they were the only ones who knew. Until Oscar got curious about the color of Blair's eyes. He want-ed to help Carol Tolliver. She'd married Blair. Secretly. Harvey Thurston came and told me. He didn't tell Mabel but he thought I had a right to know. Blair is my neph-ew . . . She was bad—bad—Carol. I had her in school—I know. Man-crazy even then. She . . . Harvey Thurston was sick about the marriage. He came to me—warned me that Carol was making trouble and that Oscar—Oscar thought that Harvey was Blair's own father and he was trying to find out who his mother could be. Harvey told me not to worry—that he'd pay the money and take care of Oscar. But Harvey was a business man, he drove hard bargains, and I was afraid. I didn't want a scandal and if that story ever came out . . . We'd always been respectable . . .

"Then it was that night and it was stormy. I decided to stay down town and eat before I went to choir practice. I went to the Café Rouge. I saw Carol there. She was with Dean MacDonald and they were talking. I wondered if she was telling him. I thought Oscar might have found out and told her . . .

"I decided to go and see Oscar. I was foolish—I know it now. It would have given him another hold over me. And then, when I got there, I couldn't tell whether he knew or not. He wouldn't talk. You know what he was like. He only grunted at me. He had a note from Carol and he was going up to fix the organ. He left me there in his apartment.

"I didn't know what to do. And then Carol came in the back door looking for Oscar. I tried to talk to her and she—she laughed at me. She called me an old maid. She asked me why I was so interested—if it was possible that I could be the woman in the case. And then she laughed. And I—I . . .

"There were knives on the table—they were beautiful sharp knives—sharp . . .

"I held my hand across her mouth. She couldn't cry out. I stabbed her twice—she fell. I wasn't sure she was dead so I cut her throat. I knew she was dead then. There was no blood on me. I'd been careful."

"Why—why're you telling me this?" Charles Dennison croaked. "I don't want to know. Why, good gollies, you— you're telling me that you're the one who—that you killed them . . ."

It was as though she hadn't heard the interruption. Charles Dennison's voice died away and the other, in emotionless monotony, went on.

"I thought about Oscar then. He'd be coming back and there was no place to hide her body, no place where he couldn't find it. And I thought about it and I knew what I had to do.

"There was a choir robe lying over a chair. I took off my coat and put on the robe. I took one of the knives. Then, just as I was going, I saw a heavy cane in a corner. I took that too. Oscar was strong. I was afraid I mightn't be able to handle him. Then I went upstairs.

"He didn't hear me coming. The organ doors were open. He was coming down the ladder. I stepped inside the doors. His back was to me. I waited until, he was down and then I—I struck him with the cane—behind the ear. He fell. Then I cut *his* throat too."

I sobbed out loud at that. I couldn't help it. Frantically came my whispered plea. "Ran—Ran, do something! stop it—!"

His hand crushed over my mouth. "Shut up! I want to hear . . ."

The voice was continuing. "I had to hurry—it was getting late. The others would be coming. I shut the organ doors, locked them. I knew where Tess King kept the keys—I'd often been in the office when she was putting them away. I hid them as I'd seen her do.

"There was blood on the robe I'd worn. I took it off and hung it in the wardrobe."

"That was my robe, dang it!" Charles Dennison exploded. "You nearly got me arrested!"

"Was it?" There was complete indifference in the voice. "I took the knife and the cane and went back downstairs. I put the knife beside Carol's body. I wasn't afraid. I knew there'd be no fingerprints on it. I'd worn gloves. But the gloves were bloody . . .

"I put on my coat again. I took the cane. . . . I was ready to go when I saw something flash in the light. It was the ring she wore around her neck—Blair's ring. I took that too. Then I turned off the lights and went up the back stairs. I knew I had to get away from the church before anyone came. No one saw me.

"I tried to think what to do. I had to clean my hands somewhere—there was blood on them too. I was afraid to throw the gloves away for fear they'd be found and traced to me. And anyway it was a cold night—I couldn't be without gloves. I went home. I walked—all the way in the cold and the snow—with the gloves on my hands, and the cane . . .

"I burned the gloves in the furnace, washed the cane clean and put it in the umbrella stand. There were other canes there—Father's—no one would notice one extra. Then I called a taxi and went back to the church. I was late but it didn't matter. The storm. They hadn't started singing yet. No one noticed anything. I was—just the same . . ."

"Look!" This was Charles Dennison, fired by some high secret excitement. "Listen—do you know what you've been telling me?"

"Yes, I know." Measured and relentless, the words came. "That I killed them."

"That isn't what I mean." He brushed that away as negligible. "What I'm talking about is—if it was the way you said and you killed Carol *first,* then—then I get the money! Oscar's money!"

There was a laugh, brief and bitter, "You won't get that money, Charles—don't you understand? I wouldn't have told you all this unless—unless I meant to kill you too!"

"Me?" It was a shriek. "Listen—you're crazy—you can't kill me! Great gollies! I didn't have anything to do with any of it—I told you I didn't know anything—"

"You do now. It's too bad, Charlie—you would have liked having that money, wouldn't you? You've never had it very easy either, have you? That money would have helped . . ."

"The dang Gregorys will get it!" Charles Dennison groaned. "What do they need more money for—you tell me that!"

"They won't get it, Charlie. No one will get it . . . Because no one will know . . ."

Things happened then, so quickly that it's hard to get them down in proper sequence. I saw Charles Dennison shrink back against the organ console, his face a mask of horror and disbelief. Ran had gone from me. I could see him, a dark shadow that crept forward—slowly, silently. I wondered if Charles Dennison saw him too, if he knew that help was coming, was even now on its way. But Ran was going slowly—too slowly. That other shadow had drawn itself together, had suddenly grown taller. Its right hand was coming up. There was something in the hand— something long and knobbed and heavy. It lifted high, began to descend . . .

My scream was lost in the crescendo of other sounds. The rush of Ran's feet, uncareful now. The outraged squeal of organ pipes as Charles Dennison's body slumped heavily down upon the manuals. The rattle of something falling. Wood striking sharply against wood.

Ran was shouting now but, underneath, I could hear the scurry of those other feet—desperate fleeing feet. Ran was running too—down the near aisle. He was too late—too late to cut off those other feet, winged as they were by fear. A door opened, slammed loudly. There was a thump—another. A single long drawn out shriek. Another thump. Then silence, save for the low rumble from the organ where Dennison's body had slipped down to lie across the open pedals.

I unfastened my fingers from where they clung to the door jamb. I took a step forward. I tried to see into the blackness where Ran had vanished. I called to him and there was no answer. Then light bloomed behind me in the choir room and with it came the blessedness of Alec's voice. "Tess—is that you? What's going on here? What are you doing here and where's Garrison? And what—what is *that?*"

I didn't stop to question his appearance. I simply grabbed for him and hung on. "It's Charles Dennison," I babbled. "I think he's dead. It was the murderer—Ran's followed her—we've got to go after him—help . . ."

It was Ran I'd meant to help but Alec hurried to Charles Dennison. He wasn't dead. There was a bloody bruise down one side of his face but he was conscious as we moved back the organ bench and lifted him out. We tried to lay him flat in one of the choir stalls but he blinked at us and struggled up.

"Did you get that she-devil? She tried to kill me, by gollies—so's I wouldn't get that money! Did you get her, hey?"

We never answered for just then Ran came up beside us, moving on silent feet, his face set and white. He glanced once at Dennison, then looked at me. "Tess, call the station and tell them to send Doc Morton and an ambulance over right away." Then as I moved to obey, he turned to Alec. "We'll have to go out and back in through the basement. We may have to take off that door—it's jammed. I'm afraid she's badly hurt. I can hear her groan . . ."

Alec straightened abruptly. "She?" he said hoarsely. "Her? What do you mean? Who is it?"

Ran looked away, spoke tonelessly. "I thought you knew. Or guessed. It's Miss Erickson."

21

Leota Erickson died that night, died without speaking or regaining consciousness although Ran, Alec and Bishop Walters all waited by her bedside. The fall down the basement stairway had broken her back and injured the spinal cord. If she could have lived, Doctor Morton said gravely, it would have been as a helpless cripple.

Sometime in the early dawning, a nurse had slipped into that quiet hospital room with a whispered message. A call had just come in from the Erickson home. Leota's mother had died in her sleep.

"And thereby wrote an end to *that* chapter," Ran said. "There's no other family so far as we can find out."

It was noon of the next day. Alec had come home at five, condensed his news into two terse sentences and then retired into his bedroom from which he had only just emerged. No one knew where Ran and Bishop Walters had been nor what they had been doing. They had only just appeared to participate in what Ruth called "bruncheon."

"Oh, well, it's terrible any way you look at it," Ruth said as she poured more coffee into Alec's cup. "Although I don't know why we should be so surprised. Don't lots of old maids—school teachers especially—go nuts? What I mean is, they get used to bossing children around, then they try it on the rest of the world and it doesn't work. It—addles them."

"Leota Erickson was a very pretty girl," Harvey Thurston said heavily.

"Oh, dear!" Ruth said in genuine distress. "I shouldn't have said that. I'm sorry, Mr. Thurston—I just didn't think."

There were six of us about the table—Ruth and Alec, myself and Ran, the bishop and Harvey Thurston. Neither Mrs. Thurston nor Blair—who might have been considered to hold a priority of interest in the discussion—had been included. It was the consensus of opinion that Blair be kept in ignorance of his relationship to the Ericksons.

"It doesn't matter," Mr. Thurston assured Ruth. "She changed sadly after Essie's—uh—tragic death. My wife noticed it. So did I. Up until the time that we took Blair, she and Mabel had been close friends. Leota was constantly at our home. After that the close relationship ceased. We were not sorry. Mabel was completely wrapped up in the boy and she distrusted predatory maiden aunts. Moreover, Leota's fear that Essie's story might in some way become known kept her away. I know, from what my wife has said, that Leota lived in constant terror lest the boy grow up to resemble the Ericksons and the resemblance be noted. As it happens, if Blair looks like anyone, it is his father. But Lawrence Benson has been gone a long time from Dorchester. No one remembers him."

"She really did a magnificent job of covering up," Ran said. "If it hadn't been for Oscar's unexpected interest in scientific matters . . ."

"Ah, yes, the eyes," said the bishop. "An element of luck was certainly present, for I doubt if Oscar really comprehended more than a fraction of what he read. Your scientist would have been more chary of jumping to conclusions, obvious though they might appear to be. We may not lay down laws for Nature. The most we dare to say, I fear, is that, over against the probable, there looms always the unpredictable possible. Oscar was right in this case. Given a different set of hereditary factors, he could have been wrong."

"It was all so unnecessary," Ruth burst out. "It only proves what I was saying—that Miss Erickson was crazy. Even Oscar was only guessing. Of course, now that Charles Dennison knows . . ."

"Charles Dennison will be silent," Bishop Walters told her. "The poor fellow is badly shaken up, understandably, but he is amenable to reason. He appreciates the futility of this story being made public. He has sent assurances of complete silence to Mr. Thurston."

"He'll get the money now. That may have something to do with it."

It was a statement so out of character that I blinked. There was no doubt that Alec's intrinsic faith in human nature had received a severe jolt.

"Not entirely, I believe." The bishop's tone gave reproof. "Dennison had known and liked Essie. For a short time she had been one of his pupils."

"Essie?" Ruth repeated, as much to draw the limelight from Alec, I suspected, as for any other reason. "Oh, yes— she was the sister. It's hard to realize her somehow and the part she played in all this. It was all so long ago."

"Essie was another Carol Tolliver," Harvey Thurston said thoughtfully. "An earlier, less sophisticated model. I think that Leota realized it and that it was behind her intense dislike of the girl. Not that I'd hand my dead daughter-in-law much myself. She never showed me that side of her. With me she was shrewd and as hard as nails. She'd estimated to a dollar what she thought she could get out of me and she meant to get it. But Leota had had her in school—hers was probably the truer judgment. I'll not forget in a hurry the way Leota raged when I told her about Blair and Carol. I thought she had a right to know and that it would be less of a shock to hear it from me. The things she told me about Carol that night—well, it opened my eyes, I can tell you!"

"And Essie was like her?"

"Well, yes and no. She was—didn't they call them 'baby vamps' in those days?—confiding, always lowering her lashes at you and slipping a hand in yours. Mabel always insisted that she'd have had a time with the boys in school if she hadn't been so frightened of Leota. Leota was bossy—" here he bowed to Ruth—"even then and she was fifteen years older than Essie. The mother'd been an invalid for years and Leota took all responsibility from her—even that of Essie."

"And she failed with Essie," Ruth said. "Poor thing! That must have been hard to bear. Trying so hard to keep her safe from boys and then this older man . . . I suppose she never suspected—never dreamed of *that!* What was *he* like?"

"Benson? Oh, he was a wishy-washy kind of fellow. Young, good-looking in a weak way. Married early and with several children. He taught Public Speaking and Debate in the high school. That's where he ran into Essie. She was graduating with honors—trust Leota to see to that!—and she had a speech for commencement. He was coaching her. I remember shortly before the whole thing broke that Leota told us how hard Essie was working on her speech and how kind it was of Benson to give her so much extra time and help. Kind! A month later that wasn't what she called it!"

"She came to you?" This was Alec.

"To Mabel rather. I was. there. This was in the summer—July. She told us the whole story. She was as near despair as I've ever seen her. She had seen Benson and he'd disclaimed all responsibility, hid behind his wife and family. He was leaving Dorchester for a better job on the west coast. Of course Leota could have made trouble for him but then the whole thing would have come out and she was thinking of Essie. So she and Mabel put their heads together. I helped where I could. I was sorry for Leota—darn sorry. She was completely crushed."

"It was a good plan," Ruth said. "It must have been. No one ever suspected."

"No. Mabel was pregnant at the time. Our baby would be born about the same time as Essie's. Mabel talked of taking Essie's baby from the start, of coming home from the hospital with twins. She'd planned to go to Hospers. It was her old home and her father had been head of the hospital there. Essie went there in September, lived there as Mrs. Esther Benson. Leota told everyone that she'd gone east to college. No one questioned that—she'd planned sending her since Essie was a little girl. She pretended she got letters and told about the good times Essie was having. Just before Essie's baby was due, Leota gave out that she was sick and she got a leave of absence from the Board of Education and went east—supposedly. In reality it was to Hospers. She was there when Essie died. Then our baby was born dead and we took Blair. That's the story—all of it."

"Essie was buried there in Hospers?" Ran asked. He was slanting marks on a piece of paper, carefully shading them.

"No. Leota took the body east. She posed as a Miss Benson in Hospers—Leota. As a sister-in-law. The death certificate was made out in the name of Esther Benson. There were no questions asked. Leota had seen to a wedding ring and such."

"No questions until Oscar asked them," Ran said. "Just how much was he able to find out, Thurston?"

Harvey Thurston's hand whacked down on the table. "Not a damn thing! Beg pardon," he said to the assembled clergy, "but it makes me mad just thinking about it. I don't mind legitimate claims on me but this was a shake-down from start to finish. Carol told me flatly that she didn't give the snap of her finger for Blair—it was simply that I had more money than anyone else in town and she thought she could get more out of me. When I didn't play easy to get, she told Oscar her troubles. He'd known all about the marriage, had even supplied the money for the diamond Blair had given her, and some of the stuff he'd been reading about heredity had stuck in his thick Norse head. I suspect he'd been wanting to get something on me for a long time—we'd had plenty of rows about church affairs and I'd had to call him down hard a few times. He was a vindictive sort of cuss. At any rate he set Dennison on the prowl."

"According to Dennison," Ran observed, "he didn't find out enough to count."

"He found out enough to convince Oscar that there might be more. The very fact that we'd kept the adoption secret convinced him. So he gave the information he had free to Carol to use as a lever in her dealings with me. And it worked—it damn near worked," he finished grimly. "It touched me where I was raw. It wasn't so much my wife or I, you understand—although it seemed a pity to keep a thing like that twenty-odd years and then have it come out. Then, too, I suspected the news would give Blair a nasty shock, might even make him harder to control. But in the main it was Leota I thought about. It would be toughest on her. That's why I went and warned her—and thereby dumped over the apple cart."

"It must have been Oscar then that Carol meant," Ruth said with some satisfaction. "That's been bothering me. You know, Alec—what she said about sowing the wind and reaping the whirlwind? Maybe she hadn't really wanted to do it this way and Oscar was forcing her . . ."

"Possible but—from what I saw of Carol—improbable," Thurston said. "We hadn't come to terms yet, remember. More likely she was saving it for her heavy artillery. She was no fluffy little angel, let me tell you. It takes nerve to face a man and accuse him of being the adopted father of his illegitimate son. And think what she said to Leota— asking her if she were the woman in the case."

"I suspect it was *that* that tipped the apple cart," Ran said quietly. "She was already half out of her mind with fear of the threatened scandal and then to be laughed at and taunted by the girl she disliked—to learn that she was actually in league with the man who was making her life a financial hell."

"Disliked is hardly the word," Thurston said. "She hated Carol, made no secret of it—at least not to me. It made her furious to think that Blair'd fallen for Carol— had dared to marry her. And then, when she found out Carol didn't even have the excuse of loving him—that he was simply a commodity with which she proposed to bargain—well, I think her brain snapped right then."

"There is one thing I should like to know," Bishop Walters interposed. "Why—when Miss Erickson was in such financial straits was she driven to Oscar? Why didn't you give her help?"

Harvey Thurston flushed a little. "I didn't know. I knew that her mother was ill but, as I told you, we saw very little of Leota after we took Blair. Mabel wanted it that way and Leota agreed. If she had come to me, I would have been glad to let her have the money. But she didn't. She was too proud. Probably felt that we'd done enough when we helped cover up for Essie. She wasn't the kind who took favors easily." He stopped and looked around at us defiantly. "Well, that's my part of the story. Now, what I want to know is this—what are you going to do about it?"

Ran was silent. "What are *we* going to do about it?" the bishop repeated gravely. That, too, was a question.

"Yes. Is it all to come out or not?"

Ran got up and walked over to the window. The rest of us just sat and watched his back. A nice straight back, square-shouldered, I thought idly. But it wasn't his back I wanted to contemplate just then—it was his face.

He turned about at last. "I think that this part of the story can be kept quiet," he said slowly. "I don't see what good it would do to publish it. We know who the murderer was. We have witnesses to her confession. We have a motive—financial worry—that will serve. Why not let it?"

"Carol too?" This was Alec. Foreseeing difficulties with the Tollivers, I supposed.

Ran's glance was impassive. "Motive for her death, do you mean? An intense, unreasoning dislike for a former pupil—it's not uncommon among teachers. Carol got in her way. No one will ask for further reason. We're excusing the woman under the cloak of temporary insanity and that's wide enough to cover many sins." He turned his eyes from Alec's face of righteous indecision to the kindlier countenance of the older man, "Surely, sir, the old tenets need not die. Justice *can* be tempered with mercy."

The bishop's silence gave agreement.

Harvey Thurston got to his feet. "Well!" he said. "Well. That's taken a load off my mind, I can tell you. Now, I think I'd better get home. Mabel has taken this very hard, but I couldn't answer her questions before without knowing just how much I could tell her. Now," he drew a long breath, "now, I know."

"One last thing, Thurston," Ran said evenly. "After I talked to you last night, you left the house. Where did you go?"

Thurston looked sheepish. "Oh, you know that, do you? I drove to Leota's—thought I'd better see her and bring her up to date. She wasn't there. I talked to the nurse and then came home."

Obviously the bishop had been thinking. "I presume," he said diffidently, "that it was Miss Erickson who—ah—felled me in the church?"

"I think so," Ran said. "No way of proving it now, of course. But she had just learned the truth about the notes. No doubt she made a desperate attempt to get possession of them. You had sent her home in a taxi. She must have taken her key to the church and returned. You got in her way, that was all. By the way, we did try to test the flashlight for fingerprints but there were none. Either she wore gloves, or—and this is a possibility—the thing she hit you with wasn't the flashlight at all but her cane."

I'd been thinking myself. I said, "Ran, what about Georgia Brastock's story? You know—about Charles Dennison being downstairs the night of the murder. Did you ask him?"

Ran shrugged. "I did and I've no reason to disbelieve what he told me. He says he was mad when he arrived at the church and found the organ open and running. He says he thought Carol might be downstairs talking to Oscar, so he started down to see. But when he reached the foot of the stairs, he found the entire basement dark, so he concluded they weren't there and he came up again, madder than ever. The door slam Mrs. Brastock heard was his shutting of the door at the foot of the stairs. I've an idea he did it rather forcefully." That seemed to finish it. Thurston said his good-bys and departed, the bishop and Alec going with him to the door. Alec came back but the bishop didn't.

There was a purposeful glint in Alec's eye as he strode in. He began to speak before he was fairly inside the room. "Now, I want you to understand I'm not asking any more questions about this—this tragedy. I know all that I want to. Except for one thing. It wasn't the kind of question I cared to ask before Thurston. But—" here he fixed Ruth accusingly—"you distinctly gave me to understand that Miss Erickson called you and told you I was with Carol in the Café Rouge. Obviously she didn't. She didn't have time and she wasn't interested in me. Then who did?"

Ruth dimpled. "*I* gave you to understand—oh, Alec! It was Tess—Tess and your own guilty conscience. Of course it wasn't Leota Erickson. As a matter of fact, it was a good thing you didn't ask while Harvey Thurston was here. It might have been embarrassing." She hesitated, dimpled again. "Darling it was Mrs. Thurston. She'd been here waiting to see you—remember? And you didn't come. So when she finally started back down town and happened to glance in the Café window and saw *you* . . . Well, she thought I really *ought to know!*"

Alec looked at her blankly. "She did! Mrs. Thurston . . . Well." Words seemed to fail him for the moment. When he recovered, he looked quizzically at Ran. "You see what happens when you take your wife into too close a partnership? I only hope you're being warned in time."

"Alec, you beast—"

"Alec, that's not fair—"

Ruth and I spoke simultaneously but Ran only laughed and patted my hand.

"You don't know me," he told Alec. "Once I put my foot down . . . Now, darling, go easy. Don't say anything you'll be sorry for . . ."

I didn't. How could I? His kiss had silenced me.

Additional classic detective fiction, suspense thrillers, and police procedurals can be found at:

CoachwhipBooks.com
(print)

Coachwhip.com
(epub)

THE
THING
IN THE
BROOK

PETER STORME

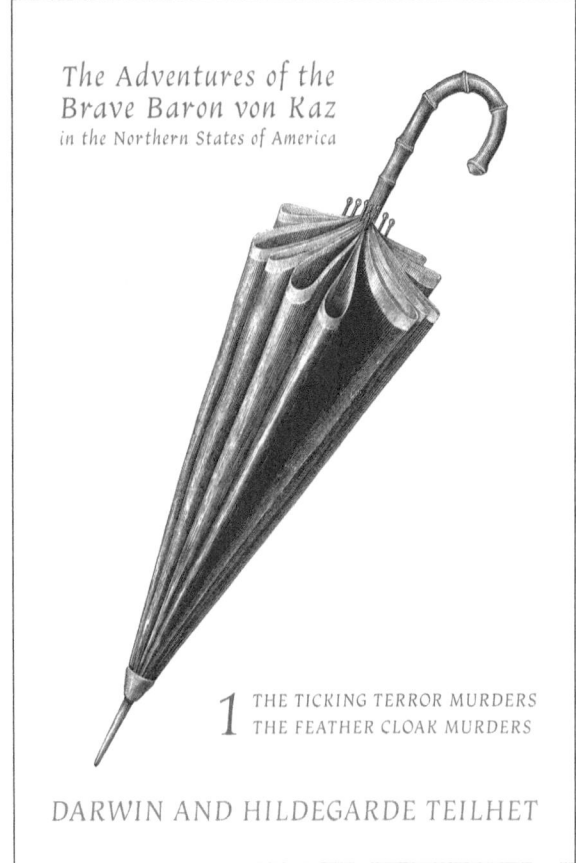

The Adventures of the
Brave Baron von Kaz
in the Northern States of America

1 THE TICKING TERROR MURDERS
THE FEATHER CLOAK MURDERS

DARWIN AND HILDEGARDE TEILHET

A Matter of Iodine

David Keith